Case Study
Graeme Macrae Burnet
The Booker Prize 2022
Longlisted
D0106675
'Brilliant ... burstingly alive and engaging.'
Telegraph
'Compelling ... I was hooked like a fish.'
Spectator

Praise for Graeme Macrae Burnet's *Case Study:*

LONGLISTED FOR THE BOOKER PRIZE 2022

SHORTLISTED FOR THE GORDON BURN PRIZE 2022

SHORTLISTED FOR THE NED KELLY AWARDS 2022

'Forensic, elusive, and mordantly funny … layered with questions about authenticity and the self.' *Booker Prize Judges' citation*

'A twisting and often wickedly humorous work of crime fiction.' *Gordon Burns Prize Judges' citation*

'A provocative send-up of midcentury British mores and the roots of modern psychotherapy … brisk and engaging.' *Kirkus Reviews*

'A page-turning blast, funny, sinister, perfectly plotted … Rarely has being constantly wrong-footed been so much fun.' *Times*

'Encourages us to look more closely at the inherent instability of fiction itself … genuinely affecting … very funny.' *Guardian*

'Indecently entertaining.' *Telegraph, Books of the Year*

'Compelling … I was hooked like a fish.' *Spectator*

'Brilliant, bamboozling … what might have been just an intellectual game feels burstingly alive and engaging.' *Telegraph*

'A riveting psychological plot ... tortuous, cunning ... clever.' *Times Literary Supplement*

'Bitingly funny and surprisingly moving … [A] barnstorming psychodrama … Consistently inventive, caustically funny … one of the finest novels of the year.' *Financial Times*

'Enormous fun … a mystery and a psychological drama wrapped up in one … magnificent – a triumph.' *Observer*

'Poses questions about the nature of the self and the authenticity of identity … fine comic passages … He is an uncommonly interesting and satisfying novelist.' *Scotsman*

'A thrilling investigation into the nature of sanity and identity.' *Alice O'Keeffe, The Bookseller*

'A novel of mind-bending brilliance … Burnet is a master of … ideas of truth and identity, fiction and documentary, and *Case Study* shows him at the height of his powers.' *Hannah Kent*

'Brilliantly depicted … intriguing … compulsive.' *Irish Times*

'You'll be completely beguiled by this sly, darkly comic offering, with its unreliable narrator and its equally unreliable author.' *Mail on Sunday*

'Fun and funny, sly and serious, a beguiling literary game.' *David Szalay*

'Sinister and cleverly done … punctures the myth-making of the period.' *Daily Mail*

'A great work of psychological suspense … Smart, entertaining character study wrapped in a thrilling mystery.' *Lori Feathers, Interabang Books (Dallas, TX)*

'Utterly compelling and slightly deranged, a fascinating psychological study of two troubled individuals.' *Lexi Beach, Astoria Bookshop (Astoria, NY)*

'Often the highest compliment for a work of non-fiction is to say that it "reads like a novel." Burnet has achieved the opposite in this intriguing work … Surprising, puzzling, and often archly funny.' *Grace Harper, Mac's Backs (Cleveland Heights, OH)*

Case Study

ALSO BY GRAEME MACRAE BURNET

His Bloody Project

The Gorski Novels:
The Disappearance of Adèle Bedeau
The Accident on the A35

Case Study

Graeme Macrae Burnet

BIBLIOASIS
Windsor, Ontario

FIRST EDITION
10 9 8 7 6 5 4 3 2 1

Library and Archives Canada Cataloguing in Publication

Title: Case study / Graeme Macrae Burnet.
Names: Burnet, Graeme Macrae, 1967- author.
Description: Previously published: Salford: Saraband, 2021.
Identifiers: Canadiana (print) 20220256780 | Canadiana (ebook) 20220256799 | ISBN 9781771965200 (softcover) | ISBN 9781771965217 (ebook)
Classification: LCC PR6102.U76 C37 2022 | DDC 823/.92—dc23

Readied for the press by Daniel Wells
Cover designed by Daniel Benneworth-Grey

PRINTED AND BOUND IN CANADA

Contents

Preface

TOWARDS THE END OF 2019 I received an email from a Mr Martin Grey of Clacton-on-Sea. He had in his possession a series of notebooks written by his cousin that he thought might form the basis of an interesting book. I replied, thanking him, but suggested that the person best placed to make something of the material in question was Mr Grey himself. He protested that he was no writer, and that he had not approached me randomly. He had, he explained, come across a blog post I had written about the forgotten 1960s psychotherapist Collins Braithwaite. The notebooks contained certain allegations about Braithwaite he was sure would interest me.

At this point my curiosity was properly aroused. A few months earlier I had come across a copy of Braithwaite's book *Untherapy* in the notoriously chaotic Voltaire & Rousseau bookshop in Glasgow. Braithwaite had been a contemporary of R.D. Laing, and something of an *enfant terrible* of the so-called anti-psychiatry movement of the 1960s. The book, a collection of case studies, was salacious, iconoclastic and compelling. My new-found fascination with the author was not satisfied by the scant information on the internet, and I had been intrigued enough to visit the small archive at the University of Durham, twenty-five miles north of Braithwaite's hometown of Darlington.

This 'archive' consisted of a couple of cardboard boxes containing the heavily annotated manuscripts of Braithwaite's books (frequently adorned with obscene though not unartistic doodles), some newspaper clippings and a small number of letters, mostly from Braithwaite's editor, Edward Seers, and his sometime lover, Zelda Ogilvie. As I pieced together the details of Braithwaite's extraordinary life, I began to contemplate writing his biography, an idea that met with little enthusiasm from my agent and publisher. Why would anyone, they asked, want to read about a forgotten and disgraced character whose work had been out of print for decades? It was, I was forced to concede, a perfectly reasonable question.

This was the context in which my interaction with Mr Grey began. I told him that I would, after all, like to take a look at the notebooks and provided him with my address. A package arrived two days later. The accompanying note attached no conditions to publication. Mr Grey did not want any remuneration and, out of respect for the privacy of his family, preferred to retain his anonymity. Grey, he confessed, was not his real name. If I did not consider the notebooks to be of interest, all he asked was that I send them back. He was confident, however, that this would not be the case and included no return address.

I read the five notebooks in a single day. Any scepticism I might have had was immediately dispelled. Not only did the author tell an absorbing story but, despite her protestations, her writing had a certain kooky élan. The material was haphazardly arranged, but that only added, I thought, to the authenticity of what she had to say.

Within a few days, however, I had convinced myself that I was the victim of a prank. What could be more calculated to entice me than a set of found notebooks alleging criminal malpractice by a person I happened to be researching? If it was a hoax, however, Mr Grey had gone to a great deal of trouble, not least of which was the writing of the documents themselves. I decided to carry out a few checks. The notebooks (actually inexpensive Silvine school jotters) were of a type commonly available at the time. They are undated, but various references in the text suggest that the action described must have taken place in the autumn of 1965, when Braithwaite was indeed resident in Primrose Hill and approaching the height of his celebrity. The pages of *Untherapy* taped into the first notebook are from the first edition, which would not have been easily obtainable later on, suggesting that the notebooks had been written contemporaneously. Many of the details corresponded with what I had read at the university archive or in newspaper articles of the time. That proved little, however. Had the notebooks been forgeries, it would only have been necessary for the author to carry out the same research as I had. Other details were less accurate. The pub that features in the narrative, for example, is actually called the Pembroke Castle rather than the Pembridge Castle, as it is referred to in the text. Such an error, though, seemed much more likely to have been made by an author innocently recording her thoughts than by one seeking to perpetuate a deception. The notebooks also contained an unflattering cameo appearance by Mr Grey himself, something he would hardly have included had he himself been the author.

Then there was the question of motivation. I could think of no reason for anyone to go to such lengths to deceive me. It seemed equally unlikely that the objective was to discredit Braithwaite, whose career had in any case ended in ignominy, and who now merited barely a footnote in psychiatric history.

I emailed Mr Grey. The material, I told him, was indeed intriguing, but I could not take things any further without definitive proof of its provenance. He replied saying that he did not know what evidence he could be expected to provide. He had found the notebooks while clearing out his uncle's house in Maida Vale. He had, furthermore, known his cousin all her life and the vocabulary and turns of phrase employed were entirely consistent with the way in which she expressed herself. It was simply not credible that they could have been written by anyone else. None of that, of course, constituted the kind of proof I sought. I asked Mr Grey if he would be willing to meet me. He refused, arguing quite reasonably that this would not prove anything either way. If, he concluded, I did not trust his 'bona fides', all I had to do was return the notebooks, for which he now provided a PO Box number.

Clearly, I did not do so. While I had done enough to convince myself that the notebooks were genuine, what I cannot attest to is the truth of their contents. Perhaps the events described are no more than the flight of fancy of a young woman with self-confessed literary ambitions, and who, by the evidence of her own words, was in a troubled state of mind. I told myself that what mattered was not whether the events had actually taken place, but simply that, as Mr Grey had said at the outset, they would form the basis of an interesting book. The fact that my receipt of the notebooks dovetailed so neatly with my own research seemed too apposite to resist. I redoubled my efforts, visiting the relevant locations, making a more detailed study of Braithwaite's work and conducting a number of interviews with persons connected to him, and now present the notebooks, lightly edited, alongside my own biographical material.

– GMB, April 2021

The First Notebook

I have decided to write down everything that happens, because I feel, I suppose, I may be putting myself in danger, and if proved to be right (a rare occurrence admittedly), this notebook might serve as some kind of evidence.

Regrettably, as will become clear, I have little talent for composition. As I read over my previous sentence I do rather cringe, but if I dilly-dally over style I fear I will never get anywhere. Miss Lyle, my English mistress, used to chide me for trying to cram too many thoughts into a single sentence. This, she said, was a sign of a disorderly mind. 'You must first decide what it is you wish to say, then express it in the plainest terms.' That was her mantra, and though it is doubtless a good one, I can see that I have already failed. I have said that I may be putting myself in danger, but there I go, off on an irrelevant digression. Rather than beginning again, however, I shall press on. What matters here is substance rather than style; that these pages constitute a record of what is to occur. It may be that were my narrative too polished, it might lack credibility; that somehow the ring of truth lies in infelicity. In any case, I cannot follow Miss Lyle's advice, as I do not yet know what it is I wish to say. However, for the sake of anyone unfortunate enough to find themselves reading this, I will endeavour to be clear: to express myself in the plainest terms.

In this spirit, I shall begin by stating the facts. The danger to which I have alluded comes in the person of Collins Braithwaite. You will have heard him described in the press as 'Britain's most dangerous man', this on account of his ideas about psychiatry. It is my belief, however, that it is not merely his ideas that are dangerous. I am convinced, you see, that Dr Braithwaite killed my sister, Veronica. I do not mean that he murdered her in the normal sense of the word, but that he is, nonetheless, as responsible for her death as if he had strangled her with his bare hands. Two years ago, Veronica threw herself from the overpass at Bridge Approach in Camden and was killed by the 4.45 to High Barnet. You could hardly imagine a person less likely to commit such an act. She was twenty-six years old, intelligent, successful and passably attractive. Regardless of this, she had, unbeknown to my father and me, been consulting Dr Braithwaite for some weeks. This I know from his own account.

Like most people in England I was familiar with Dr Braithwaite's uncouth Northern drawl long before I encountered him in person. I had heard him speaking on the wireless, and had even once seen him on television. The programme was a discussion of psychiatry hosted by Joan Bakewell.* Braithwaite's appearance was no more attractive than his voice. He wore an open-necked shirt and no jacket. His hair, which reached to his collar, was dishevelled, and he smoked constantly. His features were large, as if they had been exaggerated by a caricaturist, but there was something, even on television, that drew one's eyes to him. I was only vaguely aware of the other guests in the studio. I remember less of what he actually said than his manner of delivering it. He had the air of a man to whom it would be futile to offer resistance. He spoke with a weary authority, as if tired of explaining himself to his inferiors. The participants were seated in a semi-circle with Miss Bakewell in the centre. While the others sat up straight, as if attending church, Dr Braithwaite slouched in his seat like a bored schoolboy, his chin slumped on

* This edition of *Late Night Line-Up* aired on BBC2 on Sunday 15th August 1965. The other participants were Anthony Storr, Donald Winnicott and the then Bishop of London, Robert Stopford. R.D. Laing had been invited to take part but refused to share a platform with Braithwaite. There is, unfortunately, no surviving footage of the programme, but Joan Bakewell later wrote that Braithwaite was 'one of the most arrogant and unpleasant individuals' she had ever had the misfortune to meet.

the palm of his hand. He appeared to regard the other contributors with a mixture of contempt and boredom. Towards the end of the programme, he gathered up his smoking materials and walked off the set, muttering an expletive that there is no need to repeat here. Miss Bakewell was taken aback, but quickly recovered her composure and remarked that it was an admission of the poverty of her guest's ideas that he was unwilling to engage in debate with his peers.

The following day's newspapers were filled with condemnation of Dr Braithwaite's behaviour: he was the embodiment of everything that was wrong with modern Britain; his books were filled with the most obscene ideas and displayed the basest view of human nature. Naturally, the following day I visited Foyle's during my lunch hour and asked for a copy of his most recent book, which laboured under the unappealing title of *Untherapy*. The cashier handled the volume as though it carried the danger of infection, and gave me a disapproving look I had not experienced since I acquired a copy of Mr Lawrence's disreputable novel. My purchase remained under wraps until I was safely ensconced in my room after supper that night.

I should say that, prior to this, my knowledge of psychiatry was exclusively derived from those scenes in films in which a patient reclines on a settee and recounts her dreams to a bearded physician with a Germanic accent. Perhaps for this reason, I found the opening part of *Untherapy* difficult to follow. It was full of unfamiliar words, and the sentences were so long and convoluted that the author would have benefited from following Miss Lyle's advice. The only thing I gleaned from the introduction was that Braithwaite had not even wanted to write this book in the first place. His 'visitors', as he called them, were individuals, not 'case studies' to be paraded like sideshow freaks. If he now set out these stories, it was for the sole purpose of defending his ideas against the scorn poured on them by the Establishment (a word he used a great deal). He declared himself to be 'an untherapist': his task was to convince people that they did not need therapy; his mission was to bring down the 'jerry-built edifice' of psychiatry. This struck me as a most peculiar position to adopt, but, as I have said, I am not well versed in the topic. The book, he wrote, could be seen as a companion to his previous work, and consisted of a series of narratives based on relationships he had entered into with troubled individuals. Naturally, the names and certain identifying details had been changed, but the fundamentals of each story were, he insisted, true.

Having got past the baffling opening section, I found these stories frightfully compelling. I suppose there is something reassuring about reading about those duds who make one's own eccentricities pale by comparison. By the time I was halfway through I felt positively normal. It was only when I came to the penultimate chapter that I found myself reading about Veronica. The most sensible thing, I think, is simply to insert these pages here:

Chapter 9

Dorothy

Dorothy was a highly intelligent woman in her mid-twenties. The elder of two sisters, she was brought up in a middle-class family in a large English city. Her parents were phlegmatic Anglo-Saxons. Dorothy had never witnessed any display of affection between them. Disputes were settled, she said, by her father, a docile civil servant, acquiescing to her mother's demands. Until the sudden death of her mother when she was sixteen, Dorothy's childhood was untouched by any great trauma, yet when asked if it had been a happy one, she found it difficult to answer. Eventually she admitted that from an early age she had felt guilty because she had a comfortable upbringing when so many others did not, but still did not feel happy. She had, however, often pretended to be cheerful to please her father, whose own happiness appeared to be dependent on hers. He would constantly cajole her to engage her in games, when she preferred to be left to her own devices. Her mother, on the other hand, constantly reminded Dorothy and her sister how fortunate they were, and, as a result, from her earliest childhood she had exercised restraint, especially in relation to the treats her father liked to tempt her with: ice creams, birthday presents, sweets and so on. Even as a child, she felt a strong resentment towards her sister. This, she insisted, was not the normal jealousy felt when a younger sibling comes along and dilutes the attention and love of the parents. Instead, it was because this younger sister was often disruptive and unruly, yet still received equal treatment from her parents. It did not seem fair that while her own good behaviour went unrewarded, her sister's waywardness was unpunished.

Dorothy excelled at school and won a scholarship to study mathematics at Oxford. There, she continued to outshine her peers and, although introverted, fitted in well enough. At Oxford she found that there was no obligation to 'take part' or to appear to be enjoying oneself. She became aloof and distant. It was, she said, the first time she was able to 'be herself'. Even so, when her fellow students attended dances or held impromptu parties in their quarters, she felt consumed by jealousy. She graduated with a first-class degree and later, while studying for her doctorate, she met a junior member of the teaching staff, with whom she became engaged. She had, she said, no strong feelings towards him, and certainly no sexual desire, but she agreed to marry him because she felt that he was the sort of decent young man her father would approve of. Later, Dorothy's fiancé broke off the engagement, saying that he wished to concentrate on his career for the time being. Dorothy believed that the real reason for his termination of the relationship was because she had suffered a period of nervous exhaustion, necessitating a short stay in a sanatorium, and he feared she was unstable. She was, in any case, relieved that he had called off the wedding, as she did not herself feel equipped for marriage.

On her first visit to my office, Dorothy was well turned out and presented herself in a professional manner, as if attending an interview. Although it was a warm day, she was dressed in a tweed suit that made her appear a good deal older than she was. She wore little or no make-up. It is quite usual for visitors from the middle classes to present themselves this way. They are eager to make a good impression; to set themselves apart from the drooling lunatics they imagine frequent the headshrinker's grotto. But Dorothy took things further than most. Before we had even sat down, she declared: 'So, Dr Braithwaite, how should we go about this?'

Here was a young woman inordinately keen to be in control of the situations in which she found herself. I called her bluff: 'We can go about it however you choose.'

She played for time by removing her gloves and carefully putting them away in the handbag she had placed at her feet. She then embarked on a discussion about the practical arrangements, frequency and so on of our sessions. I allowed her to continue until she could think of nothing else to say. In such situations, silence is the therapist's most valuable tool. I have yet to encounter a visitor who can resist the urge to fill it. Dorothy touched her hair, straightened the hem of her skirt. She was very precise in her movements. She then asked if we should not begin.

I told her that we had already begun. She started to protest, but her argument fell away.

'Ah, yes, of course we have,' she said. 'I expect you have been studying my body language. You probably think I am trying to avoid telling you why I am here.'

I indicated with a movement of my head that that might indeed be the case.

'And you think that by saying nothing, I will prattle on and reveal my deepest secrets to you.'

'You're not obliged to say anything,' I said.

'But anything I do say may be taken down and used in evidence against me.' She laughed at her own clever joke.

Intellectuals are the trickiest nuts to crack. They are so eager to impress you with their own understanding of their condition that they tend to carry on their own commentary as they are talking. 'There I go again, deflecting attention from the real issues,' they will say. 'I expect you'll think that turn of phrase is rather revealing.' All this to prove that they are on an equal footing with me; that they have insight into their own problems. This is self-evident nonsense. If they understood their own condition, they would not be here in the first place. What they do not realise, is that it is their intellect—their constant rationalising of their own behaviour—that is most commonly at the root of their problems.

But, in this case, Dorothy's little joke was revealing: she felt that she was going to be accused, to be placed on trial; and, despite the fact that she had presented herself to me voluntarily, she saw me as an adversary. I did not express these thoughts to her at this point, instead merely repeating my question about how she wished to proceed.

'Well, I rather thought you would have some ideas in that direction,' she said. And then, with a silly laugh: 'Isn't that what I'm paying you for?' As so often with the middle classes: the retreat to money, the compulsion to remind you that you are their employee.

Dorothy had entered the room with every appearance of one accustomed to being-in-control, but as soon as she was actually offered that control, she wanted to relinquish it. Either that or she did not know what to do with it. I put this to her.

Her reaction was to laugh. 'Yes, yes, of course, you're absolutely right, Dr Braithwaite. You're very astute. I can see now why everyone speaks so highly of you.' (Flattery: another diversionary tactic.)

Amusing as it was, the situation was rapidly becoming tiresome, and there is, after all, nothing wrong with fulfilling a visitor's expectations. I asked her what had brought her here.

'Well, that's the thing,' she said, 'and perhaps it's why I have been wittering on so. I'm not sure I can really say.' I encouraged her to continue. 'I mean, I'm not mad. I don't hear voices or see things. I don't want to make love to my father or anything like that. I'm sure there are a lot of people crazier than me.'

'That remains to be seen,' I said.

'Perhaps there's some kind of test I could take,' she suggested. 'I'm ever so good at tests. Perhaps one of the ones with the inkblots. I'll tell you now, they all look like butterflies to me.'

'Really?' I said.

She looked down at her hands. 'No, not really.'

I was not in the least interested in administering a Rorschach test. Neither am I an advocate of the fifty-minute hour so beloved of the psychiatric profession, but a reminder of the ticking of the money-clock can act as a spur. You can be sure that every client that has ever walked into a therapist's office has already mentally played out the scene a hundred times, and the idea of leaving without having touched on the very thing that has brought them there is unthinkable. This dynamic would be particularly germane to a practical, scientific-minded person like Dorothy. Her mathematical training had likely led her to believe that if she described her symptoms to me, I would simply slot them into a formula and miraculously effect a cure. Despite what certain theories would have us believe, there is no universal formula to which human behaviour conforms. As individuals we are buffeted by a set of circumstances unique to each of us. We are the sum of these circumstances and our reactions to them.

I saw Dorothy glance at the mannish watch on her wrist. She took a deep breath. 'You'll think me awfully silly,' she began, 'but I have these dreams of being crushed; that I am being slowly crushed.'

I nodded. 'Dreams, you say? I'm not sure I'm particularly interested in dreams.'

'Well, they're not only dreams,' she went on. 'They're thoughts, too, waking thoughts. That I'm going to be crushed, by a building, by cars, by crowds of people. Even, sometimes, by the tiniest of things. Like a fly. Just the other day there was a bluebottle in my bedroom and I had an overwhelming sensation that if it landed on me it would crush me.'

Dorothy visited me twice weekly for a period of a few months. She slowly abandoned her attempts to exert control over the situation. Indeed, she soon seemed to come to relish the more submissive role she adopted. On her fifth or sixth visit, she asked if she could lie rather than sit on the settee. I told her that she could do whatever she wanted. She didn't need my permission.

'But is it better if I sit or lie?' she asked.

I did not answer and she reclined as gingerly as if she were on a bed of nails. I have never seen a person lie on a settee and look less relaxed, but within a few weeks, she would remove her shoes on arrival and stretch out with something approaching languor.

Almost everything I needed to know about Dorothy had been contained in our initial exchanges. As a child, she had been pulled in opposite directions by her parents: her father wanted to indulge her and for her to be joyful; her mother induced feelings of guilt at any pleasurable experiences. It was impossible for her to satisfy both parents at the same time, and because she was so conscious of the effect of her behaviour on these external parties, she never developed the ability to please herself. Her resentment of her sister was clearly based on the fact that she behaved the way that Dorothy would have liked to, yet was not punished for doing so.

In contrast to the cases of John and Annette, discussed in previous chapters, Dorothy had no desire to revert to an idealized 'true self' that those individuals thought they had lost. She had, in fact, never properly developed a sense of self at all. During our seventh session, Dorothy, after much coaxing, admitted that upon the death of her mother she had experienced a feeling of liberation. It was, she explained, as if the regime had collapsed and she was now free to do whatever she wanted. She jokingly compared this event to the death of Stalin and then—as was her habit—reprimanded herself for having made such an inappropriate comparison.

When I asked how this change in circumstances had altered her behaviour, she replied that it had not changed at all. It would hardly do, she explained, to appear to be rejoicing in her mother's death. I asked what it was that she would have liked to have done.

She could not tell me anything specific. 'It was not that there was anything I particularly wanted to do. It was only that if there had been, I would not be prevented from doing it.'

During her years at Oxford, Dorothy did not indulge in any of the normal experimentation of growing up, either sexually or with alcohol or other drugs. She had never so much as smoked a cigarette. It was not, she insisted, that she denied herself these 'alleged pleasures'; instead that she had no desire to try them in the first place.

I asked if she took any pleasure in her academic achievements. She shook her head. None of it meant anything to her. She did, however, admit to feeling some satisfaction in making her father proud. Similarly, in relation to her short-lived engagement, she was gratified that she had been able to attract an eligible young man. When asked what it was she liked about her fiancé, the best she could up with was to say that he was clean and had never made any inappropriate advances.

I allowed some weeks to pass before I returned to the subject of Dorothy's fears of being crushed. At first she attempted to pass this off as a joke.

'I'm afraid I was being rather melodramatic,' she said. 'I haven't had any such thoughts since I started coming here.'

Nevertheless, I persisted. These thoughts, I insisted, were real, and when she had told me about them, she had clearly been agitated.

'Yes,' she replied, 'but I am well aware that buildings are not going to suddenly collapse and bury me alive.'

I had previously explained to her that her habit of rationalising things was a way of defecting* how these thoughts made her feel. The fact that a building was not likely to collapse and bury her was irrelevant. The fear she experienced was real.

I asked her specifically about the story of the bluebottle she had mentioned on the first day. She appeared embarrassed. It was at least physically possible that a building or a car could crush you, but a bluebottle could not. Again she tried to rationalise away her fears: bluebottles were filthy insects that carried many diseases. Yes, I replied, but that was not the fear you expressed to me. Perhaps the bluebottle is a symbol, she suggested, apparently thinking she had wandered into the office of a psychoanalyst. I explained that I was not interested in symbols. I was interested in things in and of themselves. She countered by saying that in mathematics, symbols or substitutes were often used to solve problems. I told her that if her problems could be solved by mathematics, she would have done so herself.

The problem, of course, was neither one of buildings or bluebottles. It was that Dorothy felt that the external world was pressing in on her: that it was oppressing her. Her habitual way of dealing with this feeling was to tell herself that she had no desires she wanted to act upon. Dorothy denied this. The internal system of repression she had built up was so efficient and well established that she did not recognise its existence. It was easier for her to believe that she had no desires than that she herself was suppressing them. It was a simple enough matter (I needed only to appeal to her highly developed rationalism) to convince her that the external world was not, in reality, oppressing her. What was more difficult to persuade her of was that the oppression she felt came from within rather than without. She was so thoroughly repressed that her entire way of being-in-the-world was a response to a wholly imaginary set of constraints.

'So, I would be more myself if I lived in a more unfettered way?'

'It is not a question of being *more yourself*,' I told her. 'Your self is not a separate entity from who you are now. It is a question of being less yourself, of being a different self.'

Dorothy appeared to ponder this for some time. I was reminded of the stories of the inmates of Auschwitz who, when the Allies arrived to liberate them, could not bring themselves to leave the camp. 'But if I became a different self, I wouldn't be me any more. I'd be someone else.'

I told her that if she was happy being 'me' she wouldn't have sought the help of a therapist in the first place.

It served no purpose for me to further drive my point home. There would be a certain irony if Dorothy—whose entire way-of-being was predicated on pleasing others—was to change her behaviour only in order to gratify me. I thus terminated the session, knowing that, as an intelligent young woman, she was capable of reaching her own conclusions.

During what was to prove our final meeting, I asked her to imagine that she had been given a licence granting her permission to do whatever she wanted for twenty-four hours. No one would know what she had done and there would be no consequences to any of her actions. Under such circumstances, I asked, what would she do? She struggled with this concept, asking for many clarifications of the rules governing this imaginary licence. After a great deal of reassurance, she set to pondering the question. Eventually, the colour rose to her cheeks. I asked her what she was thinking. She only blushed more deeply, evidence that my objective had been achieved. It was not necessary for her to give voice to these thoughts, only to have them in the first place. For Dorothy, this was progress. I asked her to focus on whatever it was she was thinking about and asked her what the consequences would be if she were actually to do it.

'Nothing,' she said. 'There would be no consequences.'

I told her that she could do or be whatever she wanted. She seemed greatly unburdened. She did not, she told me, want to be Dorothy any longer. She thanked me and left my office with a lightness of step that I had not seen in her before.

At first, as I read this, I was amused by the similarities between 'Dorothy' and Veronica. The details Dr Braithwaite had changed threw me off the scent. Veronica had studied at Cambridge rather than Oxford; our father was an engineer, not a civil servant; his characterisation of Dorothy's relationship with her sister was entirely misleading. While Veronica and I were perhaps not as intimate as sisters are supposed to be, she had never harboured any resentment towards me. The evidence on the other side of the scales crept up on me, however. Braithwaite's description of his patient gingerly reclining on the settee was so true to Veronica it made me laugh out loud. Like Dorothy, Veronica always had an exaggerated horror of wasps, bees, moths and bluebottles. She was, furthermore, a dreadful stickler for rules. But, finally, it was the use of a single word that convinced me. When we were young and I became over-enthusiastic or upset about something, Veronica had a single and habitual admonishment: 'Oh, must you be so melodramatic?' she would say witheringly. It was the very word she had used to reprimand herself. Later, when I discovered that Braithwaite's office was only a few minutes' walk from the overpass from which Veronica had thrown herself, I became convinced that she had not left with a 'lightness of step', as he claimed, but having resolved to end her life. Or perhaps it was precisely this resolution that lightened her step. Still, having been on occasion accused of having an overactive imagination, and not wishing to rush to judgement, I returned the following day to Foyle's.

I approached an earnest young man in wire-framed glasses and a Fair Isle tank-top. He did not look the type to pass judgement on a customer's tastes. In hushed tones, I explained that I had recently read *Untherapy* and asked if Collins Braithwaite had written anything else. The young man looked at me as if I had just emerged from the ark. 'Anything else?' he replied. 'I'll say!' With a movement of his head he indicated that I should follow him and I had the feeling that we were then engaged in a kind of conspiracy. Two floors above, we arrived at the psychology section. He pulled a book from the shelves and handed it to me with the whispered words, 'Incendiary stuff.' I looked down. The cover featured a silhouette of a human body, fractured into pieces. The title of the book was *Kill Your Self*. That afternoon at work, I felt as if I was in possession of an item of contraband. I found myself unable to concentrate and told Mr Brownlee I had the most dreadful headache and would he mind awfully if I left early. Back in my room I opened the package. I'm afraid I cannot attest to the book's incendiary qualities as it made no sense whatsoever to me. I do not doubt that this was due to my intellectual shortcomings, but it appeared to be no more than a jumble of incomprehensible sentences, each having no discernible relationship to its neighbours. Still, the title chilled me, and in it I saw the method in Dr Braithwaite's apparent madness.

Naturally, my first instinct was to go directly to the police. The following morning, I telephoned Mr Brownlee and told him I would be late to work. He asked if I was still sick and I replied that a crime had been committed and I was required to present myself as a witness. I said nothing to my father, but as I buttered my toast at breakfast, I imagined myself marching into the police station on Harrow Road and declaring that I wished to report a murder. When asked to provide some evidence to support my allegation, I would calmly place Dr Braithwaite's books on the counter. 'All you need to know,' I would say dramatically, 'is contained within these pages.'

I got no further than the corner of Elgin Avenue. I pictured the puzzled expression on the face of the kindly *Dixon of Dock Green* type behind the counter. What exactly was it I was alleging? he would ask. Perhaps he would go and consult with some unseen superior, or would simply disappear behind a partition to tell his colleagues that he had a right nutcase out there. I imagined my face reddening as I overheard their laughter. In any case I realised that in the absence of any real evidence, my plan was defective and would lead only to humiliation.

It was, instead, a simple enough matter to make an appointment with Dr Braithwaite. I found his number in the *Yellow Pages* under 'Miscellaneous Services'. I telephoned from my desk at work one afternoon when Mr Brownlee was out. A girl answered brightly. I nervously asked if it would be possible to arrange a consultation. 'Of course,' she replied, as if it were the most mundane thing in the world. Aside from my name, no further questions were asked. We agreed that I would come at half past four the following Tuesday. It was as straightforward as making an appointment at the dentist's, yet when I replaced the receiver I felt that I had committed the most audacious act of my life.

I arrived at Chalk Farm Station fully an hour before my allotted time. Outside the station I asked directions to Ainger Road. The man I stopped began to describe the route, before breaking off and offering to accompany me. I declined his offer, not wishing to make small talk as we walked, far less to face an interrogation about my reasons for being in the area.

'It's no trouble,' he replied. 'On the contrary, it would be my pleasure. I'm going that way myself.' He was a handsome fellow in his late twenties, dressed in a fisherman's sweater and short black coat. He was clean-shaven but had something of the air of the beatnik. He wore no hat and had thick dark hair that rose in an impressive swell above his forehead. He had an accent I could not place, but which was not wholly unpleasant. The situation was entirely of my own doing. I had allowed several perfectly innocuous persons to pass before I had addressed him. Now I was in a pickle.

'I promise not to molest you,' he said, before adding with a laugh, 'unless of course you want me to.'

I had a vision of being dragged into some shrubbery and the man forcing himself upon me. That might at least provide some material for my conversation with Dr Braithwaite. As I could think of no way of extricating myself from the situation, we fell into step. My chaperon thrust his hands deep into the pockets of his coat, as if to reassure me that he had no intention of groping me. He told me his name and asked what mine was. Such exchanges of personal information are, I believe, quite normal, so I saw no reason not to take the chance to try out my new identity.

'Rebecca Smyth,' I replied. 'With a Y.'

I had decided on this name while sitting in the Lyons on Elgin Avenue. The names I had previously thought up felt conspicuously fake: Olivia Carruthers, Elizabeth Drayton, Patricia Robson. They none of them had the ring of truth. A van was parked on the opposite side of the street with the words *James Smith & Sons, Central Heating Engineers* painted on the side. 'Smith' was exactly the sort of innocuous name that one would never think to choose as an alias, and was thus ideal for my purpose. Then, when I decided to alter the spelling, I felt I had the beginnings of a convincing persona. 'Smyth with a Y,' I would say in an offhand manner, as if I had grown weary of repeating it all my life. And, perhaps on account of Mrs du Maurier's novel, Rebecca had always struck me as the most dazzling of names. I liked the way its three short syllables felt in my mouth, ending in that breathy, open-lipped exhalation. My own name offered no such sensual pleasure. It was a single-syllabled brick, fit only for head girls with sensible shoes. Why should I not, for once, be a Rebecca? Perhaps I would tell Dr Braithwaite that my nervous troubles were caused by the inadequacy of not living up to the image of my name. I practised presenting my hand to my own image in front of the bathroom mirror, palm downwards, fingers slightly curled in the way that women with expectations do. Then I would glance up with what I thought passed for a flirtatious smile. I had already begun to enjoy being Rebecca Smyth. And now, as I said it out loud for the first time, Tom (or whatever his name was) had batted not an eyelid. Why should he? He was not the type that girls would fob off with *un nom d'emprunt*.

'And what brings you to Primrose Hill, Rebecca Smyth?' he said.

Rebecca, I decided, would not be one to be ashamed of such a thing, so I replied that I had an appointment with a psychiatrist.

This caused my companion, if not to stop in his tracks, then to at least evaluate me afresh. His lower lip jutted out. 'If you'll forgive me, you don't seem the type.'

'The type?' I replied.

Tom looked abashed, as if he might have offended me.

'You mean, I don't look like a nut?' I said.

'Well, if you put it like that, then no, you don't look like a nut.'

'I can assure you I'm mad as a March hare,' I said with Rebecca's most winning smile.

He did not seem the least bit put off. 'Well, you're the most attractive March hare I've met,' he said.

I made no reaction to this. A girl like Rebecca would be quite accustomed to hearing such blandishments. 'And what brings you here?' I asked.

'I have a studio nearby,' he said. 'I'm a photographer.'

'Aren't you going to ask me to come and pose for you?' I asked. It was rather a lark being Rebecca.

'I'm afraid I'm not that kind of photographer,' he said. 'I take pictures of things, not people. Food mixers, sets of cutlery, tins of soup, that sort of stuff.'

'How glamorous,' I said.

'It pays the old Duke of Kent,' he replied.

'I'm sorry?' I said, taken aback that the fellow might have some connection to royalty.

'Duke of Kent. Rent,' he said, and I realised that he had been indulging in the silly custom of rhyming slang. He at least had the good grace to look as abashed as I did.

I realised with a shiver that we were that very moment crossing the overpass from which Veronica had thrown herself. I had never visited before. It was a drab place to end one's life, but I suppose as good as any other.

'Are you cold?' Tom asked. Clearly he was the solicitous type.

I pulled my coat tight around my neck and smiled at him. 'I just felt a sudden breeze.'

We turned into what resembled a village high street. Tom halted at a junction and indicated the way to Ainger Road. Rebecca Smyth held out her hand. Tom took it and expressed the view that it had been a pleasure to meet her.

'Likewise,' she said, then turned on her heel and walked off.

'You still don't look like a nut,' he called out to her retreating back. I half expected him to come after me and ask for my telephone number, but he did not do so. When, after a respectable period of time had elapsed (one does not wish to appear desperate), I looked over my shoulder, he was gone.

Ainger Road was a perfectly ordinary row of terraced houses, separated from the pavement by narrow front gardens strewn with rusting children's tricycles and overturned geraniums. A few sickly trees punctuated the pavement. The last November leaves clung sadly to the branches, as if they knew their fate but had not yet accepted it. The houses looked gloomy and unlived in. There was a general air of dilapidation. The only notable thing about the street was that the houses were numbered not with the even numbers on one side and the odd ones on the other, but consecutively, so that they formed a sort of loop. The address in question was no different from any of the others on the street*. The building must have been divided up, as there were two doorbells, one above the other. A piece of cardboard pinned to the doorpost and bearing the name 'Braithwaite' was the only indication that here was the lair of the notorious head doctor. As I still had forty minutes before my appointment, I retraced my steps. I had spotted a teashop on the little high street I had passed along with Tom.

It was called Clay's. A bell above the door announced my arrival. The place was empty, which, given that it was almost four o'clock on a Tuesday afternoon, was not altogether surprising. The likely clientele of such a place would now be at home busily peeling potatoes in preparation for their hubbies' return. A stout woman behind the counter greeted me with a thin smile and observed me as I made my way to the back of the café, where I calculated I would feel least conspicuous. She approached with a gait that suggested my presence was an inconvenience. Mrs Clay was an appropriately solid name for her. There was something of the golem about her. I ordered a pot of tea and, in an attempt to curry favour, a scone and jam. Above the counter a sign proclaimed that the establishment's baking was all made with butter rather than margarine, 'because he CAN tell the difference!' I found myself wondering whether Tom was the sort of chap who could tell the difference. I suspected not. Or, rather, that his mind would be on loftier matters than the ingredients of a scone. I shared his indifference. I have never made a scone in my life (save for one best-forgotten episode in domestic science) and have no intention of ever doing so. My husband, in the unlikely event

* The property still stands and is as described here in the notebook. I have concealed the precise address out of respect for the privacy of the current occupants.

that I ever find one, will have to go scone-less. Or get his scones elsewhere, ho ho. Nor could I imagine Rebecca Smyth sullying her well-manicured hands in a bowl of flour, although were she forced to do so, she would certainly not countenance the idea of using something as common as margarine.

The proprietress brought my tea. My attempt to wheedle my way into her good graces appeared to have been in vain. She placed the cup and saucer on the table without care and when she returned with my scone, tossed it onto the table with such recklessness that the knife fell to the floor. I was forced to fumble at my ankles to retrieve it, thanking her as I did so. I wondered if I had committed some inadvertent transgression of the establishment's rules to merit such a frosty reception. The most charitable interpretation I could muster—both to myself and to the hostess—was that I was a stranger and did not warrant any special attention. This suspicion was compounded when the bell above the door tinkled again and an elderly lady, dressed in a camel coat and woollen scarf, entered. She was wearing a man's tweed hat with an arrangement of coloured feathers at a jaunty angle, and carried a walking cane. Mrs Clay's demeanour was transformed. She greeted the newcomer—a Mrs Alexander—with such a profusion of welcomes that I would not have been surprised to see her emerge from behind the counter and scatter rose petals on the floor. The lady sat down at what was clearly her regular table by the window and was in due course brought a pot of tea and a slice of Victoria sponge, which was, I noted, placed delicately on the table before her.

I retrieved a novel from my handbag and opened it in front of me. It was a frivolous work unworthy of my attention, but I did not imagine that Mrs Clay was much inclined to literary criticism. In any case, I found myself preoccupied with the words of my erstwhile chaperon: I did not look in the least like a nut.

Ordinarily, one would be flattered by such a remark, but in view of my current mission, it was quite inapposite. That morning I had paid a good deal more attention to my attire than customarily, and before I left Mr Brownlee's I had popped into to the lavatory on the landing to retouch my make-up. This had been wrong-headed. Nuts do not have their hair done at Stephen's in St John's Wood. Nor do they match a natty scarf with their eye shadow or wear stockings from Peterson's. Nuts have no time for niceties. If I arrived at Dr Braithwaite's in my present state, he would rumble me post-haste. I entered the WC at the back of the café and examined myself in the mirror. No lipstick for nuts, I thought, and wiped it off with the back of my hand. I took my finger and smudged the mascara around my eyes, giving me the panda-eyed look of those who haven't slept in weeks. I cleaned my hands, then removed the kirby grips from my hair and roughly tousled it with my fingers. The neckerchief had to go. I took it off and stuffed it into the pocket of my coat. Then I lowered the lid of the pan and sat down. It pained me to do so (they had cost me 10/-), but I leant over and, with my thumbnails, pierced the nylon of my stocking, just below my left knee. It was the perfect touch, suggesting a negligence no woman of sound mind would countenance. I stood up and examined my appearance in the mirror above the wash hand basin. It was too much. I looked quite the madwoman in the attic. As I did not wish to be carted off to the nearest loony bin, I moistened a clump of toilet tissue and removed the smudged mascara from around my eyes. My foundation had to go, too. Finally, I was satisfied. I looked ashen, or as the Scotch are wont to say in that picturesque way of theirs, peely-wally. Men, of course, are wholly unaware of the lengths to which we go to present them with an appealing visage, but I hoped Dr Braithwaite would appreciate the efforts I had made in the opposite direction.

I flushed the lavatory and returned to my table. The sound of my chair scraping on the floor caused the proprietress to look in my direction. She stared at me in some astonishment, as if an entirely different person had emerged from the WC. My tea was cold and I was not in the least bit hungry, but I spread my scone with the butter and apricot jam provided and ate it methodically. How mad it would seem to order a scone and not eat it! As I waited at the counter to pay, not wishing to be lumped in with those ruffians who could be fobbed off with margarine, I complimented her on her baking.

She looked at me with an incredulous expression. I thought she was going to make a remark about my appearance, but she restrained herself and rang up my bill on the register. I paid and left tuppence in the saucer, in the hope that this might repair her good opinion of me.

It had grown more gloomy outside. Ainger Road now seemed more menacing than dilapidated. I stepped up to the threshold of Number -- and pressed the lower of the two bells. As there was no response, I pushed open the door and entered a narrow hallway. A bicycle rested against one wall. A note pinned to the bannister directed visitors upstairs. The carpet was worn and several stair rods were missing, making the ascent rather treacherous. How simple it would be to shove someone from the top and claim that they had merely slipped. There was a smell of damp. On the landing was a door with a panel of frosted glass displaying the words:

A. COLLINS BRAITHWAITE

The name caused me an involuntary shudder, and I suddenly doubted the wisdom of my undertaking. Up to this point, it had seemed little more than a game, but it now took on an altogether darker hue. I could hear the clack of a typewriter from within, a reassuringly familiar sound. I knocked and entered a small anteroom. A woman a little younger than myself looked up from behind a desk. She was blonde and wearing a well-laundered white blouse. Her blue eyes were mascaraed, and she wore a pale pink shade of lipstick. I felt mortified by my dishevelled state, before reminding myself that she must be accustomed to such sights.

'Hullo,' she said cheerfully. 'You must be Miss Smyth?'

'Yes. With a Y,' I said redundantly. She did not seem the least disconcerted by my slatternly appearance, and invited me to take a seat. Three mismatched wooden chairs were lined up against the wall beneath the window and there was a table with copies of *Punch* and *Private Eye*. I sat down and crossed my legs in an attempt to conceal the hole in my stocking.

'It's so maddening when that happens,' she said. 'Only yesterday, I laddered a brand new pair.'

I feigned ignorance and then looked down at my knee. 'Oh, I hadn't noticed,' I said. 'How very tiresome!'

'I keep a spare pair in my desk. You're welcome to them if you wish. You can replace them on your next visit.' She widened her eyes enquiringly.

Her suggestion struck me as inappropriately chummy. Perhaps too, her make-up was rather overdone. My mother had had a sliding scale of epithets reserved for women she judged to be excessively embellished: painted lady, Jezebel, harlot and (when she thought my sister and I were out of earshot) whore. She herself never wore a scrap of make-up, nor did she approve of any clothing that might enhance rather than detract from one's figure. 'Have you ever heard of a man eating the shell and leaving the yolk?' she liked to proclaim. My mother's pronouncements only served to ignite a curiosity in me. Whenever a woman was labelled a Jezebel, this epithet was invariably directed at the most alluring woman in the room. Heaven help my father if his gaze inadvertently fell on such a creature. The designation of 'whore' was generally reserved for French actresses, who were doubly damned by virtue of being both actresses *and* French. It was thus with a certain illicit pleasure that when I started earning a few shillings as a Saturday girl at Clark's, I was able to buy lipsticks and rouge. I would position a chair beneath the handle of my bedroom door and spend evenings transforming myself into just such a Jezebel. I would then amuse myself in front of the mirror, transfixed by my scarlet lips and whorishly painted cheeks.

I politely declined the receptionist's offer and picked up a copy of *Punch*. I turned a few pages, then let the magazine fall open in my lap and gazed blankly into space. It would not do, I supposed, to have any interest in the goings-on of the world. I was supposed to be *déprimé*. The least I could do was to affect a vacant look. No doubt Miss Spare-Stockings would later report her impressions of me to her employer. She resumed her typing. I have always enjoyed the clack and ping of the typewriter. The current practitioner's technique was sadly lacking, however, and I concluded that in accordance with the unhappy tendency of our age, she had been employed more for her looks than her clerical skills.

I concentrated my attention on the wall above the receptionist's desk. It was decorated with an innocuous floral design, presumably intended to calm the restive souls who weekly passed a few minutes gazing at it. After a short time, however, I noticed that, seven or eight feet from the floor, there was a small tear in the wallpaper, the size of a man's thumbnail. The tear was folded over like a dog's ear, revealing the lining paper beneath. This was odd. Had the tear occurred while the wallpaper was being hung, it was inconceivable that the tradesman would not have had sufficient pride in his work to repair it. Perhaps it is a reflection of my lack of imagination, but I could think of no scenario that would have precipitated such a tear occurring at a later date. In any case, the curling paper tongue began to vex me, to the extent that I felt a tightening in my throat. My breathing became shallow and I was glad I had removed my neckerchief. I had an urge to suggest to the receptionist that we might attempt to patch it up. If she was resourceful enough to keep a pair of stockings in her desk drawer, she would certainly also have some Copydex or Sellotape in there, and the tear could be easily reached if one of us were to stand on her desk. There being a limit, however, to how eccentric I wished to appear, I kept schtum.

It came as a welcome distraction when the door to Dr Braithwaite's office opened and a woman of about thirty emerged. She was slim and wearing a knee-length cashmere dress. Her hair was dark brown and artfully styled. She did not to my eye seem in need of any sort of psychiatric treatment. Quite the contrary. She retrieved a fur coat from the stand by the door and unhurriedly put it on. She did not appear remotely ashamed to be seen in a shrink's office. She glanced towards me, but I maintained my catatonic expression. As she left she said: 'Goodbye, Daisy.'

The receptionist replied in a cheerful tone: 'See you on Thursday, Miss Kepler.'

I was taken aback that a woman of such apparent poise required not one, but two visits per week. She must have been a serious case, yet if one were to see her in the street, one would look upon her with envy.

I stood up, but Daisy told me that Dr Braithwaite would be ready to see me in a few minutes. I glanced at my watch. My stomach tingled, but, as my mother would have pointed out, I had made my own bed. Now I must sleep in it. A few minutes later, without any apparent communication from within, Daisy indicated that I could enter.

The great panjandrum was sitting behind a desk scribbling in a notebook. How I would have loved to read what was written there! After a few moments, he looked up, noisily closed his book and rose to greet me. He was wearing a flannel shirt, open at the neck, and brown corduroy trousers. On his feet, he wore a pair of brown brogues, the laces undone.

'Miss Smyth!' he said cheerfully. 'Or is it Mrs?' He stepped across the room with his hand outstretched. We shook hands and I informed him that it was 'Miss'. His features were not half as repellent as they appeared on television. His eyes were bulbous but, *dans la vraie vie*, alert and twinkling. He also seemed younger, but they say that television puts ten years and ten pounds on everyone.

'Take a seat, any seat you like,' he said, in the manner of a magician asking a member of the audience to select a card. The consulting room resembled a rather cluttered lounge or, perhaps more accurately, a man's 'den'. The walls behind the desk and by the door were lined with books. Further books and papers were piled untidily on the floor. The windows overlooking the street were dripping with condensation. The only suggestion of a professional environment was a green metal filing cabinet, the top drawer of which gaped open. I resisted the urge to march across the room and close it. The selection of seating consisted of a tatty leather armchair, an uninviting wicker wingback and a settee with a rayon throw over the back. I felt a chill when I realised that this must be the settee upon which Braithwaite had described Veronica languidly reclining (an action that would have been wholly out of character, for my sister never did anything 'languidly' in her life). In the centre of the room was a coffee table on which there was an unemptied ashtray, a carved wooden cigarette case and a box of tissues. It crossed my mind to go and sit behind his desk, just to provoke him, but I did not do so. Instead, I took a seat on the right of the settee. Braithwaite nodded, as if this was exactly where he had predicted I would sit. He took the wooden chair from behind his desk and sat opposite me. He stretched out his legs and crossed them at the ankle. He was not wearing any socks. He folded his arms across his paunch.

'You find us all right?' he asked.

I nodded. His complexion was mottled, and a little grey had begun to appear about his temples. He was forty years old and had I been asked to guess his age that is exactly what I would have said.

'So Miss Smyth,' he began, in a tone suggesting that we would now be getting down to business, 'what brings you here?' He waited without impatience for me to respond. His eyes wandered from my tousled hair to my shoes. As they passed the ladder in my stockings a tiny movement of an eyebrow betrayed his surprise, and I felt that the sacrifice of 10/- had not been in vain.

'I'm not sure I know where to begin,' I said vaguely.

He unfolded his arms and spread his hands. 'Why not begin with what led you to make this appointment?'

'Yes,' I said. I realised that he must be very used to dealing with peculiar behaviour. It was, after all, inevitable in his line of work. A normal person would, for example, feel that he must make best use of his time in Dr Braithwaite's office, to make sure he got his value for money. But then, a normal person would not be here in the first place.

'Perhaps I would like it better if you called me Rebecca,' I said.

'As you wish,' he replied. 'And what would you like to call me?' He paused for a moment, before elaborating some options. 'There is "Dr Braithwaite", if you want to keep things on a formal footing, or just "Braithwaite" if you prefer. My mother called me "Arthur", my friends call me "Collins", and my enemies call me—well, we won't go into that.' He laughed at his own joke. I expect this was all a routine intended to put me at my ease. Or lower my guard. 'So, what'll it be?'

He had a curious lop-sided way of speaking.

'Well, I suppose if you are going to call me "Rebecca", then I should call you "Arthur",' I said. I glanced down at my hands, which were then resting in my lap. I had varnished my nails the previous evening and their well-manicured state must have seemed at odds with the rest of my appearance. This was good. How mad to take such care over one's nails and yet leave the house in a pair of laddered stockings. Men cannot usually be counted on to notice such things, but I already had the impression that nothing would elude Dr Braithwaite. I regretted electing to call him 'Arthur'. It suggested an inappropriate intimacy. Nor did I want him to think that I wished to associate myself with his mother, or to adopt a maternal bearing towards him. Nothing could have been further from the truth. I have never had a maternal craving in my life. I loathe children, with their sticky faces, scabby knees and noise (always their infernal noise). And that is to say nothing of the horrifying matter of giving birth, or the filthy business of copulation.

Braithwaite nodded. 'So, Rebecca?'

His tone was perfectly amiable (it was not his money after all), but I realised that I had to say something. Only a proper nut would visit a psychiatrist and pretend there was nothing wrong with them.

'I've been feeling…' I here cast my eyes about the room, as if searching for the right word. 'I've been *experiencing* a sense of malaise,' I said. 'An intense feeling of malaise.' I was rather pleased with this phrase.

'Ah, malaise!' Braithwaite repeated. 'From the French *mal à l'aise*: ill at ease. Well, I can't say I blame you, Rebecca. With everything that's going on in the world, who wouldn't feel ill at ease? I feel bloody ill at ease myself.'

'It's rather more than that,' I said. 'I suppose I feel I've rather lost myself.'

This seemed to delight him. He leapt up from his chair and theatrically began throwing aside cushions. He got down on his hands and knees and looked under the settee. He opened the door and called to Daisy: 'Did Miss Smyth leave her self out here? No?' He slammed the door shut without waiting for an answer, and turned to me. 'Perhaps it's in that handbag of yours?' he said. 'Always been a mystery to me, the contents of a woman's handbag. Far more so than the contents of your minds, ha ha.' He took my bag from the floor. I was terrified for a moment that he was going to find the dead mouse wrapped in tissue paper. But he merely handed it to me and gestured for me to look inside. 'Not in there?' he asked, as I obediently opened the clasp and gazed inside.

He sat down, adopting a puzzled expression. 'Let's think,' he said. 'This self of yours, can you remember when you last had it?'

I rather felt that he was making fun of me, and said so.

'Not at all, Rebecca. It's a serious thing, a lost self. And my question is a serious one: when do think you last had it?'

I had only been in Dr Braithwaite's presence for a few minutes, but I could already see that he was the kind of man who inspired admiration. His unkempt appearance only underlined the fact. He had no need for the suit and tie that other men use to bolster their authority. He had that mysterious thing which is so often discussed but so rarely encountered: charisma. It was clear that Collins Braithwaite could bend you in whatever direction he desired. It was at once terrifying and thrilling. I could see why Miss Kepler would wish to spend two hours a week in his company.

'I'm not sure I could say,' I said in answer to his question.

'Well, not to worry,' he replied cheerfully. 'If it had been a half decent self, you wouldn't have lost it, would you? You're probably best off without it.'

I did not know what to say to this. If he had set out to bamboozle me, he had succeeded admirably.

The remainder of the hour was spent with me telling him something about myself, or rather, about Rebecca. Rebecca and I had much in common, but in order to conceal my relationship with Veronica, it was necessary to alter certain details. (I should perhaps here point out that I do not in the least resemble my sister. She was dark, like my mother, with thick ankles and, if I may say so, rather lumpen features. I daresay I am no beauty, but my own features are rather fine. I was Joan Fontaine to Veronica's Mrs Danvers.) There is a time for the whole truth, but this was decidedly not it. To this end, I told Dr Braithwaite that my mother had passed away and I now lived with my father, a retired architect. Rebecca, I had decided, must be an only child (always so dreadfully lonely), but like me, she had a silly receptionist's job at a theatrical agency.

Braithwaite did not question me much about any of this. Indeed, when I reflected on it afterwards, he did not question me much about anything. It just streamed out of me. Afterwards I felt rather mortified that I had sat there prattling on about myself as if I were quite the most fascinating woman in London. But he never once glanced at his wristwatch. His attention did not wander from you for a moment. I had never before felt under such scrutiny. I remember little else of the conversation, only that it took an intense effort of will to feel that I was holding my own. I quite forgot the true purpose of my visit. I realised that I wanted to please him. At a certain point, he simply stood up, and it was as if a spell had been broken. I took this to indicate that the session was over. I felt that I had been in a trance and I wondered for a moment if he had hypnotised me. I gathered up my things and stood up. My legs felt a little weak.

Braithwaite was standing in the no-man's-land between the door and the settee. As I made my way towards the exit, he angled his body in such a way that I felt compelled to stop. We stood in uncomfortably close proximity. Although he had neither laid a hand on me nor attached any shackles, I felt suddenly captive.

'It's been interesting to meet you, Rebecca,' he said. 'If you would like to come again, make an appointment with Daisy.'

I was bemused. 'But what do you think?' I said. 'Do you think I should come back?'

Braithwaite threw up his hands, as if he were tossing pennies to an urchin. 'It's up to you.'

'But do you think you can help me?' I persisted.

'The question is not whether *I* think I can help you. The question is whether you think I can help you.' He looked at me with his goggly eyes. I felt rather helpless.

'I thought perhaps you might be able to cure me,' I said quietly.

He gave a little laugh through his nose. 'Miss Smyth, *Rebecca*, we are not in the business of "cures" here. Cures are for quacks, and Christ knows enough folk that think I'm one of those already. In the first place, the idea of a cure presupposes there is something wrong with you, something we have yet to establish. And in the second place, if there is something wrong with you, I doubt if it's curable.'

'But if I can't be cured, what's the point in coming back?' I said.

'That's a question for you rather than me,' he replied. 'If anything, the fact that you think there might be something wrong with you already suggests you're a good deal saner than most people.'

He took the smallest step to the side, thus authorising my exit, and I made for the door. In the anteroom, I made a new appointment. Daisy wrote my name in the ledger on her desk and said in a low voice: 'We'll see you next week then.'

Perhaps it was her use of the word 'we', or perhaps it was her conspiratorial manner, but I felt as if I had been initiated into some sort of indecent club.

Outside I paused and examined the rusting paint of a lamp-post, tipping my head this way and that, as if discerning mysterious patterns in it. I assumed Dr Braithwaite would be spying on me from his window. If I were a psychiatrist, I would certainly watch my patients leave. I do believe I would make a rather good psychiatrist. Father says I have a talent for identifying other people's flaws.

I remained for some moments fingering the paintwork, my face inches from the lamp-post, then took an emery board from my handbag and started sanding a section of the metal. How mad Braithwaite would think I was. 'Poor creature,' I imagined him thinking. 'She tried so hard to seem normal.' Perhaps he would even call Daisy over to the window: 'Take a look at this. We've got a right nutcase on our hands here.' After a while I stood back to scrutinise my handiwork, before nodding as though satisfied with the results, and put away the emery board. I walked with an awkward lurching gait to the end of the street. Once round the corner, and having checked that I was not being followed, I straightened my posture. I was relieved to be myself again. I congratulated myself on my performance. Rebecca, I felt, had acquitted herself well.

I found myself on a busy road, circumscribing a park. It is my habit—an idiosyncrasy perhaps—never to return home by the same route as I left. There is something about retracing my steps that makes me feel I am getting tangled up in myself. When I think of Theseus finding his way out of the labyrinth with his ball of thread, I always imagine his feet, then his legs and entire body, becoming ensnared, so that he is finally bound from head to foot and unable to move. So I found myself at the opposite end of Ainger Road from which I had arrived. It may seem curious but I had never before visited Primrose Hill and it had never crossed my mind that there was actually a hill there. The name seems so unLondony, more like a village in Devon or some other tedious, bucolic idyll (I loathe the countryside). But there it was: Primrose Hill. I followed the road around the park until I came to a gate.

It was around quarter to six and the sky had darkened. There was a constant growl of traffic, which made the hill seem to throb. It was like a swollen belly waiting to burst and spew forth some subterraneous pus. I felt drawn towards it. The few other figures in the park were evenly spaced, as if they had been positioned for my benefit. On the path leading towards the summit, a man walked with a black dog on a lead. Both had the resigned gait of those climbing the scaffold. I followed the path skirting the foot of the hill. The tarmac was wet from the earlier drizzle. In the gloomy twilight, the grass appeared silver. Everything was off-kilter. The horizon was in the wrong place. The hill loomed over me. I had an urge to fold myself up like a piece of paper.

I came across an object at the edge of the footpath. It was about six feet in length and consisted of four painted planks of wood. The first two were parallel to the ground at a height of about two feet, while the third and fourth were positioned at right angles to these. The structure was secured by a wrought iron carapace, consisting of four legs and two struts, these attaching the third and fourth planks to the pair parallel to the ground. Between the pairs of legs there was further ironwork; this, I suppose, to provide rigidity. Of course, I knew it to be a bench. I have seen and sat on a great many benches in my time. But at that moment it appeared to me a squat, malevolent thing, like a cockroach, or a crab lying in wait to pounce on some unsuspecting prey before scuttling into the bushes to gobble it up. I stood in front of it for a minute or longer. It did not scuttle away. It was just a bench. As if to test my conviction, I sat down on it. I placed my bag at my feet and my hand on the planks by my hips. The paint was rough on my palms. I took a series of long slow breaths. I could feel London pulsing into my body. I closed my eyes and listened to the rumble of the city. Then I lifted my feet and lay face down with my arms by my sides. The blistered wood pressed upwards against my thighs and chest. I felt the cracked paintwork against my lips. I touched it hesitantly with the tip of my tongue. The taste was bitter and metallic. The wood smelt like damp forest earth. The throbbing of the city grew more intense. I felt the bench lifting me and we began to soar high above the metropolis. I kept my eyes tightly closed and gripped the sides. The lights and streets of London were far below. We swooped and banked in slow arcs. It was exhilarating. I do not know how long the flight lasted, some minutes certainly. Then I heard a voice and felt that I was being roused from a deep sleep. I opened my eyes. A man loomed over me.

'Are you all right, Miss?' he said. His tone had an urgency suggesting it was not the first time he had asked.

I struggled into a sitting position. There was a black dog, a Labrador, by the man's side. Perhaps it was the same man I had seen earlier. He had a concerned expression on his face.

'Of course I'm all right,' I said. 'Why shouldn't I be?'

He gestured towards the bench, as if this constituted adequate explanation for his concern. 'Someone might've been off with your purse.'

That much was true. 'Yes, you're quite right,' I said. 'Thank you.'

I picked up my bag and placed it on my lap. The man nodded and wished me good evening. I remained on the bench until he had disappeared from sight.

Naturally, I had missed supper, which is served at six o'clock in our household. Mrs Llewelyn served me wordlessly and stood with her behind resting on the sideboard, watching me eat. She had not troubled to reheat the soup. She was trying to provoke me, but I drained every last drop. She waited a few moments before removing my bowl and returning with a plate of roast pork, which had been kept warm in the oven. The three stems of broccoli—a vegetable I dislike at the best of times—were the colour of hospital walls. The gravy had the flaky appearance of dried blood on a sheet. Thankfully, Mrs Llewelyn did not stand over me as I ate my main course. I chewed a few mouthfuls of meat and emptied the remains into my handbag. I would dispose of it later in the lavatory. When Mrs Llewelyn returned, she was unable to conceal her surprise that I had polished off such an unappetising dish. This constituted a victory. My reward was a bowl of blancmange with tinned mandarins. Blancmange is a favourite dish of mine. It requires no effort of mastication. I like to hold a spoonful on my tongue, before letting it slip down my throat, imagining it to be a little ship sliding from its mooring into the open sea. The segments of mandarin I left untouched, there being something obscene in their form and texture.

I fled the dining room before Mrs Llewelyn returned and went into the parlour. Father looked up from his copy of *The Times* and smiled his gentle smile.

'Good evening, Daddy,' I said.

I am aware that it is mawkish for a woman of my age to address her father as 'Daddy', but no sinister interpretation should be put on this. It is merely a habit I have never broken, and were I to do so now, I would feel that I was making some kind of statement; that I was somehow asserting a distance between us. There is, moreover, no satisfactory alternative. 'Dad' has always struck me as dreadfully plebeian, a flat grey syllable in the mouth. 'Father' is excessively formal when spoken; and the idea of addressing him by his Christian name is simply vulgar. We are not, thank heavens, all Americans yet.

'Ah, there you are,' he said. 'We were worried about you, my dear.'

I loathe it when my father refers to himself and Mrs Llewelyn as 'we', as if they are some kind of single entity. It was, in any case, poppycock to suggest that Mrs Llewelyn would be worried about my whereabouts. Nothing, I am sure, would please her more than for a policeman to call with the news that I had been run over by an omnibus.

'Out with a young man, were you?' He was teasing me, but I masked any slight I felt. I replied that Mr Brownlee had required me for a late meeting. I liked to pretend that I was indispensable, but, in reality, any cretin with a typewriter could do my job. Father expressed the hope that Mr Brownlee was paying me overtime. I sat down in the plaid upholstered armchair opposite him.

His eyes returned to the newspaper on his lap. He was doing the crossword. I enjoy the moments we spend together in the evening. We have little to say to each other, but the silence between us is comfortable. Even so, I know that I am a disappointment to him. Veronica was his favourite. I daresay he did his best to conceal this; even sometimes favouring me over her, but he looked at her in a way that he never does at me. Since her death, all the energy has drained out of him. Despite my efforts to jolly him along, it quite floored him. Naturally, the word 'suicide' is never uttered in his presence. Veronica had an accident. To suggest otherwise would be to besmirch her.

Father's condition had been brought on when he contracted malaria in India. He was an engineer, and he and my mother had moved to Calcutta shortly after their marriage. Father was to supervise the building of the Howrah Bridge over the Hooghly River. Veronica was born there and because of her dark colouring, Father liked to call her his 'little Indian'. Mother hated Calcutta and had been pleased when father's illness precipitated their return to England. They made the journey home in 1940, while she was expecting me, so I suppose there is a little part of India in me too. Mother never tired of telling me that she didn't know what was worse on the voyage, the sea-sickness or the morning sickness. For the rest of her life she blamed everything on India; if she saw a man in a turban in the street, she would turn her face away or put her handkerchief to her nose.

I asked Father if I could help with his crossword.

'I'm afraid I'm rather stuck,' he said. He read out a clue.

'Claptrap,' I said. This was a little joke between us. Whenever he recited a crossword clue, I replied with this word.

'It's nine letters, dear, second one A, seventh one A.' He repeated: 'Limb stuck in sick French jam', as if every syllable was of momentous significance. He had explained the arcane code of crosswords to me a hundred times, but he might just as well have been speaking Bengali. The solving of puzzles had always seemed to me the most futile of pursuits. On a winter's evening Father and Veronica would often spend hours bent over a jigsaw puzzle. The picture—invariably of a stately home or a railway station—was printed on the lid of the box. Why spend hours putting all the pieces together when you could already see the solution? Whenever I expressed this view, they would roll their eyes despairingly, before silently continuing to sort and sift the pieces. Once, when they were out of the room, I palmed three pieces of a puzzle and dropped them down a drain on the way to school the following day. Afterwards, when they discovered the puzzle was incomplete, I felt dreadfully ashamed. Neither of them ever accused me of taking the pieces, but I suspect they knew I was the guilty party.

Father supplemented his pension by writing books about bridges. On our return to England he had written the first, *Great Bridges of India*, to amuse himself. When it was finished he planned to publish it as a monograph but was surprised when he was approached by a publisher, who assured him that there was a market for that sort of thing. The book was something of a success and, after considerable cajoling, Father produced a series of similar volumes: *Great Bridges of Africa*, *Great Bridges of the Americas* and so on. Among bridge enthusiasts, he became something of a celebrity. He is, naturally, self-deprecating about this success. Until recently he gave occasional lectures to civil engineering societies. These talks—to which as girls Veronica and I were often taken along—took place in wood-panelled committee rooms or church halls and were attended exclusively by white-haired men in blazers and tweeds. The only woman who had ever read any of his books, he claimed with a certain pride, was Veronica. His talks all began in the same way: The difference between an engineer and a poet was that for an engineer, a bridge was a question of mathematics; for a poet, it was a symbol. He was an engineer, he would go on, and for him there was poetry in mathematics. This sentiment was invariably greeted with murmured approval, sometimes even a smattering of applause, and I enjoyed seeing my father smile modestly and cast his eyes towards the floor in acknowledgement of this acclaim. In recent years, however, his health has precluded such activities. The two flights of stairs to our residence have become an ordeal. He swears every book will be his last. He is, in any case, running out of continents.

'Marmalade!' he suddenly proclaimed. 'Arm: limb. Stuck in *malade*: "sick" in French. You see?'

'Oh yes, of course,' I said.

He wrote in the answer and began to read out the next clue. I got up and kissed him on the cheek and said that I was going to bed. Our flat is over two floors. On the lower level is the entrance hall, kitchen, scullery, dining room, sitting room, my father's study and a WC. On the upper floor, under the eaves of the building, are the three bedrooms, a box room and the bathroom. Mrs Llewelyn occupies what was once Veronica's room. My own boudoir is between this and my father's room. Mrs Llewelyn is under strict instructions never to enter, but I keep the door locked and carry the key in my handbag. At night, I leave the door ajar to make sure there is no funny business between the two of them. My laundry I leave in a wicker basket outside my door.

I changed into my nightdress and removed what was left of my make-up in front of the dressing table mirror. Tiny lines had appeared at the corners of my eyes. I stretched the skin with my fingers to make them disappear. I was turning into an old crone. I resolved to eat more fresh fruit and vegetables.

Braithwaite I: Early Life

ARTHUR COLLINS BRAITHWAITE WAS BORN in Darlington on 4th February 1925. His father, George John Braithwaite, was a successful local businessman. George was born in 1892 and came from a family of railway workers. Like his forebears, he was stocky and barrel-chested. Photographs show a good-looking young man with a shock of unruly hair and intense dark eyes. He survived two years at Verdun in the First World War, before being injured by shrapnel in 1917 and sent to a clinic in Sussex to recuperate. It was here that he met Alice Louise Collins, who was employed as a nurse.

Alice was the daughter of the vicar in the nearby village of Etchingham. She was a pretty but unworldly girl of twenty, with soft brown eyes and fair hair. George entertained her with stories of his adventures at the front and of growing up in 'Darlo'. They must have seemed an odd couple—he the voluble Northerner, she the reserved Home Counties girl—but on Alice's days off they took to walking in the surrounding countryside. George made a full recovery and, the night before he was sent back to the Front, he proposed. Alice was too timid to either accept or decline. George had not even met her father. 'But who would not approve of me?' George retorted. As it turned out, the war ended only a few weeks later and George presented himself, still in uniform, at the vicarage in Etchingham. He was canny enough to play the deferential future son-in-law, taking tea and playing down his achievements during the war (he had been thrice commended for valour), and soon he had his answer. The couple were married by Alice's father at the local church six weeks later.

The newlyweds returned to Darlington and rented a red-brick, two-up-two-down terraced house on Cartmell Terrace. George opened an ironmonger's in Clark's Yard, but within two years had moved into larger premises on the busy thoroughfare of Skinnergate. He proved to be an astute businessman and would later open branches of Braithwaite's in Durham, Hartlepool and Middlesbrough. For the first four years of his life, Arthur slept in a crib in his parents' bedroom. He claimed precocious memories of these early years. The house, he would later write, was 'all darkness, cold and damp' and at night he would pretend to sleep while his father grunted bestially in the bed next to him. He longed to climb into bed with his mother, but was afraid of the 'monster' that lay next to her.

Arthur was the youngest of three sons, the others being George Jnr (born 1919) and Edward or 'Teddy' (born 1920 and named after Alice's father). By the time Arthur was ready to start school, the family had moved into a semi-detached house on Westlands Road, on the edge of the affluent neighbourhood of Cockerton. Here Arthur had his own room, overlooking the small back garden. George never tired of reminding anyone who would listen that, despite his lowly origins, he was now a 'man of property'. He joined the local Chamber of Commerce and the Conservative Club, even standing as their candidate in the General Elections of 1931 and 1935.

Alice found it hard to adjust to life in Darlington. Her reserved nature made it hard to make friends. George was occupied with his various shops from morning to night, and on Sundays would take his three sons on long hikes on the nearby North York Moors. Alice, whose life in Etchingham had revolved around church activities, village fêtes and the tranquil pursuits of reading and letter writing, found the rugged landscapes and rough accents of the North intimidating. In a letter to her sister, composed some months after her marriage, she wrote: 'Everything is so dark here. I feel like a sparrow amongst a murder of crows.' George, who was relentlessly energetic and cheerful, grew impatient of his wife's introverted nature. 'You want to get yourself out and about, lass,' he would tell her. The very things that had attracted Alice to him in the first place must have come to seem a reproach.

George refused ever to take a holiday. His customers, he insisted, would take their business elsewhere and never return. Twice a year, however, Alice travelled south to see her family. Over the years, these sojourns became more and more lengthy. In the summer of 1935, her father suffered a stroke, leaving him bed-ridden, and Alice used this as an excuse to prolong her stay. She never returned. Ten-year-old Arthur felt her absence keenly, but his father treated the development with typical pragmatism. A live-in housekeeper, Mrs McKay, was engaged and to all intents and purposes, the routine of the household continued unchanged.

The five-year gap between Arthur and his two brothers meant that he was never close to them. George Jr and Teddy were inseparable and showed little interest in their younger sibling. If Arthur tagged along on a fishing trip or a Saturday afternoon jaunt 'into town', his brothers took every opportunity to let him know that he was an unwelcome burden. By 1935, the older boys had left school and were employed in what was now proudly called Braithwaite & Sons. Alice wrote numerous letters begging for Arthur to be allowed to visit her during school holidays, but George Snr would not countenance the idea. 'If she's so desperate to see you, she can bloody well get on a train herself.' Other than that, the matter was never discussed. Arthur, for his part, did not dispute his father's decision, but at night he sobbed into his pillow, simultaneously longing for his mother and angry with her for abandoning him.

Arthur had been born with lenticular astigmatism and from an early age wore thick glasses. For a while he was mercilessly bullied, but a certain devil-may-care attitude meant that he was not averse to taking on his tormentors, and after numerous pairs of broken spectacles, he was left alone. Like his mother, though, he found it difficult to make friends and became something of a loner. He turned to books, enjoying W.E. Johns' Biggles stories and other tales of derring-do. Years later, when he saw Hugh Edwards' portrayal of Piggy in Peter Brook's 1963 film of *Lord of the Flies*, he would comment that he felt that he had been watching his childhood self: 'a hopeless misfit, trying to reason with those who are uninterested in reason'. It's an unflattering self-appraisal. In reality, aside from his bottle-bottom glasses, photographs show quite a handsome little boy, with features too mature for his age. It was not until his late teens that he began to grow into them.

In common with many self-made men, George Braithwaite had little time for formal education, but Arthur did well at school. If he was unable to compete on the football pitch or the athletics field, he could at least excel in the classroom. He enjoyed seeing playground bullies humiliated by their inability to read rudimentary sentences or perform long division. His identity became tied up with being brainy. He was the first of the three brothers to attend grammar school. At the age of twelve, for the first time, Arthur was conscious of stepping out of his brothers' shadow; of becoming a 'person in himself'. If his father took any pride in his son's academic achievements, he did not show it. School reports were given a cursory glance and dismissed with the comment that 'none of this will mean owt when you come to work for me'. Such comments only redoubled Arthur's determination to forge his own course in life. But for the time being, there was no alternative to spending his

Saturdays working in his father's Skinnergate shop. This did at least provide him with a small income and during the summer holiday of 1939 he saved enough to take a train first to London, then onto Hastings, from where he hitched the thirteen miles to Etchingham. His mother, upon seeing him at the back door of the vicarage, dropped to her knees and started to weep. Arthur, unused to such displays of emotion, merely stood and watched. The outburst, he would later write, embarrassed him. 'I suppose I had not known what to expect. I had not yet developed the capacity to see the world from another person's point of view.' As his mother, still from a kneeling position, embraced him, he felt 'that she was not embracing me, but a version of myself that no longer existed'. Still, there was something in the smell of her hair that returned Arthur to his former self and for the duration of his stay he 'played the baby', as he sensed that this was how his mother wished him to be. It was, he said, 'pleasurable to revert to childish ways and not pretend, as I did under my father's roof, that I was impervious to the slights that came my way. It was only then that I understood that at home I had also been playing a role.'

Arthur found his mother much changed. She had always been slim, but now she was no more than skin and bone. She was often distracted and forgetful. These lapses upset her and she would witter admonishments to herself and chastise inanimate objects for not being in their proper place. Reverend Collins had died two years previously. Alice had not communicated this news to her estranged husband, presumably because it would have put paid to her ostensible justification for remaining in Etchingham.

When Arthur returned to Darlington, his father sacked him from his job at the shop. Arthur was untroubled by this. Now that he had seen his mother, he had little need of money. He borrowed books from the public library on Crown Street and spent his time reading in the Denes, an area of parkland adjoining Cocker Beck, a few minutes' walk from Westlands Road. It was a blissful and innocent summer, brought to an end by the outbreak of war in September. George Jr and Teddy enlisted immediately. Arthur was called up in 1943 but was exempted from active service on the basis of his poor eyesight. Instead, he saw out the war as an orderly in the medical corps. Teddy was killed on Gold Beach during the Normandy landings on 6th June 1944. Both Georges seemed to hold this against Arthur, as if by not seeing active service himself he was somehow to blame for his brother's death.

After the war, and to his father's displeasure, Arthur took up a scholarship to read philosophy at Oxford. He chose philosophy for no other reason than because its abstract nature represented the antithesis of his father's Northern pragmatism. Unsurprisingly, he did not fit in among the Eton and Harrow boys. It was here that he first began to use his middle name. 'Arthur Braithwaite' was incurably Northern. 'Collins Braithwaite', he thought, had a certain gravitas. Arthur made a conscious effort to lengthen his flat County Durham vowels and began to smoke a pipe, rather than the Woodbines he had grown up with. It was all affectation, of course, but in it he found a certain liberation. At Oxford he could be whatever, or whomever, he chose. He realised that the person he thought he had been was no more than a construct. You could not separate an individual from the environment they found themselves in, or the people they interacted with. His identity up to that point—or what he thought of as his identity—was no more than a reaction to his upbringing, and reading philosophy no more than a shallow attempt to differentiate himself from his father.

His first tutor was Isaiah Berlin. For the duration of the first semester, Berlin treated him indulgently, perhaps impressed by his native intelligence and fearlessness. At the beginning of the Hilary term, however, Braithwaite presented him with an essay on Descartes. After only a few sentences, Berlin laid into him: his thinking was sloppy and unsystematic; he was expressing his own unsupported thoughts rather than paying sufficient attention to the text. It was presumably a well-intentioned attempt to push his pupil to the next level, but Braithwaite did not react well. Perhaps Berlin's criticisms echoed those of his father. Or perhaps he was simply too pig-headed to listen. Growing up believing that he was a solitary genius, he had not developed the maturity to have his ideas challenged. It was the beginning of the end of his first crack at academia. Over the following months, he singularly failed to adapt to the idea that, as a first-year student, he was not yet expected to entertain original thoughts. Or maybe, more disturbingly, he was more like his father than he liked to believe, and the kind of abstract thinking required for the study of philosophy did not come easily to him. In any case, after struggling on for a year and half, he dropped out. Braithwaite did not confess this humiliation to his father. He went first to London and took a series of menial jobs.

Then, in 1948, he joined the itinerant gangs in France following the grape harvest. After the rarefied atmosphere of Oxford, he enjoyed the physical labour and the camaraderie between the workers. He picked up French and enjoyed the easy-going sexual milieu. Until that time, he would write, his sexual experiences had been solitary ones, followed 'not by a post-coital cigarette but by waves of guilt and the fear of being "found out"'. In France, no one seemed to mind if they came across a couple copulating behind a hedgerow or in an outbuilding. 'It was only after I returned to England,' he wrote with some disappointment, 'that I discovered that sex was supposed to take place indoors.' But, return to England he did.

He took a job at the British Army facility in Netley, near Southampton, where he had served during the war. Once a sprawling complex housing 2,500 beds, it was now reduced to accommodating psychologically scarred veterans. The regime was the stuff of nightmares. Inmates were kept in insulin-induced comas. For fear of provoking epileptic seizures, the wards were kept in darkness, necessitating the doctors to wear head torches. Staff were not permitted to talk to patients, and vice versa.

It was here that Braithwaite first encountered the Scottish psychiatrist R.D. Laing. Laing remembers nothing of their encounters—there was no reason that he should—but he made a lasting impression on the young orderly. Until then, Braithwaite had unthinkingly accepted that 'the mad were mad, and the men in white coats knew best and had their best interests at heart'. But observing Laing at work changed all that: 'He did not act like a doctor; he did not move like a doctor; he did not even sound like a doctor.' Laing's approach was, indeed, radical. He spoke to the patients as equals, even soliciting their opinions about their treatment; in short, treating them as individuals rather than as living corpses devoid of free will. Netley was a formative experience for both Laing and Braithwaite. Laing would later write: 'I was beginning to suspect that insulin and electric shocks, not to mention lobotomy and the whole environment of a psychiatric unit, were ways of destroying people and driving people crazy.'

For Braithwaite, Netley was where 'I came to see that I was not employed as an orderly in a hospital, but as a warder in a prison where the inmates—none of whom were guilty of any crime—were held under conditions that would drive the sanest man mad.'

Laing left Netley in 1953. Braithwaite hung on for a few more months but found that the conditions had begun to affect his own mental health. He suffered nightmares in which he was convinced he had become an inmate of his own workplace. He began to find bright outdoor spaces oppressive and menacing. His experiences inspired him to return to Oxford, where he was allowed to take up a place on the course in psychology, philosophy and physiology, which had been established within the Institute of Experimental Psychology in 1947. His studies enabled him to see his own relationships in a fresh light. In his memoir *My Self and Other Strangers*, he wrote: 'My father relayed his wartime experiences as if they were *Boy's Own* adventures, shells crashing here and there—KA-BOOM!—men blown limb from limb; knee-deep in mud, blood and entrails; bullets whistling hither-thither. But I never doubted, even as a small boy, that all this bravado was a mask, papering over the trauma he had suffered, and that his inability to sit still—to *be* still—was a kind of flight from the demons that pursued him.'

On his sixty-fifth birthday, George Braithwaite drove his Jaguar Mark VII to the North York Moors, drank a pint of bitter and a whisky at the Buck Inn, Chop Gate, before driving the four miles to Fangdale Beck, where he shot himself in the mouth with an Enfield No.2 his son had brought back from the war. He did not leave a note. George Jnr immediately sold the family business and within five years, had drunk himself to death. Even after ten years, Braithwaite could find no compassion for his brother: 'He was a bully, who realised too late he had nailed his flag to the mast of a sinking ship.'

Braithwaite continued to visit his mother at irregular intervals over the years. Alice had moved in with her sister and appeared contented, but as time passed she remembered less and less of her son. She often took to her bed for days or weeks on end. Eventually, she did not recognise Arthur at all and he discontinued his visits. If he was distressed by this, he did not show it. 'My mother was, to all intents and purposes, dead. If someone else now inhabited what had once been her body, what concern was it of mine?' Alice died in 1960. Despite his aunt's entreaties, Braithwaite did not attend the funeral.

The Second Notebook

On the occasion of my tenth birthday I was presented, as Veronica had been before me, with a five-year diary. It was a fat little book with a red leatherette cover and a clasp lock. It was only that night, as I sat on the edge of my bed, weighing it in my hands, that I realised the significance of the lock: it was an acknowledgement that I had reached the age when I was permitted to have secrets; that I was now old enough to have thoughts I would not wish to share with my family. Of course, this was humbug. I had been having nasty, malicious thoughts for as long as I could remember, but that little lock granted me licence. Here was a book in which I could record and confine them.

It is a curious thing that, as far as I know, boys are not presented with such diaries. Boys are uncomplicated creatures. They swarm around shouting, fighting or chasing balls—noisily *being*—while we girls sit demurely on the sidelines nursing our resentment. Boys have no need for secrets. Everything just pours out of them. Girls are required to keep themselves to themselves. My ten-year-old self was vaguely aware of all this as she opened her new diary on her lap. The pages were divided into four sections on the verso side and three on the recto. The space allotted for each day of my life was the width of two fingers. If I was now granted licence to have secrets, evidently I wasn't expected to have too many. It was clear, however, that my handsome new diary was a trap. It had been presented to me so that I would reveal myself to its pages. Naturally, I assumed my mother would read it, just as I read Veronica's (picking the lock required no more than the brisk twist of a kirby grip).

The contents of my sister's diary were unremittingly wholesome. She documented her marks at school (always outstanding); her thoughts on the books she was reading (always positive); and her feelings about her family (always affectionate). It never occurred to me that Veronica might not be telling the whole truth, that she might be withholding some darker, more malevolent thoughts. Veronica, you see, was good. I did not even take any great care to conceal that I had been reading her diary. In her innocence, she would never suspect that someone might be so devious as to violate her trust in this way. I did not share her naïvety. My appetite to fill the pages of my diary dissipated, but I realised that to write nothing would be taken as evidence that my thoughts were so wicked they could not be committed to paper. So, having completed the personal details on the title page, I set to work. The first entry was as follows:

> Saturday 10th June 1951
> *Today is my 10th birthday and I have been given this diary in which I shall endever to faithfully record my thoughts and feelings for the next five years. I also got a new dress that I will wear tomorrow. This afternoon we went to Richmond Park and daddy bought me an ice-cream. The whether was fine but later on it clowded over and there were a few spots of rain and we had to shelter under the trees. Mum said we should have brought an umbrela.*

For the next two years it continues in a similar vein. Each entry begins with a note of the day's weather. There then follows a series of earnest remarks about my day at school, what we ate for supper and, on Sundays, where Veronica and I were taken for a walk. For a few months I developed an ornithological bent and recorded the species of birds I observed. One would be perfectly justified, reading this insipid drivel, in concluding that I was quite the dullest little girl in the world. My diary, however, was a work of fiction. I constructed a character, much as any novelist would do, and all for the benefit of a single reader. It is not that what I wrote was untrue. At least as far as I can recall, these things did actually happen. It's just that, taken together, they create a false impression. The real truth lay not in what I wrote, but in what I omitted.

The entries peter out after my twelfth birthday. I don't remember making a decision to stop writing. I expect I simply became bored. One evening over supper, Mother asked in a casual tone if I was still keeping up my diary. 'Of course,' I replied sweetly, knowing that she could not dare to contradict me. 'That's good,' she said. 'It's important to write things down. When you're older, you forget so much.' Re-reading my youthful jottings, I see no value in remembering that on the 20th of October 1952 my eleven-year-old self saw a chiffchaff. Writing something down invests it with a kind of significance, but in general things are of such little consequence, even to those involved, that the act of recording them is no more than vanity.

Now, however, I feel differently. It's not that I think that my life has assumed greater importance, but with my room safely under lock and key, there is no longer any need to censor myself. If I want to write obscene words or filthy thoughts, I am free to do so. What, after all, is the point of a journal if one is not honest about things? I am not even sure, looking back over what I have written so far, that I am not still constrained by a sense of decorum; that I am not inhibited by the thought of my mother looking over my shoulder. I can only say that from now on I will hold nothing back.

[THE FOLLOWING TWO PAGES OF THE NOTEBOOK HAVE BEEN TORN OUT]

Suicide makes Miss Marples of us all. One cannot help but look for clues. And naturally one looks for these clues in the past, for that is all the individual in question now has. As I have said, one would have thought Veronica the last person in the world to commit such an act, if for no other reason than that she was so terribly dull. One thinks of suicides as reckless, wild-eyed, tormented beings. Veronica was none of these things. At least, she did not appear to be. But perhaps the image she presented to the world was as fictional as the one I had created in my childhood diary. Perhaps there was another Veronica that she kept carefully under lock and key. When a person like Veronica jumps from the overpass at Bridge Approach, one cannot help but appraise them afresh. They are all of a sudden more interesting. And when one begins to place things under the magnifying glass, the most innocuous events can take on a new complexion.

I am not proud to admit it, but I greeted the news of my sister's 'breakdown' with a secret hurrah. She was twenty-three and had embarked on her doctorate at Cambridge. She had graduated with a first and was engaged to be married to a square-jawed don with whom she appeared to enjoy nauseatingly harmonious relations. A few weeks previously, she had brought the Lunk home for Sunday lunch. This was, in itself, unheard of, but when Peter asked my father if he might have a word in his study, I realised that something altogether more sinister was afoot. Veronica and I sat silently in the parlour while the men conducted their adda. I looked at her accusingly, but she avoided my gaze. Mrs Llewelyn set out glasses and the crystal sherry decanter, which during peacetime remained in the dining room sideboard from one Christmas to the next. This made me wonder if she had had advance warning of what was to come. Certainly, she would not have taken it upon herself to authorise the serving of sherry. Not ten minutes elapsed before the men re-joined us. Veronica rose and looked expectantly at Father. He smiled and, in a display of affection hitherto unprecedented in our family, embraced her. He then made a brief speech welcoming Peter to the family and wishing the conspirators many years of happiness. They sat together on the settee as if posing for a spread in *Tatler*, Veronica clasping Peter's meaty paw on her lap. Father insisted that Mrs Llewelyn join us in a glass of sherry, which she agreed to only after the mandatory display of reluctance, before bustling off to the kitchen to baste her roast.

I suppose I should have been happy for my sibling, but I could not help but think that she was motivated solely by a desire to best me. Not only had she conquered academia, but she had also somehow acquired a husband of unimpeachable eligibility. So, when the news of her 'breakdown' reached us, I could hardly be blamed for feeling anything other than a certain glee. Here, at last, was a crack in the veneer.

One Sunday morning Father and I drove to the sanatorium on the outskirts of Cambridge in which Veronica had been confined. The journey passed mostly in silence. Father kept his unlit pipe clenched between his teeth and drove with his customary adherence to the Highway Code. He expressed the view that Veronica must be over-tired on account of her great achievements. I kept my gaze fixed on the featureless landscape of Hertfordshire. I entertained an image of Bedlam, inmates shackled to the walls, clothed only in smocks soiled with vomitus and faeces, amid air riven by bloodcurdling screams. The corridors would be patrolled by burly wardens in greasy leather waistcoats, pausing now and again to administer beatings to the grovelling wretches. Veronica, I imagined, catatonic and drooling, insensible to the mayhem around her, muttering mathematical formulae incoherently under her breath. I imagined myself too in a cell, writhing on a plank bed, trussed up in a straitjacket, the strap between my legs affording surreptitious gratification. The pleasures of such restraints would undoubtedly be lost on Veronica.

How disappointed I was as we pulled into the drive of Burlington House. It was more Manderley than Bedlam. As we pulled up on the gravel outside the porticoed entrance, I half expected Max de Winter to bound out and greet us, spaniels capering at his ankles. Still, I told myself, appearances can be deceptive. Who could tell what horrors lay within? Fresh fruit being a remedy for all disturbances of the mind, Father had ordered a basket from Fortnum & Mason's and this he instructed me to retrieve from the back seat of the car. He rang the bell and we stood at a respectable distance from the door, lest we be taken for tinkers. A wide-hipped woman with her hair secured in a bun answered and Father stated our business. We were ushered into a chequerboard-tiled hallway with a wide staircase and asked to sign a guestbook, which I did under an assumed name. The matron then led us along a corridor to a large drawing room with French windows giving out onto a terrace and sloping lawns.

Veronica was sitting in a leather armchair, reading. I had the impression that she had deliberately adopted this pose in anticipation of our arrival. On seeing us, she feigned surprise, stood up and strode across the room. She was wearing a cream blouse, woollen skirt and flats. Regrettably, she did not appear to have soiled or vomited on herself. She had at least lost weight, I noted with satisfaction, so that her eyes appeared sunken in their sockets.

She stretched out both hands. 'Daddy!' she said. 'You really shouldn't have come all this way. I'm quite well, you see. It's all a fuss over nothing.'

I lurked behind my father, clutching the fruit basket.

'And you!' she said when she saw me. She held out her hand and I clasped her fingers for a moment.

The handsome fiancé loomed up behind her. He greeted my father with a firm handshake, then said my name and kissed me on both cheeks, as if he were French. 'Isn't she doing well?' he proclaimed. 'We'll have her back on her feet in no time.'

'Actually, I rather like it here,' Veronica said. 'Perhaps I'll act a bit more doolally and extend my stay.' She stuck her tongue out of the side of her mouth and rolled her eyes in a demonstration of lunacy. We all laughed.

There followed an extended kerfuffle of drawing up armchairs until the four of us were seated in a loose circle around a small coffee table, upon which I placed the fruit basket. Veronica proceeded to go through its contents, naming each article as though she were Eve in the Garden of Eden. One would think she had never set eyes on a pineapple before.

'You're ever so thin, my dear,' Father said. 'I'm sure that's what must have brought this on.' He turned to the Lunk: 'You will make sure she eats, won't you?'

'Absolutely, sir,' he replied, as if she were a piece of livestock to be fattened for the abattoir.

I gazed around the room. There was a young fellow in pyjamas and dressing gown sitting by the window, reading a book. He seemed oblivious to the commotion. If one saw him in mufti sitting in the corner of a café, one would never have taken him for a nut. As Father quizzed Peter about the catering arrangements of the establishment, I stood up and took a turn around the room, purposefully concluding at the French windows.

'You should be outside,' I said to the young man. It was the sort of irritating remark my mother would have made.

He raised his head slowly, but did not seem to be properly looking at me. I was standing with my legs crossed at the ankle.

'It's such a lovely day,' I said, by way of explanation.

He directed his gaze vaguely towards the window. 'Yes,' he said. 'I suppose it is.'

I pulled up a chair and sat down with my back to my family, who did not in any case appear to have noticed my absence. He leaned forward in his seat, as if he was about to whisper something to me. His book fell to the floor. It was in French. How thrilling! He did not appear obviously deranged, but it seemed indecorous to ask him what he was 'in' for. There was something of the Romantic about him. Perhaps he was suffering from a broken heart.

I told him my name. 'That's my sister over there,' I whispered. 'She's had a nervous breakdown.'

'Ah, Veronica,' he replied, visibly perking up. 'She seems a good sort.'

'Yes,' I said, 'but very disturbed.'

'I thought she was at Cambridge.'

'Oh dear, is that what she told you?' I said, shaking my head sadly. 'You mustn't believe a word she says.'

The fellow glanced towards the family gathering. 'What about her fiancé?' he said.

'Her fiancé? That's her doctor. Her *private* doctor. Our father is a millionaire.'

He looked at me blankly.

'You didn't tell me your name,' I said.

'Are you a nurse?' he asked suspiciously.

'No,' I said, 'I'm from the outside.'

'It's Robert.'

'Well, *Robert*'—I pronounced it the French way—'what would you say to a little turn on the terrace?'

He glanced over his shoulder. 'I'm not sure that's permitted.'

I stood up. 'Well, *I* am going to take a turn around the terrace.'

I imagined he would stand up to join me, but instead he

merely retrieved his book from the floor. I rattled the handle of the French window. It was locked. I gazed at it for a moment, then tried again. It would have been too much effort to make my way back along the corridor, out the front door and round the back of the building, just to prove a point.

'It's clouding over anyway,' I said.

Robert gave no indication that he had heard me. His attention had returned to his book, which he was holding upside-down. I re-joined my family, none of whom so much as glanced at me as I sat down. A doctor in his mid-fifties was addressing the group. He had a florid complexion and there was a small shaving cut at the corner of his mouth. All Veronica required, he was saying, was a good long rest. She would be back to her old self in two or three months. This sort of thing was quite common in young women who over-did things. It was not clear what 'this sort of thing' was, but I did not ask and nor did my father. Veronica smiled beatifically, as if she was rather proud of having over-done things.

Afterwards, Father insisted that we stop for a late luncheon at an inn we had passed en route. He was in better spirits. He ate a steak and kidney pudding and drank half a pint of beer. I had a pork chop with new potatoes slathered in enough butter to add a pound to my hips. Aside from passing some remarks about our surroundings, we ate in silence. We have never, Father and I, had much to talk about, but it is precisely in this that our bond lies. We have no need to fill our time together with meaningless chit-chat. I gazed around the dining room and wondered if the other patrons might take us for lovers.

At the time I gave little thought to this incident. It was principally notable for having constituted a trip out of London. Veronica, as predicted by the Lunk, was back on her feet in a matter of weeks. The episode was never mentioned again. But after her death I could not help wondering if it had been an augury of things to come. We are inclined, I think, to sift the past for explanations of the present. From the little I know, this rummaging of the past is a pillar of the black psychiatric arts. There lie the buried clues that can be deciphered only by the inscrutable, bearded physician.

Dr Braithwaite was not bearded, and had thus far shown little interest in any buried treasure of mine. I confess that after my first visit, I thought myself a frightful clever-clogs. He seemed entirely taken in by Rebecca. In the intervening week, however, I had come to see that my scheme was flawed. Aside from experiencing the power of his personality, I had discovered nothing of substance. Rebecca Smyth must arm herself with something more than a vague feeling of malaise. She must, I decided, acquire an inclination towards self-destruction. All week I mentally played out the conversations we might have. When I went to sleep, it was of Collins Braithwaite that I dreamt and he was my first thought when I awoke.

There would be no more play-acting. No more torn stockings or tousled hair. From now on I would stick, as far as was practicable, to the truth. It was with some pleasure that I readied Rebecca for her second visit. The natty scarf was retrieved from the pocket of my coat. Her make-up was immaculate. When I examined myself in the mirror of the WC on the landing outside Mr Brownlee's office, she looked quite the girl-about-town. Were it not for the gravity of my mission, I might have thought the whole thing a bit of a jape.

On the train to Chalk Farm, a man dressed in a light grey suit smiled at me. I did not avert my eyes, as I normally would, but returned his look. That was what Rebecca would do. He was entirely unabashed. He seemed perfectly respectable. He was in his forties, his hair greying a little at the temples.

Over one arm was a folded raincoat, and in his right hand he carried a copy of *The Times*. His eyes lingered on my knees for some moments before progressing slowly up my body to my face. A quizzical smile played on his lips. He raised one eyebrow. I touched my hand to my face to conceal the blush that rose to my cheeks. I directed my gaze towards the end of the carriage, but for the remainder of the journey I felt his eyes on me. Was this, I wondered, how assignations began? As we approached my stop, I glanced in his direction. To my disappointment, he was engrossed in his newspaper and appeared to have forgotten me. He did not even look up when I got off. I expect I had failed to play the game properly. Nevertheless, I felt a certain frisson, as if for a moment we had reached a sort of secret understanding. Perhaps later, as he lay in bed next to his wife, it would be Rebecca of whom he was thinking.

None of the floods, fires or other assorted catastrophes for which I had made allowance came to pass, so I once again found myself in the environs of Ainger Road with time to spare. The bell above the door of the teashop announced my arrival, as before. The sole customer was a young woman in a pillbox hat who was gazing sadly at a half-eaten chocolate éclair. Her dejection, I suppose, was either because there was only half left or because she now regretted consuming the first half. The table at the window was unoccupied, but I returned to my place at the back. I ordered, as before, a pot of tea and a scone and jam. I had no desire for the scone, but having previously praised the establishment's baking it would have been peculiar if I did not have one. Mrs Clay mustered a thin smile when she brought my order and succeeded in placing it on the table with no forfeiture of cutlery. My desire to sit at what was established in my mind as Mrs Alexander's table had not sprung from a vague yearning to gaze out of the window, but because I secretly hoped that Tom (or whatever his name was) might pass by on the way to his studio. Indeed, I was obliged to admit that I had never really believed that my journey would be delayed by fire, flood or pestilence, but instead that I had left prematurely in the hope that I might contrive a meeting with him. As I forced down my scone, I kept my eyes fixed on the window, but he did not appear. I do not, in any case, know what I would have done if he had. The woman in the pillbox hat got up and left. From my vantage point, I could not see whether she had finished her éclair, but I imagined she had, if only to avoid incurring the disapproval of the fearsome Mrs Clay. When the appointed time approached, I settled my bill, leaving tuppence in the saucer on the counter as before.

As I was about to cross the street, I heard the name Rebecca being called. It was not until I heard it a second time that I turned my head. Tom was approaching with his right hand raised in greeting.

'Rebecca,' he repeated as he came to a halt before me. Not being sure of his name, I returned his greeting with a smile. I could not help hoping that Mrs Clay was observing this scene from within.

'So, you haven't been carted off to Bedlam?' he asked.

'Evidently not,' I replied drily.

He paused for a moment, before saying: 'Actually, this is rather serendipitous. I wondered if you might like to have a drink with me sometime.' He blurted out those words as if they had been lodged in his gullet and a passer-by had just slapped him on the back.

I looked at him as though surprised at his audacity. He really was a handsome fellow. He ran a hand over his chin. He did not appear to have shaved and it was speckled with dark stubble. My father shaved every morning without fail. As a little girl I would stand on a stool in the bathroom and he would let me soap his face with the stubby little brush that reminded me of a neatly trimmed ponytail. I would imitate the faces he pulled to tauten his skin and watch with rising tension as he drew the razor across his throat. On the rare occasion that he drew blood, he would react with no more than a soft tutting, before asking me to pass him a flannel to dab the wound. Afterwards he would splash his face and the water in the basin would turn pink, like the mouthwash at the dentist's. For years I believed that dental water was mixed with blood and refused to use it.

'Well?' said Tom.

'I don't see why not,' I said, as nonchalantly as I could muster.

'Super,' he said. There was a pub, the Pembridge Castle, at the top of the street. 'Shall we say half past six?'

As I could hardly admit that I had never once been in a London pub, I nodded my assent, or rather Rebecca did.

'See you there, then,' he said, as if all this were perfectly commonplace. He strode off down the street, his hands shoved into the pockets of his coat. I expect he was already thinking about something else.

Daisy greeted me cheerfully. She was one of those good-natured sorts who exist in ignorance of the turmoil experienced by the rest of us. Her looks were of the unthreatening, girlish variety so appealing to the male sex, but it would be unjust to hold that against her. As I sat down, I reflected that if I were ever to have a friend, I would want her to be like Daisy. Daisy would not mock or ridicule me. She would lend me stockings and ask nothing in return. If we went to the pictures, she would let me choose the film, and when we had tea she would insist on 'going Dutch'. I found myself picturing us as a pair of septuagenarian spinsters, dissecting the bill in a shabby country hotel, despising ourselves for having frittered our lives away on each other. Even so, given the task at hand, it struck me that I might do worse than make an ally of her. To this end, I complimented her on her cardigan (which was, in fact, mint-green and rather hideous). She raised her head from her typing, evidently having not heard me over the clacking, and I repeated my statement.

She thanked me pleasantly enough, but did not venture any further information about the garment. Nor did she, as is customary in such exchanges, make a reciprocal remark about my attire. Nevertheless, I persisted.

'It's not, by any chance, from Heaton's, is it?' It clearly was not, but my comment had the desired effect.

'Goodness, no,' she said. 'I knitted it from a pattern in the *Journal*.'

'Clever old you!' I said.

'I'd be happy to lend you the pattern.'

'I'm afraid I've never been much of knitter,' I said, before adding nonsensically, 'Perhaps if I was, I wouldn't be in need of a shrink.'

The smile she now gave me contained a trace of pity. She returned to her typing. I consoled myself with the thought that, as I was supposed to be a nut, asinine remarks like this were only to be expected. Still, I was ashamed of dragging Rebecca down to my level. A well-adjusted girl like Daisy would never befriend a clot like me. Her offers to lend me stockings and knitting patterns were not made out of friendship, but because I would clearly be paying many visits and would have numerous opportunities to return them.

The tear in the wallpaper above Daisy's shoulder had not been repaired. I stared at it, wondering if it had become a little larger. The loose triangle of paper lolled like a pale tongue. As I have resolved to hold nothing back, I must record the thoughts that I then had. I have read of a practice (a sexual practice, I mean) involving the application of the tongue to the private parts. Whether this is apocryphal, I do not know. Certainly I cannot imagine anything more alarming than having another person's genitals near my mouth. Sometimes though, when I am amusing myself, I moisten the tip of my middle finger and imagine it to be a tiny tongue engaged in just this practice. I imagined Dr Braithwaite's delight if I were to tell him this, psychiatrists being, as is well known, obsessed with sex. The thought caused me to giggle to myself. Daisy looked up from her work. She smiled in the same condescending way as before. Nuts, as we all know, are prone to laughing for no apparent reason.

The door to the office opened and Miss Kepler emerged. As she pulled on her fur, she turned towards me. Our eyes met, but her expression did not alter. I expect it is not the done thing to make small talk in a psychiatrist's waiting room, and as I was the neophyte, I did not want to be the one to commit a breach of etiquette. As before, there was an interval of some minutes before Daisy indicated that I could enter.

Dr Braithwaite was sitting in the centre of the settee beneath the windows, his arms stretched across the back, his legs indecently splayed. He greeted me affably but did not get up. I stood before him and he gestured around the room for me to take a seat. I appraised the various options but remained standing. Braithwaite observed me, and I felt I was being subjected to some sort of test.

'Is something the matter?' he asked after a few moments.

'You're sitting in my place,' I replied.

'Am I?' he said innocently.

'You know you are,' I said. 'And you are doing so to try to throw me off.'

Rebecca, I had decided, would be the sort of person who said what was on her mind. In this way, she was my opposite. If I have something on my mind, I keep it to myself. Sometimes, this is for reasons of decorum (there are some things one simply doesn't say), but at others I feel that I would be showing my hand; that by revealing myself, I would be handing an advantage to my opponent. In any case, I daresay people have little interest in knowing what I am really thinking. If Mr Brownlee asks me how he looks as he runs out to a meeting (he's always late), he does not want me to tell him that his shirt does not go with his suit or that there is a soup stain on his tie. He wants me to tell him that he is very handsome, and that is what I do. But it is not what Rebecca Smyth would do. Rebecca would tell him that he looked like an unkempt mendicant. But then she would not be working for Mr Brownlee in the first place.

'"Throw you off"', Braithwaite repeated. 'That's an interesting phrase. Why don't you tell me what you mean by it?'

I had remained in the centre of the room. 'First, I should like my seat back,' I said.

He made a face, as if impressed by my resolve, then stood up and indicated with an open palm that I was free to sit down. When I had established myself on the settee, he repeated his question. I replied that I thought it was perfectly obvious what I meant, and if he was going to make a habit of dissecting my every utterance, we would never get anywhere.

'And where is it you want to go?' he said.

He had remained standing, his eyes fixed on mine. I rummaged in my bag for my cigarettes and lit one. He sat down in the uncomfortable-looking wicker chair. I noticed, for the first time, that he was bare-footed. He crossed his legs at the ankle and waited.

'Well, I don't exactly know,' I said eventually.

'But you would like to go somewhere?'

'I wouldn't be here otherwise,' I said.

'And yet when you arrived, you became uncomfortable when you found that I was sitting in the place you think of as your own merely by virtue of having sat in it once before. Another person might have been happy to sit elsewhere, but your instinct was to return to where you had been before.' He paused for a moment, then held up his hands. 'I admit it. I was trying to throw you off, Rebecca. It's my job to throw you off. You have your malaise and, assuming you want to get rid of it, something has to change. Yet you cling to the same routines and habits, even though you know that these are the very things that make you unhappy. And the longer you persist in these behaviours, the more entrenched they become. I don't believe that you have any love for that settee—it's actually bloody uncomfortable—but despite that, you return to the place you know rather than try somewhere new.'

It was true. The settee was exceptionally uncomfortable. I could feel a spring insinuating itself against my buttock. He got up from his seat and invited me to do the same. I stayed put. I felt quite skewered by his assessment, but to comply would be to admit that he was right. Rebecca Smyth was not one to be pushed around. I told him I was perfectly happy where I was.

'How do you know you wouldn't be even happier somewhere else?'

I held his stare for a few moments. 'You've made your point,' I said. 'But I hardly think forcing me to move would serve your purpose.'

Dr Braithwaite assured me that he was not forcing me to do anything. He was merely offering me a choice. If I didn't want to take advantage of it, that was my look-out. After a few moments he shrugged and sat down cross-legged on the floor. He fixed me with his protruding eyes, a quizzical expression on his face. He did not say anything. In such situations, the passing of a few seconds can seem an eternity. Without the aid of a clock, it becomes impossible to know how much time has passed. I became aware of everything: the tuft of hair sprouting from Braithwaite's nose; the parsnip-shaped stain on the threadbare rug beside him; the blistered paint on the doorpost beyond his shoulder; a faint hissing sound, like a distant kettle, perhaps emanating from the iron radiator beneath the window; a vague herbal aroma from the flat below. I began to wonder if he was hypnotising me; if this was what hypnosis felt like: a monumental slowing down of time. Certainly, I felt what will I had drain away and become subsumed to his. When my gaze returned to his face, he pursed his lips almost imperceptibly. I understood what he was communicating through this tiny movement. He was telling me that he could remain silent for as long as necessary and would do so until I changed my seat; we both knew that this was the case and that the impasse would last until I moved.

For myself, I had no desire to offer any resistance, but Rebecca Smyth would not readily accept being pushed around in such a manner. She was made of sterner stuff. There was, however, no alternative. I stood up and surveyed the room. My instinct was to make for the wicker chair, but I thought better of this. The wicker chair was a snug carapace. Braithwaite would interpret this as an attempt to cosset myself. Instead, I selected the least appealing option: the straight-backed chair Braithwaite had occupied during our previous meeting. It was positioned a few feet behind his right shoulder. Naturally, I now expected him to get up and sit on the settee I had vacated, but instead he merely swivelled round, so that he was sitting at my feet, like a child awaiting a story. I realised how clever he was. This was precisely the outcome he intended. I felt a momentary feeling of dominance from my elevated position. Then I became aware that, from where he was sitting, he might be able to see up my skirt, and this had likely been his motive for manipulating me to sit on the straight-backed chair. I inclined my legs to the right and kept my ankles and knees clamped tightly together.

'Now that we're sitting comfortably,' he said, 'why don't we play a game?'

'I don't like games,' I replied.

'You'll like this one,' he said firmly. 'You tell me your earliest memory and I'll tell you mine.'

'What if I don't want to hear yours?'

He gave me a look. I realised that in order to establish my credentials as a patient I would have to offer him something. It did not make sense to pay him five guineas an hour to say nothing, and I daresay the sort of narcissists who visit psychiatrists are only too happy to prattle on about their childhood experiences.

'I'm not trying to be difficult,' I said in a more agreeable tone, 'but how can one tell what one's earliest memory is? I mean, it's all a bit of a jumble, isn't it?'

'What matters is not whether what you tell me is actually your first memory. As you rightly point out, how could you know? What's important is that it is something that has fixed itself in your mind. I can see that you're already thinking of something, so stop fucking about and tell me what it is.'

I pretended not to be shocked by his language. Rebecca was a worldly sort. And besides, he was, as usual, correct. An ugly incident had, indeed, already made an appearance in my head. I was wary of revealing too much of myself, but as I have no talent for dissembling, there was no question of making something up on the spot. In any case, Dr Braithwaite would be sure to see straight through such a stratagem.

I must have been three or four years old, I began. I was in Woolworth's with my mother. As we passed along the aisle where the sweets were sold, I asked if I could have a bag of dolly mixtures. Mother refused. I would only spoil my appetite, she said. She marched me through the shop. It must have been winter as I was wearing red wellingtons, and my mittens, which had been sewn onto a cord passing through the sleeves of my duffel coat, dangled against my thighs. The linoleum was slippery and streaked with mud. When we reached the sewing department at the back of the store, I started to cry. I wanted a bag of dolly mixtures. I had never wanted anything as much in my life, and my mother's refusal felt like an act of gratuitous cruelty. I bawled. I bawled out of frustration and because I wanted the other customers to know that my mother was a callous despot. People stared. Mother, who hated any sort of public scene, bent down and spoke to me in an emollient voice while simultaneously pinching the flesh at the back of my arm. This only had the effect of increasing my wailing. A woman stopped and asked if everything was all right. Mother increased the pressure on my flesh. It was a battle I could not win. My sobbing subsided. Mother returned her attention to the book of sewing patterns and I stood at her feet, rubbing the back of my arm.

Presently I slipped away and found my way back to the confectionery aisle. Standing on tip-toe, I reached my hand over the counter. I clutched a handful of dolly mixtures and stuffed them into my mouth. I reached for another handful, this time shoving them into the pocket of my coat. I must have thought myself invisible. As I reached for a third then a fourth handful, a pair of legs appeared beside me. I looked up. A man was looking at me sternly. He asked if I was planning to pay for the sweets I was secreting about my person. I cannot remember if he used precisely that phrase, but it was something to that effect. I did not reply. I pushed the sweets in my hand into my mouth. Most of them fell on the wet floor. I crouched to pick them up. The man took me by the wrist and drew me back to my feet. He asked where my mother was. I told him I didn't know. Then, hoping that he would take pity on me (his tone had not been unkind), I told him I was an orphan. The man took me by the hand and led me to the office at the back of the shop. This was accessed through a corridor that smelt of damp sawdust. I had the feeling that I would never emerge again. The man lifted me up and sat me on a mustard-coloured chair. There was a desk strewn with papers. The walls around the office were stacked with empty cardboard boxes. He asked my name and, not being of an age to have the wherewithal to make one up, I told him. He left the room. I thought about effecting an escape. There was a small window high on the wall above the desk. If I climbed onto a stack of cardboard boxes, I would be able to squeeze through it. But I knew I would not get far before I was apprehended. So I sat awaiting my fate. I imagined that I would be sent to prison and would never see my family again.

A few minutes later, Mother was ushered into the office. She made profuse apologies for the trouble I had caused. She took my hand and I slipped off the chair, thinking that the ordeal was over. It was not. The man explained to my mother that he had found me stealing, and asked me to turn out my pockets. I felt the need to let my water go and tightly pressed my knees together. He held out his palm and I meekly emptied my pockets into it. I did not dare look at my mother. The little coloured cubes were covered with fluff from the inside of my pocket. Mother offered more apologies. I had never done anything like this before, she said. She gripped my wrist painfully and started to pull me towards the door. The man blocked her path.

'I'm afraid the goods will have to be paid for,' he said. 'We can hardly sell them after they have been in your child's dirty pockets, can we?' He gave a little laugh.

Mother must have taken great umbrage at the accusation that the inside of her child's pockets were dirty. She wordlessly took out her purse and handed him the tuppence he asked for. The man then reminded her that she must also provide a coupon from her ration book. My mother protested, but, the man insisted, stealing was one thing, black marketeering quite another. F.W. Woolworth's could not be party to the latter. My mother handed over her ration book and the man searched for a pair of scissors to cut out the relevant coupon. Failing to find a pair, he passed back the ration book untouched, his point sufficiently made. Outside, Mother took me into a lane and held me by the arm while she smacked my bottom. Over supper that evening, the incident was related in detail to my father, with great emphasis placed on the mortification caused. Father responded by telling me in a mild voice that I must try my best not to upset my mother. The following night when I went to bed, I found a little bag of dolly mixtures under my pillow.

Shortly after this incident, a set of reins was procured. They consisted of an arrangement of thin white leather straps that fitted across my chest and were held from behind like a horse's bridle. Mother's motivation in acquiring these reins was, I am sure, less that she was afraid of me running off, than that she might avoid any repetition of the humiliation I had caused. For many years afterwards, I was warned against reckless behaviour with the words: 'We don't want another Woolworth's on our hands, do we?' This adage passed into family argot to such an extent that its origins became forgotten. It became a catch-all caution against any action that might have unforeseen consequences. It was only when my schoolmates greeted the phrase with bewilderment that I realised it was not in common parlance.

But it was the reins that had the most lasting effect on me. If my mother's purpose had been to subdue me, the reins had the opposite effect. I liked nothing more than to feel those straps across my chest and to strain against them like a dog on a lead. Whenever we were out, I would stray a few steps too far from my mother, so that she would be forced to tether me, muttering about 'another Woolworth's' as she did so. The feeling of being thus restrained engendered a tingling feeling between my legs akin to that which I experienced when I needed to pass water but was unable to do so. Later, when I learned the word 'frisson', it perfectly encapsulated what I felt.

At a certain point, however, Mother declared that there would be no more reins. They were not for big girls. 'If you want to run off and get hit by an omnibus, so be it,' she declared. Even at the time I did not think that she was really so indifferent to my fate, but instead wished to deny me the pleasure of being thus shackled.

I had become completely absorbed in the relating of this silly anecdote. For the duration of its telling, Dr Braithwaite had remained absolutely still. His eyes never left me, yet I did not feel self-conscious. When I reached the end, I had the sensation of coming round from a fainting fit and I understood for the first time why apparently rational people would willingly part with five guineas an hour for the privilege of sitting in Braithwaite's office. The story I had told held no particular significance for me. As soon as I had 'come to', I said as much. I felt that I had revealed too much of myself, and that Braithwaite would read all sorts of things into what I had said. In this, I was not wrong. He prevailed on me to tell him more about the reins.

'There's nothing to tell,' I said. I neglected to mention that they hang to this day on a hook in the scullery. Nor that, for years after their proscription, I would prevail upon Veronica, under the guise of playing pony-and-trap, to fasten me into them. I still, truth be told, hanker after them.

Braithwaite did not press me. His previous quarrelsome tone had given away to something softer. Even his voice had lost its edges. 'But you used an interesting word,' he said. '"Shackled". A very interesting word. Why do you think you enjoy being shackled?'

'I didn't say I enjoy being shackled,' I replied. 'I was talking about a childhood experience. It's of no significance.'

'And yet this is the story that came into your mind to tell me,' he said.

I felt terribly exposed.

'"To deny me the pleasure of being thus shackled",' he repeated. 'Very nicely put, if I may say so. Have you ever thought of writing down your thoughts in some kind of journal?'

I was secretly gratified that my words met with his approval. 'I don't have any ambitions in that direction.' Instead, I suggested that he could use them in his next volume of case studies.

He ignored this arch comment. 'I'm not suggesting that anyone else would want to read it,' he said. 'But you might find it a valuable exercise.'

I tapped a cigarette from my packet, lit it and exhaled a plume of smoke.

'Your mother sounds like a curious character,' he said. 'Were you close?'

'One doesn't have much choice when one is a child, does one?' I replied.

Braithwaite averred that this was an interesting response.

'She died when I was fifteen,' I explained.

'Why don't you tell me about that?'

I realised we were venturing into dangerous territory and protested that my hour must be nearly up. Braithwaite replied that he wasn't one for watching the clock.

It was out of the question to describe the circumstances of

my mother's death as they were so extraordinary that they could not fail to reveal my connection to Veronica. It happened while we were on holidaying in Devon. Father called it the English Riviera, which only made it seem more drab. If Mother and I had one thing in common, it was that we both loathed holidays. I found Father's insistence that we should always be 'doing something' tiresome, while Mother found fault with everything from the food in the hotel to the cleanliness of the sheets and the price of a cream tea. Father ignored her plaints and, for his sake, I pretended to enjoy myself.

It was a sunny but breezy day. We were walking on the cliffs at Babbacombe. Veronica and my father had disappeared round a bend in the narrow path. They had been discussing the geological character of the area, and I had deliberately slowed my pace to avoid listening to them. Mother, who disliked any physical activity, was a few yards ahead of me. It is impossible to walk behind someone on a narrow cliff path without the idea of shoving them over the edge crossing one's mind. I had been imagining just this (two firm hands to the back) when Mother, turning round to check that I was there, went over on her ankle. For a few moments she vainly flailed her arms in an attempt to regain her balance, before falling backwards over the cliff. Her expression was not one of fear, but rather of weary disappointment, the same look she wore whenever I embarrassed her in public. It is surprising how many thoughts can flit through one's mind in a short space of time, but in the interval between Mother losing her balance and beginning to fall backwards, I reached the conclusion that were I to attempt to save her, the most likely result would be that I too would be pulled over. So I just stood and watched. It was not so much an instinct of self-preservation that determined this course of action as the thought of dying so inelegantly. It was not my mother's broken body I pictured on the rocks below, but my own; my skirt rucked around my waist, knickers exposed to any sniggering schoolboy who happened to pass by. As it happened, I was at the time going through a silly infatuation with Keats and had, like him, fallen half in love with easeful death. I had resolved to kill myself before the age of twenty-five. But this was to be accomplished at a time and place of my own choosing, not by clumsily falling from a Devon cliff (where was the poetry in that?). The method I had settled on was to walk slowly but determinedly into the sea, pockets filled with stones, eyes fixed on the horizon. Afterwards, the only trace of my existence would be a turquoise scarf undulating on the swell.

I stood completely still for some time, before looking round to see if there had been any witnesses to the incident. The path was deserted. I stepped tentatively forward and peered over the edge. Mother was lying on her back on the rocks below, her arms at her side. Were it not for the fact that she was fully clothed, she might have been sunbathing (although this was a pursuit she abhorred). Clearly she was dead. It would later be remarked upon that I had behaved with great calm. I did not call out for help. What would have been the point? Nor did I run off along the cliff path in a manner that might have endangered my own life. Instead, I walked at a brisk pace until I found Father and Veronica waiting on a bench. When I reached them, Father asked where Mother was and I told him. He looked at me in disbelief and then ran off back along the path in such a reckless fashion that I almost called after him that there was no point in hurrying. When he returned, all colour had drained from his face. He grabbed Veronica and me and marched us along, gripping my wrist so tightly that I felt he somehow thought I was to blame. Veronica started to cry and, as this seemed appropriate in the circumstances, I aped her breathless little sobs. When I told my story to the police, they appeared satisfied. Later, at the inquest, I repeated this version of events (I had it off pat by then) and the magistrate, a middle-aged woman who might have been attractive were it not for the hideous horn-rimmed spectacles she wore, told me I had behaved in an exemplary fashion and that I must not hold myself responsible for what had happened. I lowered my eyes and nodded solemnly.

When Veronica and I returned to St Paul's after the holidays, I found my status among my classmates greatly elevated. I was treated with a degree of reverence normally reserved for girls who claimed to have 'done it'. The High Mistress, Miss Osborn, called Veronica and me into her office and told us that, should we need to excuse ourselves from the classroom, we were free to do so, but we must nevertheless not use our misfortune as an excuse to neglect our studies. At this point she directed her gaze towards my sister and said: 'Especially you, Veronica, for whom we have such high hopes.'

Needless to say, the matter was never discussed at home. Father's policy was to behave as if nothing had changed. Mother's clothes hang in the closet to this day, and her dressing table remains as she left it. Had it been up to me, I would have burned the lot, but he seemed to derive a melancholy pleasure from the presence of these items. Once or twice, I have spied him through the bedroom door, sitting in my mother's place fingering the objects there, and I felt terribly guilty, as if his unhappiness was all my doing.

As I could not divulge this, I told Dr Braithwaite that Mother had been struck by a bus on Oxford Street. A Number 7. I had no idea whether the Number 7 bus even went along Oxford Street, but I felt this detail lent authenticity to my story. I didn't imagine that Braithwaite was one for using the omnibus.

'The Number 7?' he said.

'Well, I'm not sure it was a Number 7. I wasn't there. Apparently she just stepped off the pavement without looking and that was that.'

'You don't seem very upset about it.'

'It was ten years ago,' I said.

'And at the time?' he asked.

'What do you mean?'

'Were you upset at the time?'

'I suppose I was. I don't remember.'

Braithwaite looked at me for perhaps a minute. I was sure he did not believe a word of it. And why should he?

He rose from his cross-legged position like a puppet drawn upwards by invisible strings. I took this as indication that my visit was at an end. He allowed me to gather up my things and make my exit in silence. There did not appear to be any question that I would be returning the following week.

Outside on the pavement, I did not feel there was any need to repeat my silly antics of the previous week. I was sure I had done more than enough to convince Braithwaite that I was not of sound mind. Nevertheless, I paused to inspect my handiwork. I took off my glove and ran my fingertips over the polished portion of the lamp-post. It was agreeably smooth. It was just then that the street began to list. It was no more than a gentle undulation at first, just as if the pavement was lifted on a swell. It was sufficient, however, to cause me to flatten my palm against the lamp-post and plant my feet in order to maintain my balance. Then the listing grew more severe. The street tilted, first to the left and then the right. I was forced to step forward and throw both arms around the lamp-post. I closed my eyes and pressed my cheek to the metal. There was no need to panic, I told myself. It would pass. And it did. The tumult subsided almost as quickly as it had arisen. I opened my eyes. A woman, wider than she was tall, was looking at me disapprovingly. Her girth must have provided her with ballast. I gingerly stepped back from the lamp-post and bid her good evening. She did not reply. She probably assumed I was drunk.

I walked off in the direction of Primrose Hill. Ignoring my mother's maxim that only whores smoked outdoors, I took out my cigarettes. Ever since I took up the habit, I have loved smoking more than anything. Smoking is a veil. I adore every aspect of it: the tapping with a gloved finger of the cigarette from the packet; the metallic rasp of the lighter; the pungent whiff of Ronsonol; the first deep inhalation and the blue plume of exhaled smoke; the minor obscenity of lipstick on the filter; the snug pleasure of just holding the thing between index and middle finger. I love to watch women smoke. A woman smoking is never lonely; she is solitary. She is sensual, worldly. Men do not know how to smoke. For men, smoking is a utilitarian business, like using the lavatory or getting on a bus. It is always incidental to another activity, never a thing in itself. I had not seen Tom (or whatever his name was) smoking. I imagined he opted for those thin Russian cigarettes, or perhaps for a pipe, as certain young men do in order to cultivate an intellectual air. But Tom had no need for such fripperies. What was the word he had used? Serendipitous. It had slipped off his tongue as though it had been lurking there, awaiting the moment to pounce. And then, as he pronounced the last syllable, he had glanced directly into my eyes. It was like the clash of a tiny cymbal. Had that been serendipity too? Or did the very fact that he had used this word suggest that the opposite was true: that he been lying in wait for me, armed with mellifluous, seductive words. What woman could resist serendipity?

There was a telephone box at the corner of the street. I called to say that I would not be home for supper. It was, as usual,

Mrs Llewelyn who answered. There are two telephones in the house, one on my father's desk, a second in the hall. No matter where she is, however, Mrs Llewelyn manages to pick up within a couple of rings. I asked her to tell Father that I would not be home for supper and that he should not wait for me. Of course, this information was more relevant to Mrs Llewelyn, as it was she who prepared and served the meal, but I took a childish satisfaction from treating her as if she were a mere conduit, unworthy of being informed as a person in her own right. The snub would not be lost on her. I would, furthermore, have felt obliged to tell Father why I would be late. 'Oh, that's splendid, well done, my dear,' I imagined him responding, as if I were a toddler successfully using its potty. Then, later, there would be the tentative inquisition into 'how it had gone'. Father is always enquiring if I have met any Nice Young Chaps, and I am hurt that he seems to so relish the idea of me in the arms of another man.

It was only when I had replaced the receiver and wiped it clean of my fingerprints that I began to contemplate how 'it' might go with Tom. I began a slow turn around the park. I had accepted his invitation without any thought to the consequences. As I orbited the eastern boundary, I contemplated the indignities to which I might be expected to submit. I imagined Tom dragging me into the shrubbery to my left and attempting to prise open my legs. I have no doubt a good-looking fellow like him had prised open the legs of many a young woman, and there might even have been some hussies who had willingly opened them for him. I thought of poor Constance Chatterley debasing herself with Mellors. There was a limit to what I would endure. At St Paul's there was frequently excitable talk about The Penis, this chiefly concerning its dimensions. It was not always possible to steer clear of these discussions, nor afterwards to banish from one's mind the images conjured. I cannot myself see why any woman would wish to have her private parts violated by the male member, whatever its magnitude. I understand this part of the sexual act exists solely for the gratification of the man, and it is afterwards left for the female to finish herself off.

Before I need concern myself with any of that, however, there would be the equally perplexing business of conversation. As will have become apparent, this is an activity for which I have little aptitude. In public places, I sometimes eavesdrop in an effort to learn the knack. Later, in my room, I repeat phrases to myself like a child practising scales, but they never take. I blame my mother. 'Empty vessels make the most noise,' she was wont to declare, and I naturally absorbed the lesson. Talkative types were invariably dismissed as 'garrulous', an adjective which to my young ears conjured images of gargoyles and drunkards.

By the time I had completed my circumnavigation of the park, I greatly regretted having accepted Tom's invitation. I came to the bench upon which I had taken flight the previous week. No matter how long I gazed at it, it resembled nothing other than an ordinary bench. It showed no sign of scuttling off into the bushes, nor of having any ability to do so. It was an inanimate object. Rebecca mocked me for the silly thoughts I had had. 'It's just a bench, you ninny!' she sneered. I replied that she was quite right. I was a ninny. I learnt long ago that bullies are often disarmed when you admit they are right. We sat down together. Rebecca told me that she would deal with Tom. It was, after all, her he had invited. All I had to do was hold my tongue and not mess things up. I nodded solemnly. If any legs were to be prised apart, they would be Rebecca's rather than mine.

The tarmac of the path glistened like ink. I imagined stepping into it and slowly sinking up to my waist, then to my shoulders, before it enveloped my head, leaving no trace of me. The man with the black dog approached and paused in front of us. The dog cocked his leg against the metal struts of the bench and a rivulet of urine trickled towards my shoes.

'Feeling better, are we?' he said.

Rebecca responded with language I would have blushed to use. The man shook his head and went on his way, muttering to himself.

I arrived at the Pembridge Castle at twenty minutes to seven. Tom had not made it clear whether we would meet outside or inside the pub, but as he was not at the door, and I had purposefully arrived ten minutes late, I assumed he must be waiting inside. The only public houses I had visited before were the genteel country inns of Devon or Hertfordshire. My image of the interior of a London pub resembled a Hieronymus Bosch canvas populated by prostitutes, stevedores, dipsomaniacs and queers, all blind drunk and engaging in the most licentious acts. A Modern Independent Woman like Rebecca Smyth, however, would have no qualms about entering such a place. I took a deep breath, straightened my back and pushed open the door.

The lighting inside was agreeably bright. The furniture and fittings were of dark wood. At a table to the right of the door, a man in a flat cap sat with a pint of beer and an open newspaper. Two men in pinstripe suits stood close together at the bar, holding glasses of whisky and conversing in hushed tones. Three navvies stood round a pillar, with pints of beer in their filthy paws. Tom was nowhere to be seen. Behind the counter, the landlord was hunched over a newspaper. Thus far, no one seemed to have registered my presence, so it would still have been feasible to beat a retreat and wait outside, but the sound of the door swinging shut caused the landlord to look in my direction. His expression remained impassive, as if he was quite accustomed to unaccompanied women entering his premises. This reassured me somewhat, as did the fact that his shirt, at least from a distance, appeared well laundered. I glanced at my wristwatch and then, conscious of his eyes on me, took a seat on the banquette that ran the length of the wall to my right. I placed my bag at my feet and, in order to give the impression that I was at ease, slowly removed my gloves. I was now close enough to hear that the conversation of the two men at the bar concerned the sale of some nearby property. The shorter of the two had a florid complexion. The chain of a fob watch traversed his paunch. As I was sitting in his eyeline, he inclined his head in my direction. This caused his companion to look over his shoulder, and he openly appraised me before raising his eyebrows momentarily, as if to express approval of what he saw. He turned back to his companion and made a remark that I was unable to hear. I felt my scalp prickle. Perhaps they thought I was soliciting for business and the act of removing my gloves was the opening salvo of a striptease routine. After some minutes the landlord, with a theatrical puffing out of his cheeks, raised the hatch at the side of the bar and approached my table.

'What can I get you, Miss?' he asked. His tone was neither friendly nor hostile.

I told him that I was meeting a friend.

He informed me that the establishment was not a waiting room.

'Yes, of course,' I replied. I asked for a gin fizz, as this was what I understood they drank in Paris.

The landlord gave a little chuckle and asked me if a 'G and T' would do. I said that would be perfectly satisfactory. The men at the bar followed our exchange with amusement. When the landlord returned to his post, the short one with the florid complexion teased him about his inability to make a gin fizz.

'The serving of gin fizz,' he retorted, 'has been prohibited in England since the Licensed Premises Act of 1902, section 19, paragraph 2.'

'And is it also prohibited to refill this?' the man said, proffering his glass.

All this was delivered in exaggeratedly comic tones, as if the men were performing a music hall skit. The landlord freshened their glasses before preparing my drink, which he ostentatiously brought over on a tray.

'That'll be 2/6, Lady Muck,' he said. He was, I believe, making it known that I was receiving special treatment but that he was, nevertheless, not unduly put out. The conferring of nicknames, even uncomplimentary ones such as this, is a way of demonstrating acceptance. I had never been given a nickname before and felt rather pleased with myself. I gave the landlord three shillings and told him to keep the change.

'Ta muchly,' he said. 'Keep that up and I bloody well will make you a gin fizz.'

I felt a warm glow. I envisaged a future in which I had become a Regular at the Pembridge Castle, known to everyone as Lady Muck. The landlord would make me gin fizz, and this drink would become known as a Lady Muck, at first only in the Pembridge Castle, then all over London. I would be given a column in the *Woman's Journal* called 'Lady Muck Writes', in which I would dispense wisdom about etiquette, The Arts and fashion. I would be invited to film premieres and West End shows, and dine with Laurence Olivier, with whom it would be rumoured I was having *une liaison*.

I watched the bubbles of tonic rise to the surface of my drink and burst. If Veronica had been here, she would have embarked on a scientific explanation of the process. As the landlord was watching me, I took a sip. It was the bubbles I felt first, like pinpricks on my tongue. This was followed by an acrid taste, like overcooked sprouts, and then, as I swallowed, by a burning sensation in my throat. It was most unpleasant and caused me to cough. But still, here I was in a London pub drinking a gin and tonic with (as yet) no calamities.

The place was filling up. The landlord was drawing pints for the three navvies, whose accents betrayed them to be Welsh. As he waited for his beer, the largest of them gawped openly at me. He was a huge fellow, over six feet, with great round shoulders and a belly that obscured the top of his trousers. He stared at me with his chin on his chest and his mouth half-open, like a Saint Bernard. I looked away. Every time the door opened I cursed Tom for putting me at the mercy of these brutes. It was only a matter of time, I felt, before one of them came across to 'try it on' with me. What would be more humiliating, however, would be if, despite being the only female on the premises, none of them paid me this dubious compliment.

One thing I had learned from sitting at my desk at Mr Brownlee's is that I am neither plain enough nor pretty enough to flirt with. Men flirt with plain girls because they feel sorry for them, and because they know that a plain girl will never be so foolish as to take their compliments seriously. Plain girls know they are plain. Men flirt with pretty girls to test their mettle. They do not expect to be given anything other than the go-by. This reckless tilting is a buttress against the thought that, years later, when they are stuck at home with their middling wife and their middling brats, they should have had a go. But just as plain girls know they are plain, pretty girls know they are pretty. A plain girl has no alternative but to grab the first chap whose advances are not made in jest, but the pretty girl's dilemma is different. It is this: that she might, on the assumption that her well of suitors will never run dry, become so accustomed to giving men the go-by that she suddenly finds she is thirty, no longer pretty and destined for a life of rueful spinsterhood. Men, for their part, have no such dilemmas. Just as pretty girls know they are pretty, handsome men know they are handsome. Ugly men, however, do not appear to know that they are ugly. I have often seen the most frightful-looking men approach the prettiest girls, oblivious to fact that they are upsetting the natural order of things. This lack of self-knowledge would be grotesque, were it not for the fact that we women encourage them. I cannot recall the number of times I have seen a pretty girl on the arm of the most dreadful homunculus. Yet I have never once seen the situation reversed. The explanation for this is simple: the curse of the pretty girl is that she is thought to be dim-witted. The assumption is that she need do nothing other than look pretty in order to attract a mate. But in my experience, there is no correlation between brains and beauty. I have met pretty girls who are perfectly capable of taking part in intelligent discourse, and have, by the same token, encountered plain girls whose minds are every bit as defective as their looks. The pretty girl on the arm of the homunculus is doing neither more nor less than declaring her cleverness to the world. And the world looks on in admiration, both for her and for him. Yet, there seems to me to be no more proof of stupidity than to choose an ugly man when one could have a handsome one. If, on the other hand, one were to see a handsome man with a plain girl on his arm, one would look upon him with pity. And we would look upon her with loathing for having the gall to take what she does not merit.

I, however, am neither plain enough nor pretty enough to flirt with. I am the middling type, for whom flirtation is neither a demeaning jape nor an Icarus-like tilt at the sun. Flirting with a middling girl is a dangerous business, because we might—indeed, we probably will—take it seriously. And before the poor chap knows it, there'll be a bun in the oven and a hastily arranged rendezvous at the Registry Office.

All of which made Tom's behaviour towards me mystifying. Needless to say, I had endlessly parsed our first brief conversation, and, no matter how one looked at it, it was impossible to avoid the conclusion that he was flirting with me. His insistence on accompanying me from the station might, at a stretch, be construed as innocent, but not so his assurance that he had no intention of molesting me. In order to make this statement, some thought of molestation must have crossed his mind. Rather than keep this to himself, however, he implanted the idea in my head, cunningly under the guise of insisting that he had no intention of acting upon it. All this, of course, was done in a light-hearted manner. A joke can always be passed off as such, which is why it is the stock-in-trade of the flirtatious exchange. I myself have no sense of humour. I lack the speed of thought to interject a witty remark into a conversation, and have an idiotic tendency to take jokes at face value. Had I been practised in the art of flirtation, I would have replied—archly, of course—that I could think of nothing I would like more than to be molested by him. We would both have laughed this off, in a demonstration that we were neither of us serious, while knowing that we had entered into a kind of pact.

The fact, if we can now accept it as such, that Tom had been flirting with me demanded explanation. Tom is unquestionably a handsome man (the more I think about him, the more handsome he becomes), and I am a middling girl. The thing was this though: Tom wasn't flirting with me. He was flirting with Rebecca, and Rebecca is not a middling girl. Rebecca is a pretty girl. She is the sort of girl who is accustomed to being flirted with, and who is not expected to take it seriously.

I opened my handbag and retrieved my lipstick and compact. A frowsty odour emanated from within. I quickly touched myself up. If I was to be a pretty girl, I would have to take the trouble that pretty girls take. From the corner of my eye, I saw one of the brutes by the pillar nudge his cohorts. I turned towards the door, which just at that moment opened. It was not Tom. Two men and a girl with fashionably cropped hair entered, the three of them arm-in-arm. The girl, dressed in a blue and white-striped smock and toreador pants, was of the middling type, but of the sub-group who attempt to make up for their physical inadequacies by acting in a jocular, tomboyish way. They were laughing excessively, clearly with the intention of demonstrating to all and sundry what jolly sorts they were. The trio greeted the landlord by name (Harry) and ordered their drinks. Their conversation continued unabated as they took the table next to mine. The girl sat facing me. One of the men nodded a greeting in my direction, a hint of pity in his eyes. I sat rigidly staring at my barely-touched drink. Was it worse, I wondered, to be thought a solitary dipsomaniac or to have been given the go-by? The latter, I decided. My neighbours chattered away with such bonhomie that I could have burst into tears. How I envied them their easy familiarity. And how I wished them every conceivable misery. I was tempted to lean across and whisper to the girl that she might be popular now, but no man would ever marry a little hussy like her. She would die a dried-up husk, just like the rest of us.

Then Tom appeared. I was so relieved to see him that any umbrage at his tardiness instantly dissipated. He made no apology, declaring only that he was parched. He asked what I was drinking, before answering his own question: 'Ah, gin! Mother's ruin. Let's the two of us get sloshed, eh?' His lack of contrition led me to wonder if I had been mistaken about the time of our meeting, but it was more likely that in the Bohemian circles in which he no doubt mixed, punctuality was regarded as incurably 'square'. I must, I resolved, not be a square. Rebecca Smyth was not a square. What mattered was that he was here. I had not been given the go-by, and I was now safeguarded from both the unsolicited advances of the brutish navvies and the pitying looks of my neighbours.

While Tom was at the bar, I took another sip of my gin. I rarely touched what my mother referred to as 'the demon drink'. For a man to be drunk was frowned upon, but an inebriated woman was the very definition of degeneracy and merited no sympathy for whatever ill fortune she brought upon herself. It was not that my mother did not drink (a teetotaller being every bit as suspect as a drunk), but whenever a social gathering called for her to indulge in a glass of sherry, she would always declare: 'Just a small one for me,' with heavy emphasis on the last two words, while casting a meaningful look in my father's direction. After her death, Father would allow Veronica and me a small glass of sherry at Christmas. It seemed implausible that this sickly stuff could be associated with any demonic behaviour.

My second sip tasted a little better than the first, but even so, it was hard to see what might possess a person to voluntarily imbibe such stuff. When Tom returned from the bar, I saw with dismay that, along with a pint of beer for himself, he had bought me a second gin. He placed these drinks on the table and sat down on the chair opposite. We clinked glasses. 'Bottoms up,' I said. He repeated the phrase in a way that made it clear he thought it comically antediluvian. I congratulated myself on having inadvertently made a joke. He took such a deep swallow of his beer that one would think he had spent the day toiling in the fields. I dutifully took a mouthful of gin. These preliminaries concluded, Tom placed his half-empty glass on the table and leant in towards me, as if we were about to engage in a conspiracy.

'So, Rebecca Smyth,' he said, 'tell me about yourself.' He cupped his chin between his large hands and cocked an eyebrow. His hair was thick and well oiled. Dark hairs spouted from the backs of his fingers. If one were required to describe him to the police, the word 'hirsute' would certainly be employed. I wondered if he might even be a certain part Greek.

My instinct was to reply that there was nothing much to tell, but Rebecca Smyth would never make such a limp response. She took an enthusiastic swig from her glass.

'Well, you already know I'm a nut,' she said.

'Yes, but I don't know what kind of nut.'

'Just a common or garden nut.'

'Ah,' he said, 'I was hoping for something a little more exotic. A brazil or an almond, a monkey nut even.'

'Sorry to disappoint you,' said Rebecca. 'I'm more of a hazelnut.' I myself could never have come up with such a witty response.

'Nothing wrong with hazelnuts,' he said. 'As a matter of fact I'm quite partial to a hazelnut.'

I was unsure whether he was still talking about nuts or was, once again, flirting with me. There was a lull in the conversation. Normally, I would have been inclined to fill such a silence with a banal remark about the weather, but Rebecca told me to keep schtum. It was for Tom to make the running. I made a start on the second gin. It did not taste half as bad as the first one. I lit a cigarette and leaned back on the banquette. I let the smoke flow from my mouth in its own time.

'But being a nut can't be a full-time occupation,' Tom said.

As it was clear that a conversation had to be had, Rebecca told him all about her job at Mr Brownlee's. Of course, she embellished shamelessly. Her life was an endless round of premieres and cocktail parties. She referred to Laurence Olivier as 'Larry' and said that he was the most charming chap. Only the other night, she blathered on, she had been at a party with Richard Burton and Claire Bloom, where everyone had been smoking pot. Later on, it had turned into a veritable orgy and she had walked home through Hyde Park at daybreak. Rebecca delivered this stream of claptrap, pausing only to guzzle her gin. When both the gin and the claptrap dried up, I felt ashamed to be associated with her. Tom, however, looked decidedly impressed. He really was a striking fellow. His brown eyes shone as if they were covered in a film of moisture. I caught the tomboy at the next table looking admiringly at him. He was considerably more handsome than either of her chaperons.

Two of the cardinal sins of my childhood were Staring and Asking Questions. I have observed, however, that the latter, at least, is not nearly as offensive as I had been brought up to believe. Indeed, in social situations such as the one in which I now found myself, it is regarded as nigh on compulsory. So I said: 'And what about you?'

Tom shrugged. This, it seemed, was his characteristic gesture, but it could signify all sorts of things. At this point it implied something like, 'Well, it's not very interesting, but since you ask—' He told me he came from a small town in what he called The Black Country. His father was dead in the war. His mother was a schoolteacher. He had two younger sisters. When he was twelve he had been given a box brownie and from that moment had wanted to become a photographer. That's why he had come to London. He didn't want to be doing the kind of stuff he was doing now, but it was better than nothing. He asked if I had seen an advertisement for the Sunbeam Mixmaster. Rebecca fibbed that she had seen it in the *Woman's Journal*. He shrugged again, dismissively this time, but actually revealing himself to be rather proud. 'I took the pictures for that campaign,' he said.

'How marvellous,' she said.

'I took the ones for Bon Vivant Soup as well.'

I was suitably impressed. The idea that I was in the company of a man who took photographs (even of something as dull as soup) for the *Journal* was thrilling.

'I'm meeting a chap about some fashion pictures next week,' he said. 'That's where the money is.'

'And the girls,' said Rebecca puckishly.

He had finished his beer. Over his shoulder, the pub was now a throng of people. They were spinning as if they were on a merry-go-round. The din of conversation was deafening. Tom pushed back his chair and stood up.

'Same again,' he said, pointing to my glass. It was more a statement than a question. Still, gin did not seem half as bad as it had at first. I might even grow to like it.

While Tom was gone, I took the opportunity to retouch my make-up. The face that looked back at me from the mirror of my compact was not really so ghastly. I stretched my lips into a wide 'O' and re-applied my lipstick. As I snapped the compact closed, I saw that one of the men at the adjacent table was watching me. Rebecca gave him a haughty stare and he looked away.

Tom reappeared with the drinks. He settled himself in and took a swig of his beer, leaving a caterpillar of foam on his top lip, which he licked off, the tip of his tongue lingering a moment in the corner of his mouth, before retreating like a surprised mouse. When he spoke again, it was with a new seriousness.

'So,' he said, 'what's he like?'

I knew perfectly well whom he meant, but I feigned ignorance. 'What's who like?'

'Braithwaite,' he said. 'The great Collins Braithwaite.'

I felt put out, as if our conversation up to this point had been a mere preamble; that this was his real motive for asking me for a drink. 'Why do you ask?'

Tom explained that he had seen Braithwaite in the area now and again. 'Curious sort of fellow,' he said. 'You hear all sorts of stuff about him.'

'Such as?'

Another shrug. 'You know, the usual sort of stuff: girls, parties, drugs.'

Rebecca made a face, as if such things were of no interest to her. 'If you're so fascinated by him, why don't you go and see him yourself?' she said.

Tom glanced down at his pint. He started mumbling something, but his sentence trailed off. He drank more beer.

'I'm sorry?' said Rebecca.

'Well,' he said, 'I don't really have any reason to.'

'You mean you're not a nut like me?'

'Well, you're not really a nut, are you? I mean, not a proper nut,' he said. 'I mean, it's quite the thing these days to sit and tell some shrink all about your dreams. Especially if the shrink is Braithwaite.'

'He doesn't believe in any of that nonsense about dreams,' I said. For some reason, I felt the need to defend him.

'Oh no?' He was eager for more information. 'So what does he believe in?'

'I wouldn't know. But I do know that he's unlike anyone I've ever met.' I was annoyed that this turn in the conversation had spoilt the convivial atmosphere between us. I took a sip of gin. 'You seem more interested in him than you are in me.'

'Not at all,' he said. 'I couldn't be more interested in you, Rebecca.'

I lit a cigarette and exhaled a stream of smoke into his face.

More drinks were procured. Tom apparently decided that he was on safer ground talking about things he had photographed. These included vacuum cleaners, sets of cutlery and central heating boilers. The boiler had been a tricky job, he told me. It was difficult to make a boiler look interesting. I was by that time having difficulty concentrating. And I was having difficulty remembering to be Rebecca. It took a great deal more effort to be Rebecca than to be myself. But if it had just been down to me, I wouldn't be there in the first place. This was what people did. They sat in pubs drinking beer and gin and listening to each other talk. They pretended to be interested and then took their own turn at talking. It was difficult to see the point of any of it. I was sure the navvies were not in the least bit interested in what their companions had to say. They were here only to drown themselves in beer, and yet even they felt obliged to maintain some semblance of conversation. At the neighbouring table, the repartee was merely a joust between two young men to win the favour of the girl sitting between them like a prize in the church fête raffle. The man at the table by the door was still there with his newspaper. He had been sitting silently with the same glass of beer all this time. I envied him.

I had lost the thread of what Tom was saying. I looked at him. His mouth continued to move, but his words were subsumed in the general din. I decided I needed to use the powder room and stood up. Tom pointed to a door on the other side of the pub. I moved unsteadily on my feet, as if I had received a blow to the head. I felt the same sort of numbness too. I had often seen men in the streets around Soho staggering from one side of the pavement to the other. I had always assumed that they were not really drunk, but were merely, for reasons of their own, acting drunk. Clearly, I had been wrong, for I now found myself lurching across the bar in precisely the same manner. I was, I realised to my horror, inebriated.

I managed to push open the door to the Ladies. There was a single cubicle and a small washbasin. I thought I was going to faint and steadied myself on the wall. Then I felt myself gag and swiftly vomited down the front of my blouse. There wasn't much to it. Some yellowish slime and the remains of the scone I had forced down at Mrs Clay's. I clung to the washbasin. There was a small towel, hanging from a hook. Congratulating myself on my clarity of thought, I dampened it in the sink and started to wipe my blouse. The pieces of scone were easily dealt with, but I succeeded only in working the slime further into the fabric. The blouse, for which I had paid £1 15/-, would be ruined. Then I felt a second heave, and more vomitus welled into my mouth. I swallowed what I could, but that only brought on further spasms. When the tomboy from the next table came in, I was bent over the sink with a thread of spittle hanging from my mouth. She was commendably business-like. My boyfriend, she explained, had asked her to check that I was all right, as I had been gone for some time. Even in my abject state, I felt a thrill that she had referred to Tom as my boyfriend. She stood me upright and wiped my mouth. I had made a proper mess of myself, she told me. I nodded sadly and started to cry. The girl told me there no need for that. These things happened to the best of us. I stood there like a child as she unbuttoned my blouse and made me take it off. Then she turned it inside out and instructed me to put it back on. It was with some difficulty that we buttoned it from the inside. 'Men never notice things like this,' she said. She pushed my hair back from my face and told me there was no harm done. I reprimanded myself for the unkind thoughts I had earlier had about her. She led me back through the pub by the hand. Tom asked if everything was all right. I said I was fine, but it was late and I was ready to go home. He downed his pint and led me through the crowded pub by the elbow. After he had put me in a taxi, he ran after it and knocked on the window. The driver pulled up. With some difficulty, I managed to wind down the window. He had forgotten to ask for my telephone number. I obediently gave it to him. This Rebecca, I reflected, must be quite something.

Braithwaite II: Oxford

It was during his second spell at Oxford that the character of 'Collins Braithwaite' properly came into being. Now twenty-eight, Braithwaite was both older and more worldly than the majority of his cohort. He had lived in France, seen a bit of life and, most importantly, had his experiences at Netley to draw on. He no longer felt the need to fit in with his privately educated peers and, if anything, now exaggerated his Northern drawl and coarse manners. It was at this time that he evolved the curious speaking pattern that would later be so frequently commented upon. When presenting his work or reading a passage aloud, he would place the emphasis on unimportant words, typically prepositions or articles, before leaving a long pause. 'Sentences,' noted one of his tutors, 'staggered from clause to clause like a drunk along a corridor.' The effect was 'both comic and mesmerising'. Of course, it was an affectation: merely by altering his manner of speech, Braithwaite had found a means of beguiling his listeners. Psychology was still regarded, along with English literature, as a 'soft' subject and the majority of students were female. Braithwaite used his new power to seduce to good effect. Post-war mores were loosening and the female students at Oxford were beginning to detach themselves from their parents' ideas about sex and class.

From the outset, Braithwaite found himself at the centre of things. He did not have to go out of his way to woo girls, using the licence afforded by the novelty of being Northern and working class to dispense with traditional courtship rituals. Sara Chisholm, later a successful BBC radio producer, was one of those who fell for his questionable charms. 'He was generally aloof and dismissive towards women,' she told me, 'but somehow that only added to the attraction.'* At the end of a particularly wild party, held in the lodgings of one of his circle, he suggested she come back to his room to fuck. 'I had never even heard this word spoken aloud before,' she recalls, 'but, of course, I went with him. At the time, it seemed liberating. He was challenging you to prove that you were above all the middle-class guff about courting we'd been taught by our parents. Afterwards, he made it clear that he couldn't care less about you, but you kept going back because you knew there were any number of other girls willing to jump into bed with him.' Also, she confesses, he knew how to please a woman sexually. There was none of the frustrating timidity she had experienced with young men of more conventional Oxford backgrounds.

Sara Chisholm saw Braithwaite off and on for a year or so, though they never considered themselves a couple. In retrospect, she sees the relationship as borderline abusive, but at the time she was enthralled. 'Everyone—men and women—just wanted to be in his orbit.'

Every second Sunday, Braithwaite held a gathering in his rooms. The Wagstaff Club was named after the Groucho Marx character in *Horse Feathers*, who, after being appointed head of Huxley College, sings the song *(Whatever It Is) I'm Against It*, while lampooning the ancient faculty members. Each meeting of the Club ended with a shambolic rendition of the song performed by Braithwaite and whoever else was still conscious. The title represents a fair summation of his intellectual position, which was essentially destructive and oppositional. Whatever argument one of his adversaries put forward, Braithwaite would take up a contrary, or more extreme, position. Nor did he have any qualms about contradicting himself

* Telephone interview with the author, 17th January 2020.

from one week to the next. As such, no one ever knew what he actually believed. The truth was, he didn't believe in anything. The only thing worth believing in, he said, was the here and now, and that was, by its very nature, transitory: existence had to be recognised as fleeting and meaningless. Anything else was a form of self-deception.

Each meeting of the Wagstaff Club was structured round a text proposed by Braithwaite. Students from a variety of subjects, and even some junior members of staff, attended. The readings were drawn from philosophy, literature or psychology, depending on what Braithwaite happened to be into at the time. A great deal of beer and whisky was consumed and the debate would continue into the small hours. Braithwaite would read passages aloud before inviting responses. Men and women attended, but, according to Sara Chisholm, the girls were there to nod earnestly and were not expected to voice opinions of their own. Braithwaite would appear to listen patiently to other views, before delivering a verdict that was invariably adopted as orthodoxy. Attendees measured the success of their own contributions according to how closely they aligned with Braithwaite's. It was, says Chisholm, 'all rather pathetic'.

Despite this coterie, Braithwaite appears to have had few intimate friends. The closest person to him was Stuart Macadam, the son of a Dunfermline GP, who was reading English literature, and was the only person to whom Braithwaite ever seemed to defer. Macadam would later publish two novels (the first of which, *A Cloistered Life*, features a character clearly inspired by his friend) before taking up a position at the University of St Andrews. Like Sara Chisholm, he has mixed feelings about his relationship with Braithwaite. I met him in his home in Anstruther in February 2020. 'Of course he was a bully,' he recalled. 'He was older than the rest of us and he used that to his advantage. But if he solicited your opinion about something, you felt that you were one of the elect. He didn't like to be challenged, but if you had the guts to call him out on something, he respected you for it.' Once, after a particularly long and bruising Sunday night session, Braithwaite was railing against what he saw as the effete tradition of the English Romantic poets. In response, Macadam stood up and drunkenly recited some verses of Shelley's *Men of England*. When his performance petered out, there was a pause, before Braithwaite got to his feet and lurched across the room towards him. Macadam didn't know if he was going to embrace him or thump him. Instead, he got him in a kind of headlock, which could be interpreted either as aggression or affection. It was an archetypal Braithwaite gesture: you never knew where you stood with him, but if he sensed weakness, you were doomed.

With regards to his relations with women, Macadam has one word to describe him: shameless. 'He said things that no one else would dare to say, the sort of things that would usually earn a guy a slap in the face. But he got away with it. More than that, women, or at least a certain proportion of women, fell for it.' And if someone turned him down, he just laughed it off and shifted his attention elsewhere. Macadam admits to having felt a certain envy towards Braithwaite's power over the opposite sex, but he never had the nerve to replicate his methods. In his memoir, Braithwaite explains his unconventional brand of feminism: 'Women don't want to be *treated* as equals; they *are* equals; in fact, they're our betters in many ways. They deserve to be treated with the same honesty as men. If you want an ice cream, don't ask for a banana. If you want to fuck someone, why ask them to a poetry reading?'

There appears to have been one exception to this brutal credo, however. Alice Trevelyan was the daughter of Andrew

Trevelyan, the London barrister who would later successfully defend Iain Stott in the *Red Rooster* obscenity trial of 1962. She was a pretty and exceptionally bright girl, always near the top of her class at St Paul's Girls' School in Hammersmith. At Oxford she was reading English literature, the favoured subject for female students who would never have any need to earn a living. She was an earnest, dreamy girl with a fondness for Keats, Spenser's *Faerie Queen* and the Pre-Raphaelite painters. She was introduced to Braithwaite by Macadam one sunny afternoon on the lawns at Balliol College. Macadam was surprised to observe that Braithwaite was unusually civil to her and went as far as to enquire about her background and studies. His usual bluster was entirely absent. Macadam had to leave to attend a tutorial and was surprised to find the pair still deep in conversation when he returned over an hour later. He had never seen Braithwaite behave so solicitously towards anyone. He even seemed to have softened his usually gruff tones and nodded earnestly as Alice told him about her childhood in London and Cornwall, where her family had a second home. At first, Macadam found all this amusing. The wild beast had been tamed by the sort of privileged girl whom he ordinarily made a point of insulting or shocking with some display of boorish behaviour. When he jokingly pointed this out, Braithwaite dismissed his remarks by saying that Alice was 'nowt but a lass'. Later, however, Macadam would greatly regret ever having introduced them.

During the Trinity term of 1955, Braithwaite and Alice often went for walks or for a ploughman's lunch together. He conducted himself with relentless chivalry. Alice was never invited to attend the Wagstaff Club. Clearly Braithwaite could not reconcile the contrasting personas he adopted for these different compartments of his life. During the summer of that year, Braithwaite even spent a week at the Trevelyan property near Truro, where he and Alice slept in separate rooms and he behaved respectfully towards Alice's parents, as well as to her younger brother, Anthony, with whom he played tennis and discussed poetry. In short, he did everything he could to ingratiate himself into the good graces of the family. When university reconvened in the autumn, Braithwaite took Alice for a weekend walking on the North York Moors. Bizarrely, they stayed in the Buck Inn—the same pub George Braithwaite had visited on the day of his suicide—and it was here that the relationship was finally consummated. Although no marriage proposal was made, Alice must have felt that this was what Braithwaite's courtship of her was leading up to. Although sexual mores were loosening, the vast majority of women were still virgins on their wedding night or had only ever slept with their fiancé. After the trip to the Moors, however, Braithwaite's ardour cooled. He told Alice that he had no intention of marrying her, or anyone else for that matter. Nor had he ever given her cause to believe otherwise. Alice was humiliated. On Christmas Eve at the family home in London, she swallowed a quantity of pills. It was, it must be said, a half-hearted suicide attempt, necessitating no more than a couple of days' recuperation in hospital. But in Andrew Trevelyan, Braithwaite had made his first powerful enemy.

Although Braithwaite spends over forty pages of *My Self and Other Strangers* on his years in Oxford, much of it recounting his sexual exploits, Alice Trevelyan does not merit a single mention. She suffered no lasting damage and married a young solicitor named Fredrick Drummond in 1960. The couple had four children and remained married until her death in 2016. It would be facile to indulge in a pseudo-psychoanalytic explanation of Braithwaite's behaviour. Such an analysis would point to the fact that Alice shared his mother's name and, to some extent, resembled her both in appearance and character. Braithwaite either wanted, in classically Oedipal fashion, to fuck his mother, or was unconsciously seeking to punish her for abandoning him as a child. The truth, however, is probably more reprehensible. When Stuart Macadam heard what Alice had done, he made some consoling remarks to Braithwaite. His friend's reply chilled him: 'It's kind of the ultimate thing, innit,' he said, 'to have a girl try to top herself over you.' Macadam still remembers the spiteful tone in which this verdict was delivered. From that point, Macadam did his best to distance himself from Braithwaite, although he did not have the courage to explicitly break off the relationship.

Braithwaite graduated with a first-class degree in 1956. He did not attend the graduation ceremony and made it plain to anyone who would listen that he did not place any value on such baubles and had done only the minimum necessary work. This was nonsense. The then Professor of Psychology, Dr George Humphrey, had long recognised Braithwaite's talents. It was precisely Braithwaite's aversion to authority and received wisdom that set him apart from his peers. Even if he was knee-jerkingly iconoclastic, he had the ability to think things that no one else was thinking. 'He was,' Professor Humphrey wrote, 'undoubtedly the most gifted student I came across during the nine years I was in charge of the department.' It was he who persuaded Braithwaite to continue his studies. That Braithwaite chose to remain in the rarefied atmosphere of Oxford for another three years might seem incongruous. In his own memoir, he passes over the decision without comment. The fact is, however, that his degree qualified him for little, he had no money and Oxford provided something akin to a home. He was a big beast on campus. People deferred to him, and there was no shortage of girls willing to sleep with him.

In a single week in the May of that same year, John Osborne's *Look Back in Anger* premiered at the Royal Court theatre in London and Colin Wilson's survey of existential literature, *The Outsider*, was published. Osborne was born to middle-class parents in London and brought up in Surrey. The twenty-six-year-old Wilson was from a working-class background in Leicester and, following a succession of dead-end jobs, had written *The Outsider* in the British Library reading room while allegedly sleeping rough on Hampstead Heath. Osborne and Wilson had never met, but courtesy of a *Daily Express* headline, the era of the Angry Young Men had dawned. Both were lauded as the voice of the post-war generation. There followed a spate of works, both in fiction and film, depicting life in the North of England, written by working-class writers like John Braine, Alan Sillitoe, Stan Barstow and (the sole angry young woman) Shelagh Delaney. Regardless of how much the writers lumped together under this banner actually had in common, there is no question that the movement represented an assault on the established traditions of British culture.

Both *Look Back in Anger* and *The Outsider* had a considerable impact on Braithwaite. In his memoir, Braithwaite describes reading *The Outsider*: 'There was no doubt that, despite its faults, here was something electrifying.' He immediately wrote to Wilson and asked if they could meet. Wilson, who had no qualms about declaring himself to be 'the most important thinker of the age', accepted.

Two weeks later, Braithwaite hitch-hiked to London and the two men met in the Three Greyhounds pub on Greek Street in Soho. Also present were Wilson's friend Bill Hopkins and Edward Seers, an editor at Methuen. Wilson had become used to holding court and expected due deference from a mere graduate student from Oxford. After an initial exchange of handshakes and round-buying, Braithwaite launched into a critique of Wilson's work, accusing him of being enslaved to nebulous ideas about spirituality and an out-dated concept of morality. Far from being an outsider, Wilson was actually buttressing established ways of thinking. Any admiration he had for Wilson's book, or for Wilson himself, was completely eclipsed by the need to establish himself as the dominant male in the group. Wilson reportedly looked at him across the table for some moments, assessing his opponent. 'And have you brought me a copy of your own book?' he asked. Braithwaite blustered that, when he did write a book, it would be a damn sight better than *The Outsider*. Hopkins intervened with an offer to get another round in. The session continued for some hours and, when the conversation stuck to neutral topics, was good-natured enough, but the intellectual rutting was never far from the surface. Eventually, however, Wilson accused Braithwaite of being no more than a nihilist, intent on destruction. Braithwaite responded that he was a nihilist, but that was better than being a mithering spinster like Wilson. Wilson then told Braithwaite to fuck off back to Oxford. Braithwaite grabbed Wilson by the lapels, spilling several pints in the process, but before any proper blows were landed, the two were separated and Braithwaite was thrown out. He could be heard loudly decrying 'soft London ponces' from the street. Years later, Wilson took his revenge in an *Observer* review of *Untherapy*, calling it (among other things), 'the degenerate outpourings of a third-rate mind'.

During the same trip, Braithwaite went to see Osborne's play at the Royal Court on Sloane Square, and while he had never been much interested in politics, he recognised something of himself in the play's protagonist, the hectoring Jimmy Porter. More importantly, however, this was the beginning of a fascination with the stage and with the people that inhabited it: actors. Growing up in Darlington, theatre was not part of the

Braithwaite family landscape, and at Oxford the drama society was the preserve of the sort of upper-middle-class dilettantes he despised. He considered the whole enterprise effete. But, in *Look Back in Anger*, he found a theatre that was visceral and connected to a world he recognised. After the performance, he spotted Kenneth Haigh, who had played Jimmy Porter, in the nearby Fox and Hounds pub. 'I was fascinated,' he later wrote. 'Half an hour before, I had been watching him ranting on stage, *being* Jimmy Porter. Yet here he was, talking affably in an accent I recognised [Haigh was from Mexborough in South Yorkshire]. I wondered which of the performances was more real.'

Braithwaite returned to Oxford reinvigorated. His bruising encounter with Colin Wilson had had no effect on him. He thrived on conflict and the good opinion of others meant little to him. There was a sense that something was shifting in Britain, that culture was becoming less enslaved to traditional ideas; that the class system was becoming less rigid; in short, that the time was ripe for a Northern grammar school boy with ideas above his station. The sense of foment he had encountered in London had not yet filtered through to Oxford, however, and the stuffy atmosphere and unchanging demographic of the student body began to rankle. The Wagstaff Club was a thing of the past. It no longer interested Braithwaite to have a coterie of fawning acolytes. His mind was elsewhere, and every few weeks he would hitch-hike to London and sleep on the floor of Stuart Macadam's tiny bedsit in Kensington. Macadam was working in a bookshop on Charing Cross Road and writing his first novel. Braithwaite, he explained, would turn up unannounced, often drunk, and then grumble that Macadam hadn't got any beer in for him. He ate whatever food was in the flat and refused to clear up after himself. If Macadam had to work, he gave his key to Braithwaite so that he could come and go as he pleased. On more than one occasion, he returned to find himself locked out because Braithwaite was in his bed with a girl. When Macadam complained about this, Braithwaite simply told him to get another key cut. Eventually, Macadam had no option but to move to new digs. For years he lived in dread of bumping into his erstwhile friend, but he never saw him again. 'No doubt he found other people stupid enough to put up with him,' he said.

The only person willing to tolerate Braithwaite at this time was Zelda Ogilvie, the daughter of two middle-class schoolteachers, Robert 'Rab' Ogilvie and Diane Ogilvie (née Carmichael). Aside from his teaching duties, Rab was a minor poet who published three pamphlets in the 1920s and whose poem *Yon Scunnered Lands* met with the approval of Hugh MacDiarmid and became something of a rallying call for the then nascent Scottish nationalist movement. Diane was a decent watercolourist and member of the Edinburgh Art Club, at which she frequently exhibited. The walls of the family home in Morningside were hung with numerous examples of her work. Once a month the couple held a salon to which artists, writers and students were invited. It was an unconventional upbringing, and one in which Zelda was encouraged to pursue her own artistic and creative endeavours. She was an only child and fantasised about having a brother named Zeno, with whom she carried on frequent, earnest conversations. At mealtimes she would eat only half her food, leaving the rest for Zeno. Her mother addressed this issue by setting a place for Zeno and including him in conversations. Zelda then became jealous and a few weeks later announced that there was no longer any need to set a place for Zeno as he had died of pneumonia. She was seven years old.

Zelda went to Oxford in 1954 to read history of art. She dressed eccentrically in over-sized men's tweed jackets, plus fours and sometimes even sported a monocle. She wore no make-up and had her hair cut in a mannish short-back-and-sides. She was widely assumed to be a lesbian, but, she told an interviewer in 1988: 'I never even dabbled. I always liked men.' In 1956, the year Braithwaite embarked on his doctorate, she was entering the final year of her undergraduate degree. She was aware of Braithwaite by reputation and had attended the Wagstaff Club on a couple of occasions. 'I found him insufferable,' she said, 'and I could not understand the pull he seemed to exert on people.' When, inevitably, Braithwaite propositioned her in his usual crude way, she told him in equally blunt terms where to go.

Zelda's reluctance only had the effect of inflaming Braithwaite's interest in her. With the astuteness that would later characterise so many of his relationships with clients, he wrote a series of letters to Zelda under the name of 'Colin Arthur'. The letters were not intended as a deception, but to appeal to someone he recognised to be self-consciously adopting a persona. In these letters, 'Colin' expressed his admiration for the manner in which Zelda had dealt with the advances of 'that lout Braithwaite'. 'He's a phoney, but no one except you seems to see through him. I commend your perspicacity!' he wrote. He had himself long admired Zelda, he went on, but had been too bashful to make her acquaintance. The letters appealed to Zelda and she agreed to meet her correspondent in the Three Goats Head pub on St Michael's Street.

Zelda turned up in her usual garb, on this occasion with the addition of a pair of pince-nez and a flat cap. Braithwaite explained that Colin Arthur had been called away but that she had, in any case, had a lucky escape. Colin Arthur was a rogue and not to be trusted. Zelda gazed haughtily at him with the characteristic tilted way of holding her head, apparent in many later photographs. She explained that she had not yet decided whether she was going to sleep with him. Braithwaite asked if there was anything he could do to help her make up her mind.

'Nothing at all,' Zelda said. 'I'm capricious.'

'In that case, I can assume that at a certain point you will,' Braithwaite replied.

Zelda shrugged.

Braithwaite rose and bought some drinks. As the pub would not serve a woman a pint, she insisted that he buy two halfs and bring her a pint glass into which she could decant them. The evening was spent in conversation about various authors and artists. Their tastes were dissimilar. Zelda loved Brueghel. Braithwaite did not know his work. He championed Picasso on the basis that he continually reinvented himself. Zelda contended that this was only because none of his work was any good. Later, they exchanged stories of their respective upbringings. Braithwaite called her a 'little Scotch bourgeois'. 'If it wasn't for the bourgeoisie,' Zelda retorted, 'you proles wouldn't have anyone to blame for your misery but yourselves.'

The pair went their separate ways at closing time, but Braithwaite was taken with Zelda in a way that he had never been taken by anyone before. 'I had met plenty of folk who were smarter than me,' he later wrote, 'but Zelda was the first person who knew she was smarter than me.' She was, in short, a person who could not be bullied, cajoled or browbeaten.

They met again, in similar circumstances, a few weeks later. It was approaching the end of the Hilary term, and Zelda explained that she would be going to Edinburgh to visit her parents. They were worried that she 'was Lesbian', and he would be doing her a favour if he visited for a few days and played boyfriend. Braithwaite agreed and followed her up the East Coast line a few days later. Needless to say, the Ogilvies, keen to demonstrate their Bohemian credentials, insisted on the couple sharing a bedroom.

Things continued in a similar vein over the next three years. The relationship was never exclusive. Zelda studiously avoided anything that might resemble routine. Sometimes, they would spend a Sunday in Braithwaite's rooms, reading and intermittently fucking. Occasionally, they would go away for a weekend. At other times, weeks passed when they did not so much as speak to each other. Such studied randomness might be thought to constitute a routine of its own, but regardless of the eccentricity of the arrangement, it seemed to suit both parties well.

Braithwaite's doctoral thesis, *Phantasms and Hallucinations*, written during this period, takes as its starting point a discussion of Josef Breuer's 1895 case study of Anna O. This opening chapter is mischievously titled 'Histoire d'O', after Pauline Réage's erotic novel of 1954, which Braithwaite had procured on a trip to Paris (he was a lifelong aficionado of pornography). According to Breuer, Anna O, 'complained of the deep darkness inside her head…of having two selves, her real self and a bad one […] The two states of consciousness existed alongside one another: the primary state in which the patient was quite normal; and the "second" state which might well be compared with dreams, given the wealth of phantasms and hallucinations, the large gaps in her memory, the lack of inhibition and control over her thoughts. In this second state the patient was alienated.'

From the outset, Braithwaite takes issue with Breuer's hierarchy between the primary and secondary state. Who is to say, he asks, in which state—or if indeed in either—the patient is alienated? Breuer's contention depends on his dismissal of Anna's 'phantasms and hallucinations' as invalid experiences and his championing instead of being 'in control' of one's thoughts. For Braithwaite, the secondary state represented in the case of Anna O should be regarded as every bit as 'real' as the primary state. While for Breuer, the situation could be described thus: 'It is difficult to express the situation other than by saying that the patient had two personalities, one of which was psychically normal and the other mentally ill'; for Braithwaite, the solution to Anna O's problem was not for the 'illness to run its course' until the patient sees herself as 'a single undivided personality', but instead to embrace the idea that a person is not a single self, but a bundle of personae, all of which should be valued equally. 'One does not expect a mother to favour one of her children over the others,' he writes. 'Why should things be any different with our selves?'

He then takes examples from the literature of the doppelganger. There is a lengthy discussion of Dostoyevsky's *The Double*, the gist of which is that if the story had been told from the opposite point of view it would be Mr Golyadkin who is seen as the interloper, rather than the 'double' who shares his name and physique. So it is, says Braithwaite, with the self: we take the part of the one we know first and dismiss all others as imposters.

Braithwaite develops his argument with a discussion of Edgar Allan Poe's 1839 short story *William Wilson*. This concerns a man dogged from childhood by a figure who shares his name, date of birth and appearance. After describing his schooldays, the narrator recounts how, in order to escape this double, he descends into wickedness. The double appears throughout the story as a moralising influence, attempting to restrain the narrator from committing his base acts. There is a constant battle between them: 'Wilson continued his attempts to command me, while I continued my attempts to rule him.'

William Wilson ends when the narrator confronts his double and puts a sword through his heart. But it is not his double he has run through: it is himself. Wilson's final words, and those of the story, are: 'I have lost. Yet from now on you are also dead. In me you lived—and, in my death…you have killed—yourself!'

Braithwaite's thesis is chaotic, inconsistent, sometimes dazzling, often baffling. The range of references is eclectic, reflecting his own wide reading, but this is part of the problem. He drags in Sophocles, Plato, Freud and Jung, but he never truly engages with any of the authors he quotes. Their words are mere gewgaws for Braithwaite to adorn his arguments. He is dismissive of others' theories, but fails to propose any systematic alternative of his own. The whole thing is a kind of bonfire of other people's ideas ('Whatever it is, I'm against it'). And yet it contains the seeds of everything that would find its way into the book that would soon make him famous: *Kill Your Self*.

The Third Notebook

I confess I have come to look forward to sitting down with my notebooks of an evening. They have given me a sense of purpose. Previously, I would keep Father company in the parlour; he with his crossword, I with a book or magazine. Other than habit, there was no real reason for this. All topics of conversation were invariably exhausted over supper, but if I withdrew to my room, I felt I was abandoning him to the clutches of Mrs Llewelyn. In the early days of her occupation, Mrs Llewelyn asked why I did not have a hobby with which to amuse myself. Naturally, I considered her question impertinent and said so.

I have always detested the ghastly pastimes upon which girls are encouraged to squander their lives. Spending hours squinting over an embroidery ring does not strike me as a worthwhile use of anyone's time. For the lower classes, sewing or knitting may be a necessity, but we are not paupers and there is no need for me to go about in homemade togs. Of course, there is the piano, but since Veronica's death it has been no more than an ornament. The sum of musical talent in our family resided in her stubby fingers. Father loved listening to her play and I would feel that I was cruelly summoning her ghost were I even to raise the lid of the keyboard. So I spent my evenings in the brocade armchair reading novels about Modern Independent Women who throw it all up at the first whiff of matrimony.

I long ago resolved never to become a Modern Independent Woman. I do not myself understand this current mania for freedom. It seems to me that we would all be a good deal better off if we accepted our lot in life, rather than struggling to throw off some imagined shackles. I realise that not everyone is as fortunate as me, but this constant striving for things above one's station is no more than a recipe for discontent. I want nothing more than to look after my father and be able to treat myself now and then to a new coat or a pair of stockings. That is not to say that when I am out and about, I do not sometimes feel a stab of envy towards those to whom success comes easily, but we cannot all be tip-toppers. It is better all round to accept one's allotted portion in life. All the needlepoint and pianoforte in the world cannot alter the fact that, for most of us, quiet despair is the best we can hope for.

I have not always felt this way. There was a time when I felt more optimistic about life. This embarrassing interlude occurred in the months shortly after my twenty-first birthday. Mother had been dead for six years and Veronica was off conquering Cambridge. Over supper one evening, Father told me that I mustn't sacrifice myself on his altar. When I asked what he meant, he said that I should go out into the world and not feel that I had to stay at home ministering to him; that was no life for a young woman, especially in these emaciated times. I expect he meant 'emancipated', but I did not correct him. Nor did I tell him that that I had no desire to 'go out into the world', that I was perfectly happy staying at home to look after him. No one objects to a woman staying at home to care for her husband. Why should it be any different if that man is her father? But I knew he was right. On the rare occasions when I attended a social gathering, people changed the subject when I told them what I did, or looked at me as if I was not right in the head. The truth was, I was scared. I was scared of everything. Women with jobs seemed to me to belong to an entirely different species. They inhabited a world in which people Achieved Things, exchanged *bons mots* over cocktails and blithely indulged in extra-marital affairs. The chief benefit of my employment at Mr Brownlee's has been the realisation that the world of work is populated by clots and ninnies just like me.

The business of 'finding a job' proved more straightforward than I had imagined. I waited until the following Monday and, having spent the weekend being physically sick with nerves, left the house at eight o'clock. I bought myself a copy of the *Standard* and marched along in my best suit and heels, repeating my new mantra to myself: I am a Modern Independent Woman. I AM a Modern Independent Woman. By the time I reached the Lyons on Elgin Avenue, I had almost begun to believe it. I ordered a pot of tea and turned to the Situations Vacant. I had given no thought to the kind of 'situation' to which I might apply. Clearly, it would have to be something for which no particular talent or aptitude was necessary, for other than the typing skills St Paul's forced on its less academic pupils, I had little to offer. I determined, however, not to let this lack of credentials stand in my way and circled every advertisement from which I was not explicitly disqualified. Having finished my tea, I refreshed my lipstick and proceeded to the telephone box on the pavement outside. The first three situations I enquired about were not vacant at all. On being told this for a fourth time, I asked rather snootily why the notice was still in the paper. I was informed that, although the advertisements ran for a fortnight, positions were usually filled within a few hours. Nonetheless, I persevered. A Modern Independent Woman cannot allow herself to be easily disheartened, and a few calls later I had secured an appointment for half past three that afternoon. The advertisement read only: 'Agency seeks Girl Friday. Wages commensurate with experience.' I had no idea what a Girl Friday was, but as my only previous job had been as a Saturday Girl, it seemed a good omen.

In the intervening hours, however, the get-up-and-go I had so determinedly nurtured ebbed away. I was no Modern Independent Woman. All I wanted was to stay at home, looking after my daddy, reading novels and amusing myself in front of my bedroom mirror. I cursed Emmeline Pankhurst and her gang of Jezebels for ruining everything. Nevertheless, at the appointed hour I presented myself at the offices of Charles Brownlee, Theatrical Agent, on Old Compton Street. I gave my name to the moderately attractive receptionist and was told to take a seat next to two other candidates; Mr Brownlee would see me shortly. In order to bolster my dwindling confidence, I made an inventory of my rivals' shortcomings. The first was a middle-aged woman with fat ankles and an unsightly bruise on her shin. Her coat was frayed at the hem and she sat with her knees apart. The second contender presented a greater challenge. She was a little hussy of no more than eighteen; pretty and long-haired, wearing a tight yellow sweater, white knee-length boots and a skirt that in any other era would have been deemed an obscenity. She smiled condescendingly at me, no doubt assured that her state of undress would win over the as-yet-unseen Mr Brownlee. I smiled back, girding myself with the thought of the carefully folded typing certificate in my bag.

When my turn came, I took the seat in front of Mr Brownlee's desk and sat up straight with the palms of my hands resting on my knees. Mr Brownlee looked at me for a few moments, not without disapproval. I judged him to be somewhere in the no man's land of his late forties or early fifties. He was dressed in an unfashionable brown suit with a narrow pinstripe and a kipper tie with a motif of Grecian masks. His hair was thinning and combed across a flaky scalp. He had a neatly clipped moustache, which, along with a kindly air, went some way towards making up for the shabbiness of his attire. He stubbed out his cigarette in a pewter ashtray. The interview consisted of a single question:

'Do you think you could do what Miss Evans out there does? She's leaving, you see.'

'That would rather depend on what it is she does,' I replied.

Mr Brownlee nodded approvingly. 'A sensible answer, Miss —?'

I reminded him of my name.

'You've no idea the number of girls that come in here and assure me that they could do whatever Miss Evans does before I've even told them what it is.'

'How very imprudent.' I replied modestly.

'Quite so.'

'So, what is that she does do?' I asked.

The duties enumerated did not seem particularly challenging: answering the telephone, typing letters, greeting clients, running errands. I took out my typing certificate and passed it across the desk. This seemed to greatly impress Mr Brownlee. He shrugged, as if inwardly coming to a decision, and said: 'Can you start on Friday? Evans is getting married on Saturday. She can show you the ropes. £6 a week do?' Then he added, 'You're not planning on getting hitched any time soon, are you?'

I assured him that I was not. He came out from behind his desk and we shook hands, like Roosevelt and Churchill reaching an accord.

I had never before understood the phrase 'a spring in one's step', but as I strode along Charing Cross Road, I did. I smiled at passers-by. I passed an espresso bar. I had never been in such a place, but I went in and sat at a table in the window. I ordered a cappuccino. At the next table, three young men with tousled hair and elbow patches on their jackets were huddled over a manuscript. At another, a distinguished-looking gentleman was reading a copy of *The Stage*. Perhaps he was a theatre critic. He caught me looking at him and, for the first time in my life, I did not avert my eyes. I was Girl Friday to Charles Brownlee, Theatrical Agent. I was drinking a cappuccino and would soon be earning £6 a week. I had become, almost by chance, a Modern Independent Woman. The waitress was a pretty girl with eyes thickly painted with kohl. She moved as if at any moment she expected to be photographed. I assumed she was an aspiring actress. Perhaps when I had established myself at Mr Brownlee's, I could pull a few strings for her, and years later she would mention in her memoirs that she was eternally grateful to the woman who had spotted her in an espresso bar on Charing Cross Road. The cappuccino was all froth and cost twice as much as a pot of tea in a Lyons. I resolved, despite my new-found wealth, not to be seduced by such fripperies again.

Father was so delighted by my news that I felt he must have thought me incapable of such a thing. I had waited until I had served the soup before telling him.

'That's excellent, really excellent,' he kept repeating. He gazed at me across the table, his spoon suspended over his plate. 'I'm very proud of you,' he said, as if I was retarded.

'It's only a stupid receptionist's job,' I said. 'A chimpanzee could do it.'

'Yes, but all the same,' he said. 'You never know where it might lead.'

I was rather offended by this remark, but I merely collected the soup bowls and went to the kitchen to ladle out the tinned stew I had heated.

Life at Mr Brownlee's was rather less glamorous than I had envisioned. My days consisted of typing letters and contracts, opening the mail, visiting the Post Office and lending a sympathetic ear to Mr Brownlee's down-at-heel clientele. This raggle-taggle band consisted for the most part of novelty acts, third-rate magicians and crooners whose heyday in variety shows had long passed. The Great Dando dropped in at three o'clock every Wednesday. He would lean across my desk, his breath rank with whisky, and produce a florin from behind my ear, before making it vanish and reappear in his other hand. One time in ten, he pulled it off. The other nine times, the coin would fall from his sleeve and he would be left scrabbling on the floor to retrieve it with shaking fingers. Regardless of the outcome, I feigned wonder, it not being my role to further undermine his confidence. The Great Dando refused to perform at children's parties and, these being the only engagements Mr Brownlee could offer him, he plied his trade in pubs, in exchange for drinks bought out of pity or, more likely, to persuade him to scram. For myself, I grew rather fond of him and looked forward to his visits. Once, while he was waiting to be admitted to Mr Brownlee's office, I asked his real name. 'My real name,' he proclaimed majestically, 'is The Great Dando.' He emphasised the point by pulling a bunch of plastic flowers from his sleeve and presenting them to me with a low bow. When he emerged from his fruitless audience, he asked for his flowers back and clumsily shoved them back where they had come from. 'I could get thrown out of the Magic Circle for that,' he said, tapping the side of his nose. I assured him that his secret was in safe hands. He then clasped my cheeks between his palms and told me I was a good sort.

Aside from The Great Dando and his ilk, the greater part of Mr Brownlee's business consisted in supplying girls to various clubs in Soho. Three or four times a week a girl, invariably from some beastly Northern town, would present herself at my desk, plonk her suitcase at her feet and declare herself to be an actress looking for work. Often they came bearing letters of recommendation from such-and-such a repertory company, or carefully cut-out reviews from the *Bradford Bugle* or similar. Although he was originally from Manchester himself, Mr Brownlee cheerfully detested these girls. 'Fat ankles and fat accents,' he would declare. 'I can't put such trollops on the London stage.' He was a master of persuasion, however. 'If only you had turned up yesterday,' went his spiel to them, 'there was a part going at the Old Vic that would have been perfect for you. I'm sure something will come up soon, but in the meantime—' And with that, the poor wretch would be packed off to an address in Walker's Court to demean herself for as long as she could stand it, before realising her mistake and hitch-hiking back up the A1 to marry Billy, Dick or Arthur and move into the spare room of her in-laws' two-up-two-down. It was on this dismal cycle that Mr Brownlee's trade depended. Turnover was rapid and there was a seemingly unending stream of girls to keep him in business. I kept a box of Kleenex in the top drawer of my desk.

Still, for the first time, I felt that I had found a place in the world. I was no longer invisible. I earned money by my own labour. This is not to say that I blossomed into a normally-functioning member of society, but as Mr Brownlee's clients were all, to a greater or lesser degree, peculiar, I fitted in.

I continued to pass my evenings in the parlour, but I had grown impatient with the drivel I read. There seemed no reason why I could not do better, or at least have a stab at doing so. I began to write little sketches of the characters I encountered at work. Then for a week after supper, I took myself to my room and, in a specially purchased notebook, wrote what was to become my one triumph: *An Agreeable Reception*. My heroine was Iris Chalmers, a receptionist at a theatrical agent's, and the story concerned her liaisons with the men who frequented the agency. It began:

> *Iris Chalmers was not the sort of girl to settle for second best. Her mother had always told her, 'Don't let your flat caps go by you waiting for your top hat.' But Iris had no intention of settling for a flat cap. No, it was to be top hat or bust for Iris*

Chalmers, and one day her top hat walked right into the offices of Brownstone Associates Theatrical Agents where she worked. His name was Ralph Constable. He was tall enough, wealthy enough and more than handsome enough. The trouble was: he was also married enough.

I wrote it in three evenings, lost entirely in the drama of Iris's scrapes (she was always in a pickle). I typed it up during quiet moments at work, concealing my notebook on my lap, lest Mr Brownlee suddenly enter and enquire as to what I was doing. I posted it off and heard nothing for several weeks. I had almost forgotten about it, until I returned home one evening to find an envelope on the hallstand addressed to my chosen nom de plume. Along with my manuscript, it contained a letter written in flamboyant hand from a Mrs Patricia Evesham explaining that, while my story was likely to appeal to the readers of the *Woman's Journal* and was adequately well written, certain aspects meant that they were unable to publish it in its current form. They could not, she went on, publish a story featuring a heroine who so casually entered into an adulterous liaison. Were I to make the amendments indicated on the manuscript, however, they would reconsider. 'Adequately well written' was an undreamt of accolade. I was, moreover, secretly thrilled to learn that my heroine was too depraved for the readership of the *Journal* and immediately set to work to repair my errors. Ralph Constable became a young widower. Iris was divested of her unladylike tendencies and more wanton thoughts. If I felt I was somehow compromising my 'artistic vision', that swiftly dissipated when the story was accepted for publication. A cheque for two pounds constituted ample recompense for my integrity.

In the weeks that followed, I filled more notebooks with stories. When *An Agreeable Reception* appeared, I was sure to be inundated with offers and I had to be ready. My writing, I believed, went from strength to strength. I abandoned the florid prose of my first effort in favour of a more restrained, literary tone. I lingered over descriptive passages, rather than rushing breathlessly from one scene to the next. I invested my protagonists with an inner life, hoping that they might achieve a certain complexity for the reader. I convinced myself that I was destined to be the Nancy Mitford of my generation.

On the Thursday that *An Agreeable Reception* appeared, I rushed to the newsagent's on Charing Cross Road to purchase a copy of the magazine. I stood on the pavement outside and turned the pages. A rather vulgar illustration portrayed Iris in a short skirt with her legs crossed provocatively behind her desk, which was not at all how she was described in the story, but even this liberty did not dampen the thrill of seeing my words in print. As I stood on the pavement, magazine in hand, it seemed inconceivable that passers-by could be oblivious to the fact that they were in the presence of a celebrated authoress. Somewhat deflated, I went back into the shop and bought three more copies of the magazine. The newsagent made no comment, but I felt compelled to explain myself. 'It's just, you see, that I have story in it,' I said. He gave a shrug of indifference. 'It's nine shillings all the same, duckie.'

I did not know it at the time, but this was to prove the zenith of my literary career. For the next few days, I waited in vain for the arrival of fan letters and further offers of publication. One lunchtime the following week, I walked to the offices of the *Journal* in Russell Square. A girl of about twenty asked brightly how she could help. I explained the situation. Perhaps, I said, my address had been misplaced. She went through the motions of looking through a pile of letters, but there was nothing for me. Undaunted, I typed up several of the stories I had written and sent them to various magazines. They were returned accompanied by almost identically worded letters of rejection. One evening, I re-read *An Agreeable Reception*, thinking that, in my attempts to elevate my style, I must have strayed too far from the winning formula. With each passing sentence, I cringed more deeply. It was hackneyed and lifeless. The following morning, not wishing to leave behind even the evidence of ashes in the fireplace, I dropped my notebooks in a litter bin on Maida Vale.

Within a fortnight of starting at Mr Brownlee's, Father had installed Mrs Llewelyn in the house. Of course, he made it seem quite reasonable. 'Now that you're working, you won't have time for all that shopping and cooking.' I protested that, in fact, I spent very little time on these activities. These days, all one had to do to produce a nutritious meal was open a few tins. 'Even so,' Father said, and I realised that he had not been satisfied with the meals I had provided for him. It is true that I am not much of a cook and he had grown rather thin of late. His suggestion that I should find myself a job had been nothing more than a pretext to replace me. I had failed him and my silly job at Mr Brownlee's suddenly meant nothing to me. I also reflected that in the six years since my mother's death, my father had never sought any female company. When I was younger, it had never crossed my mind that my father might have physical needs (of the sexual kind, I mean), but as I had grown more worldly myself, I realised it was natural that he would. And while it might have been acceptable for his daughter to keep house for him, it would have been inappropriate for me to take care of his carnal requirements. Such things might be tolerated in the colonies, but in England they are simply not done.

I did not take to Mrs Llewelyn and, I daresay, she did not take to me. I know that in this age of equality one should not hold the mere fact of being Welsh against anyone. It is, after all, no more than an accident of birth (more to be pitied than despised), but I do think that if one is expected to be tolerant, it is only fair that the afflicted do what they can to try to mitigate the handicaps with which they have been born. No such consideration seemed to trouble Mrs Llewelyn, however. Despite the fact that she had come to London with her late husband shortly after the war, her accent remained well-nigh incomprehensible. Once or twice I attempted to educate her in the correct pronunciation of some everyday words and phrases, but she proved a most unwilling pupil. Indeed, on our first meeting, she had the temerity to inform me that her name was pronounced 'Thoo-elin'. If that was the case, I retorted, why not spell it that way? On top of all this, as if to ensure that I was never able to forget her presence in the house, her every activity was accompanied by a lamentable singing. Knowing that it was not my place to upbraid her, I asked Father if he might have a word with her, but he seemed to find my request amusing. It was rather refreshing, he said, to have a cheerful presence around the house. The slight was not lost on me.

It was the first of many occasions on which Father took the housekeeper's side against me, and I resolved to do everything in my power to undermine her. This proved difficult. Mrs Llewelyn, it must be granted, was a most able cook. When I returned from work, the house was filled with the comforting smell of simmering stock. Within weeks they were addressing each other by their Christian names, and Father invited her to join us at the table while we ate. It would not do to have her waiting on us like a servant, he said. She was one of the family now. He looked at me for affirmation of this ludicrous sentiment, but I merely pushed my plate aside and said that I for one was watching my weight.

Mrs Llewelyn did not conform to the image conjured by the word 'housekeeper'. She was neither stout nor matronly. There was a certain ruddiness to her cheeks (a vestige, no doubt, of her lowly origins), but her features were pleasant enough and her figure elegant. I began to suspect that Father had not employed her merely to keep house but to attend to those needs from which a daughter is debarred. I took to padding around the house in my stocking-feet, so that I might surprise them together. Once, I caught them in the study. Mrs Llewelyn was standing behind the desk, at my father's shoulder. His explanation that they were looking over the household finances did nothing to assuage my suspicions. I began to leave my bedroom door ajar at night. I am a light sleeper and was sure to be roused by any nocturnal shenanigans. I lay awake, waiting to hear the click of a bedroom door. Sometimes I rose and wandered around the house in my nightdress. Often I would spring the mousetraps that Mrs Llewelyn set in the larder, or remove the sad little corpses to deny her the satisfaction of victory. She has an abhorrence of mice wholly disproportionate to any mischief they might cause.

I sensed a cruel streak in her and, if I sought to drive a wedge between her and my father, I was motivated solely by concern for his well-being. One morning before I left for work, I placed a pound note half concealed behind the leg of the telephone table in the hallway. When I returned in the evening, it was gone. Over supper I mentioned casually to my father that I seemed to have mislaid a pound. I had looked everywhere for it, I said. 'Ah, it was yours,' he replied brightly. 'Margaret found it under the hall table this morning.' He took it out of his trouser pocket and handed it to me. When Mrs Llewelyn brought in the dessert, he informed her that the mystery had been solved. She replied that she was glad to hear it, but her expression made it clear she was alert to my skulduggery. I am aware that none of this reflects well on me. I daresay I was jealous.

When I arrived at Dr Braithwaite's for the third time, Daisy told me to go directly into his office. This deviation from established custom unnerved me. I had become habituated to having those minutes in the anteroom to shed the last remnants of myself and become Rebecca. I paused at Daisy's desk.

'Is there no Miss Kepler today?' I asked.

She looked at me with her gentle blue eyes. How uncomplicated it must be to be Daisy. She looked as if a gloomy thought had never troubled her pretty head. Perhaps spending one's days overseeing the comings and goings of the well-heeled nuts of London was a recipe for solid mental well-being. She ignored my question, replying instead that Dr Braithwaite would be with me in a moment.

'Is she sick?' I persisted.

Daisy's face took on a surprisingly obdurate expression. 'You know, Miss Smyth, that I can't discuss other visitors with you.' She leaned forward and added in a stage whisper: 'You shouldn't even know her name.'

The manner in which she delivered this remark created, I felt, a certain complicity between us. 'I understand,' I replied. But still I lingered at the desk. I had a presentiment that something dreadful had occurred; that Miss Kepler had been overcome by an urge to harm herself. 'It's silly I know,' I said, 'but I would hate to think that something had happened to her.'

Daisy lowered her voice even further. 'You have no reason to think anything of the sort.' But she did not deny that something had occurred.

At that moment Dr Braithwaite appeared, not at his office door but at the entrance from the landing. The effect was as though I was meeting his double. He looked even more dishevelled than usual. He was barefoot and his shirt was not tucked into his trousers. Daisy drew away from me and began to type.

Her cheeks flushed. Braithwaite glanced between us.

'If you prefer to spend your five guineas consulting Daisy, Miss Smyth, that's all right with me. I'll eff off to the pub and leave you to it. Otherwise—' He stepped across the anteroom and threw open the door to his lair. As I passed him in the doorway, he remarked that I was wearing a new perfume. It was true. That lunchtime I had tried a sample at the counter in Boots on Tottenham Court Road. It confirmed my feeling that there was something preternatural about Braithwaite. Not only had he detected my scent, but he knew it to be different from what I had worn before. The idea made my skin crawl. He followed me into the room so closely that I could feel his breath on the back of my neck. He closed the door behind him with what seemed studied finality. I had the feeling that he somehow knew everything about me; that I was not who I claimed to be.

Instinctively, I quickened my pace, making for what seemed like the sanctuary of the settee. I sat down with my bag on my lap. He stood for a few moments with his back to the door, then walked very slowly across the room, his eyes fixed upon me. If it was his intention to menace me, he succeeded. I pictured his hands on my neck, slowly tightening their grip until he had squeezed the life out of me. I would not resist. But he did not strangle me. Instead, he pulled up the straight-backed chair and sat down so close that our knees were almost touching. He leant forward, his elbows resting on his thighs. His nostrils flared. He was, I realised, inhaling me. I felt quite violated. I opened my bag and took out my cigarettes and lit one, the smoke creating some semblance of a barrier between us. I was struck by a disturbing thought.

'I hope you don't think that I am wearing a different scent for your benefit,' I said.

Braithwaite leaned back slightly. 'The thought hadn't crossed my mind,' he said. 'At least until you saw fit to deny it. But the fact is, you *are* wearing a different scent. You must have some motive for doing so.'

Rebecca took the reins. 'I expect you're going to say that I unconsciously want to make love to you.'

'And do you?'

'If it was an unconscious desire, I wouldn't know, would I? But I can assure you that my conscious mind finds the idea quite repulsive.' I felt that Rebecca had overstepped the mark, but Braithwaite appeared to find her remark amusing.

'Repulsive or not, the thought has evidently crossed your mind,' he said.

I explained with some satisfaction that my new perfume was merely a sample from a cosmetics counter. I neglected to mention that I had then surreptitiously dropped the bottle into my bag, not because I was so enamoured with the scent, but out of an infantile desire to defy my mother's cautions against 'another Woolworth's'. Nonetheless, I felt that Braithwaite somehow knew the little bottle was nestling in there. I could conceal nothing from him. He knew that I was not Rebecca Smyth; that I *was* Veronica's sister and that my entire presence here was a charade. I awaited his accusations. Had they come, I would have denied nothing. I almost wanted to be found out.

'Well, for what it's worth,' he said instead, 'it suits you. It's more earthy. More sexual.'

This last word he stretched out well beyond its natural duration, somehow finding an extra syllable in it. He leaned against the back of the chair, looking at me. My cheeks flushed. I cursed myself. Rebecca was not the type to be so easily discomfited. I hid behind my cigarette.

'Even by your own brittle standards, you seem tense,' Braithwaite said eventually.

There is nothing more calculated to make one feel tense than having one's unease drawn attention to. 'Of course I'm tense,' I replied. 'You're making me tense.'

He pulled an innocent face. 'And what am I doing to make you tense?'

'You know very well.'

He shook his head. 'Believe me, I don't.'

'You're sitting too close to me.'

'Ah,' he replied, nodding slowly. 'And the proximity of another person makes you uncomfortable, doesn't it? If you feel I am too close, Rebecca, you are free to sit elsewhere.'

He leaned back on his chair. He massaged the lower part of his face, folding and unfolding his unshaven jowls. His lips were red and engorged, and I was put in mind of a tray of offal in a butcher's window. I stayed where I was. It was not for me to move. I had been there first. It was he who had encroached on my territory. After some moments, he leant forward again, his fingers formed into a steeple.

'Here's what I think, Rebecca,' he said. 'It's not me that's making you tense. You were tense from the moment I caught you in cahoots with Daisy out there. When I appeared, the two of you acted like I had caught you *in flagrante delicto*, but rather than taking responsibility for whatever the two of you were cooking up, you blame me for catching you in the act. A bit unfair, wouldn't you say?'

'We weren't cooking anything up. As a matter of fact, I'm a terrible cook. He would never admit it, but that's why Father had to engage Mrs Llewelyn,' I prattled on irrelevantly.

Braithwaite exhaled noisily and looked at me the way one might at an elderly dog no longer in control of its bowels. He stood up and wandered round the room for a few moments. 'Still,' he said, 'we don't want you to feel tense. We won't get anywhere if you're feeling tense. Why don't you lie down? Try to relax.'

'I don't want to relax,' I said.

'Well, I can't force you.'

'If you're so desperate for me to relax, why don't you hypnotise me?'

'I don't go in for that sort of mumbo-jumbo,' he said. 'And anyway, I'm pretty sure you'd be unhypnotisable. You're what's called "resistant". You'd be petrified I found out all your secrets.'

I told him I didn't have any secrets.

'Everyone has secrets. Come on, you tell me one of yours, I'll tell you one of mine. Quid pro quo.'

'If I told you, it wouldn't be a secret anymore, would it?' I said.

Braithwaite's circumnavigation of the room had taken him back to the door. I suspected he was going to open it and tell me to skedaddle. Instead, he slumped to the floor and sat cross-legged with his back to it. I felt like a hostage.

In order to deflect the conversation from the subject of my alleged secrets, I put down my bag and removed my shoes. I felt quite naked without them. I swivelled round and gingerly stretched out on the settee. Then, remembering Dr Braithwaite's description of Veronica performing the same action, I let my arm fall loosely towards the floor and stretched my neck back.

'The Ice Queen melteth,' he said, with more than a hint of sarcasm.

I rested my head on the arm of the settee and gazed at the ceiling. I noticed for the first time that the cornicing extended only around three walls of the room. There was a stain above one of the windows, like a mustard-coloured jellyfish. I have always disliked jellyfish. Once, as a child, I stepped on one at Paignton beach. I still remember the sensation of my toes sinking into its gelatinous corpse. I was horrified and for months afterwards suffered nightmares in which I was engulfed by these flaccid creatures. I have no doubt this would be precisely the sort of thing that Braithwaite would be interested in, so when he asked me what I was thinking, I told him that I had been recalling our conversation of the previous week.

'Ah, the shackles,' he said. 'I suspected we might come back to the shackles. You used a very interesting word.'

'I did?'

'"Frisson",' he said. 'You said that those shackles gave you a "frisson"; a certain thrill, a shiver. An unmistakeably sexual word, yet is has its roots elsewhere, in the Latin *frigere*: to be cold. Or frigid. Perhaps that is what you wanted to express to me, Rebecca; that you are frigid.'

Of course, it is well known that shrinks place an inordinate degree of importance on sex. I have always assumed that the motivation for entering this profession is the licence it grants to ask improper questions. I do not blame them for this. The fact that I have no sexual life to speak of does not mean I am not curious about the activities of others. Nor do I doubt the centrality of sex experiences to life. It is the poor who are fixated on money. The well-off never speak of it. In a similar way, it is the deprived who are most obsessed with sex.

While Braithwaite's accusation might not be a grievous insult to me, Rebecca would never admit to such a disorder. 'I can assure you that is not the case,' she said.

'My instinct tells me, Rebecca, that you are not half as worldly as you pretend.'

'That would rather depend how one measures worldliness,' she replied.

'Well, here's one way to measure it: how many lovers have you had?'

The blush that rose to my cheeks betrayed me. 'I hardly think that's an appropriate topic of conversation.' I found myself worrying at a loose thread on the cuff of my blouse. I gazed rigidly up at the jellyfish stain on the ceiling.

'A most unworldly answer.' His tone was one of amusement. He was a cat toying with a half-dead mouse. 'You become agitated at the mere mention of sex, yet the story you chose to tell me last week had an unmistakeably sexual edge. It seems to me that you were inviting me to probe you about these matters.'

I could not help but think that his choice of verb was intentional, but he was, as always, correct. Even as a child I knew that the sensations prompted by having those reins tight around my chest were illicit and dirty and not to be spoken of. For as long as I can remember, I have been able to incite such feelings in myself. As a child I would roll myself tightly in my bedsheets and then, with increasing agitation, struggle to free myself. When I was older, I discovered that by placing my hand between my legs I could provoke the most intense excitement. As a teenager, when amusing myself in front of the mirror, I augmented my pleasure by binding my knees together with a scarf or a belt. There is, unquestionably, something in the feeling of being restrained that sets me aflame. Naturally, I did not share these thoughts. Instead, I limply stated that, on the contrary, I had no desire to discuss such matters.

'All the more reason to do so,' he replied. 'If you don't want to enumerate your lovers, why don't you tell me about your earliest encounter?'

Whilst I might be resigned to being branded an unworldly virgin, Rebecca would not wish to be thus slandered. I thought of Constance Chatterley being brutishly mauled by Mellors, but Maida Vale is no Wragby Hall. There are no woods or gamekeeper's huts there. As I was incapable of conjuring up a Mellors for myself, there was no alternative but to resort to the truth, or some version of it.

After my mother died, I began hesitantly, Father would pack me off to stay at his sister's in Clacton-on-Sea two or three times a year. When I was younger, we saw little of The Clacton Lot. They never came to London, and Mother would not countenance the idea of visiting the provinces. They lived in an ugly semi-detached house on Recreation Road. Aunt Kate was a brisk woman, who affected a cheerful air, but I suspect this was her way of concealing her disappointment with life. When she was not elbows deep in flour, vigorously scrubbing the front step, or pegging out the never-ending rounds of washing (the lower classes seem to believe that they can make up for their shortcomings through excessive cleanliness), I would often catch her with an expression of deep weariness etched on her face. Uncle Brian's most notable trait was his incessant whistling; this consisting of a breathy, tuneless emission, accompanied by a slight waggling of his head, as if he was at pains to demonstrate how affable he was. He was an ineffectual sort of man, which made spending weekends under his roof quite pleasant. Not for The Clacton Lot the regimented excursions of my own family. If I wanted to lie in bed all morning or spend the weekend with my nose in a novel, no one censured me. And if I failed to grace the family with my presence at mealtimes, Aunt Kate would not look askance if I later helped myself to a ham sandwich or a slice of cake.

The only blot on these agreeably dull weekends was the presence of my cousin, Martin, who was two years my junior. Martin was not physically unappealing. His features were passably symmetrical and, by the time he was fourteen, he was as tall as his father. He had sand-coloured hair, which fell in a natural parting across his forehead. These positive features were, however, offset by a dreadfully stooped posture, as if he were constantly afraid of hitting his head on a low beam. He had, moreover, inherited from his father the habit of announcing his presence with his own characteristic sound; in this case, a constant snuffling emitted from his nose. At first, Martin and I had little to do with each other, but later he began to take an interest in me. When I was in the garden, I often caught him squinting at my legs while pretending to occupy himself with some non-existent task. If I was in my room, he would lurk outside on the landing, betraying his presence with his horsey exhalations. Needless to say, he could barely bring himself to speak to me, and if I addressed him, his cheeks immediately reddened. I daresay he was in awe of me, and I took advantage of the situation by talking in a loud voice about what my aunt (not without a hint of admiration) called my 'London ways'. Sometimes when I was in the bathroom, I would leave the door ajar, and the knowledge that he was surreptitiously watching me brush my teeth excited me.

At this point, I turned my head to look at Dr Braithwaite. He was still crossed-legged with his back to the door. His expression was impassive, but he encouraged me to continue with a circling gesture of his hand. I returned my gaze to the ceiling and did so.

On what was to prove to be my final visit, I found Martin quite transformed. He was by then sixteen or seventeen. He had acquired both the gait of Homo erectus and a black leather jerkin, which he wore even at mealtimes. He had conquered his snorting and was now able to look me squarely in the eye without blushing. As a consequence, it was I who became flustered. He played the latest records loudly in his room and, outside his parents' earshot, informed me that he smoked cigarettes with girls 'down the Esplanade'. Naturally I feigned indifference. In London, I told him, I smoked marijuana and stayed out all night at jazz clubs. When he asked me if I liked certain groups,

I concealed my ignorance with dismissive shrugs, neglecting to tell him that I preferred Chopin.

I was due to leave on the Sunday afternoon and, over supper on the Saturday, Martin—or 'Marty', as he now preferred to be known—asked if I'd like to 'hang out' with him at the Esplanade. As it was clear that he wanted to show off his London cousin to his friends, I saw no reason to deprive him of this pleasure. Before we left, I spent some time in my room, making myself up and primping my hair. Martin was waiting in the hall when I came down. He had turned up the collar of his jerkin. His thumbs were hooked into the thin leather belt he wore around his denims. As soon as we were out of sight of the house, he took a packet of cigarettes from his pocket and handed me one. I could hardly refuse. There was a breeze blowing up from the sea front and he had to stand close to me to light it. I could smell the macaroni cheese we had had for supper on his breath. The lighting of the cigarette was not achieved without difficulty. He instructed me that I had to breathe in when he lit the match. I reminded him that I only normally smoked joints. He nodded earnestly and said: 'Yeah, of course.' I held the cigarette, pinched between my thumb and first two fingers, the way women in advertisements did. Martin held his with the lit end cupped in his hand.

We rendezvoused with three boys, dressed in identical fashion to Martin. They were leaning against the Esplanade railings, appraising the knots of girls who walked past affecting not to notice them. No introductions were made and none of the boys made any effort to speak to me. It was clear that they knew who I was, however, and I felt secretly gratified that Martin must have told them about me. I asked him for another cigarette and he was only too happy to oblige. This time, the ritual of lighting up was achieved without incident. The five of us stood in a semi-circle, facing loosely onto the promenade, the silence broken only by the occasional naming of a passer-by. 'There's Mikey Deans' or 'Is that old Corky in his motor?' Old Corky was evidently one of their teachers and, once he was a safe distance away, the boys yelled some tepid insults in his wake. Perhaps my presence had dampened their normal repartee. Or perhaps this was all that 'hanging out' entailed. When my cigarette burned out (I had made only a minimal attempt to actually smoke it), I let it drop to the pavement and ground it out with the toe of my shoe. It was a pleasing, assertive action, and I resolved to take up the habit in earnest.

Presently, we were joined by two girls wearing surprisingly fashionable short macs and a great deal of make-up. Martin remembered his manners and introduced us. The shorter one (Cynthia) had a round face, small piggy eyes and a snub nose, but the taller of the two girls was strikingly pretty, like a dark-haired Brigitte Bardot. She stood with her clutch bag clasped in front of her, gently swaying her hips, her eyes wandering towards the horizon behind us. I could barely take my eyes off her. After a few minutes, in which little was said, someone suggested we 'hit the Atlanta'. I fell in with the two girls. The boys paid no heed to us and were soon out of earshot.

The small, dumpy one said: 'So you're from London?'

'Yes,' I replied.

'I'm planning to move up there as soon as I can get out of this dump.'

'Good for you,' I said.

She asked me how old I was and I told her. We walked a little in silence. Then she asked me what I age I thought girls should 'do it'. I looked at her.

'Do what?' I asked innocently.

'You know.' She leaned in closer to me, and repeated with as much urgency as can be invested in such a blunt monosyllable: 'It!' The two girls exchanged a glance.

'That depends.'

'On what?'

'Well, there are a number of factors,' I said, rather enjoying my apparent status as a sex guru. 'But it really only boils down to one thing: whether you want to.'

Cynthia nodded earnestly. She lowered her voice to a conspiratorial whisper. 'Have you done it?'

'Of course,' I said with a dismissive laugh. 'Dozens of times. Once even with a coloured man.'

They looked suitably impressed.

'My boyfriend wants to do it with me,' said Cynthia. 'Only, I'm worried it might hurt.'

'Best to get it over with as soon as possible,' I said. 'It always hurts the first time, but no one likes a demi-vierge. The most important thing,' I continued, warming to my theme, 'is never to go with the same man twice. Otherwise they get ideas.'

'What sort of ideas?'

'Oh, you know the sort of ideas men get.'

Cynthia nodded earnestly. Bardot rolled her eyes. They couldn't have been more than fifteen.

Martin and his friends were waiting at the entrance to the Atlanta, which turned out to be a shabby-looking cafeteria with a tatty awning and a number of unoccupied metal tables arrayed on the pavement. We went inside and, as all the booths were occupied, took a table in the centre of the room. I took off my coat and hung it on the stand by the door. I sat between Martin and one of the other boys.

A grey-haired man with wire-framed glasses and a cardigan came to take our order. He looked more like a church organist than a café-owner. 'What'll it be, kids?' he asked.

I felt offended to be thus lumped in with my juniors, but I said nothing. Everyone ordered Coca-Colas, which arrived with straws protruding from the bottles. The boys discarded their straws and drank straight from the neck with affected machismo. I sipped mine gingerly and surveyed my surroundings. Three youths with extravagantly back-combed hair were leaning on the jukebox in the corner. Two girls in pedal pushers danced together, slowly gyrating their hips and gazing vacantly over each other's shoulders. The close proximity in which we were now sitting seemed to have the effect of lessening the boys' reticence. The one next to me asked if I liked the Everly Brothers.

'The Everly Brothers?' I repeated. 'I don't believe I've met them.'

He sneered and gestured towards the jukebox to indicate that they were responsible for the record that was playing. It sounded like a children's song and I said so.

Martin leaned across and jabbed his thumb towards my chest. 'She prefers jazz.'

'Yes,' I said. 'I prefer jazz.'

The boy opposite said, 'Jazz is for queers.'

'*I* like jazz,' Martin said.

'Case closed,' said the boy. He took a swig from his bottle of cola, before placing it emphatically back on the formica tabletop. Then he brazenly looked me up and down, as if I were a prize in a school tombolo.

I was touched that Martin had taken my side. Now that I saw him among his peers, he seemed quite grown-up. I took a ten bob note from my purse and asked him to buy me a packet of cigarettes from behind the counter.

He leapt to his feet, delighted to perform this service for me. 'What do you smoke?' he asked.

I scanned the array of packets behind the counter. Navy Cut

did not seem very ladylike, Rothman's too working class. I settled on Craven 'A'. I had seen them advertised and I liked the picture of the little black cat on the packet. Martin returned with the cigarettes and I offered them around, playing the munificent Londoner. We all lit up and a cloud of smoke enveloped us. The boy who had asked me about the Everly Brothers told me that he liked jazz as well. I said that he and Martin should come up to London sometime and I would take them to a club.

'You would?' he said.

I told him that they would have to wait until they were old enough. He assured me that they were already old enough. They began to discuss when they might be able to take up my offer and I regretted my silly showing off.

Another record came on. 'I like this one,' said Martin. He pushed his chair back and asked if I would dance with him. The other boys sounded an ironic chorus of oohs. Martin shot them a look and as I felt sorry for him and wished to curtail the discussion of the excursion to London, I agreed. We stood facing each other in the space in front of the jukebox reserved for this activity. Another couple already had their arms draped around each other's necks. Martin bent his arms upwards at the elbow and moved his hands slowly back and forth in front of his chest. He swayed his hips slightly, shifting his weight from one foot to the other in approximate time to the beat. I mirrored his actions and we continued in this fashion for some time. The melody was repetitive but inoffensive. On the third verse, Martin took a step closer to me. He mouthed the words of the song, which appeared to mostly involve the endless repetition of the sentiment, 'Yes, I'm the great pretender', accompanied by much harmonic ooh-ing.

He placed his fingers lightly on my hips and continued his arrhythmic swaying. Other than backing away, I had little alternative but to place my hands on his elbows. He took this as encouragement and slid his hands further round my body. His fingertips rested on my back, just above the waistband of my skirt. Our chests were almost touching. It was quite indecent, but given my earlier boasting about jazz clubs and coloured men, I could hardly start acting the squeamish virgin. As the song reached its insipid climax, Martin drew our bodies together, accompanied by a cattle-like lowing from the boys at the table. Our hips now moved in unison, his chin resting on my left shoulder. Then I felt a firmness in his groin pressing against the front of my skirt. I pushed him away, though not violently. The song ended. Martin looked at me. Despite the fact that our dancing had hardly been energetic, he was breathing in short, shallow gasps. I resumed my seat. Martin visited the WC. When he returned I told him I was ready to leave. He nodded.

As we walked home, he attempted to make conversation, as if nothing irregular had occurred. I answered as best I could, as this was preferable to confronting what had taken place in the café, and somehow our dialogue acquired more spontaneity than it had ever had before. When we reached Recreation Road, the house was already in darkness. We stood listening to the silence in the cramped hallway. The knowledge that we had, albeit unwittingly on my part, engaged in something illicit made accomplices of us. Having established that his parents were in bed, Martin cast his eyes towards the 'front room', as they called it. I followed him in. It was a horrid little room, in which Aunt Kate spent her evenings knitting and watching television, while her husband dozed over his newspaper, or muttered the answers to quiz shows under his breath. The curtains were open, but Martin did not bother to draw them. Instead, he closed the door and turned on the lamp on the nest of tables next to the settee. He then knelt on the floor in front of the walnut-veneered cabinet under the television. I sat down on the settee. He glanced over his shoulder at me with a conspiratorial look. He threw open the little doors of the cabinet and rubbed his hands together: this was where The Clacton Lot kept their booze.

'What'll it be?' he asked.

I shrugged.

He took out a dark brown bottle and, with an exaggerated show of not making any noise, two glasses. He poured out the drinks and handed one to me, before carelessly tossing his mother's knitting on the floor and sitting next to me. We clinked glasses and drank. It was sherry, the sickly taste of Christmas. Martin knocked his back and poured himself another. I resisted the urge to ask whether his parents would notice. That was his look-out. I had no desire to be there, but in the atmosphere of low lights and hushed voices it was hard not to feel a sense of intimacy. I reminded myself that, as the elder, I was in command of the situation and could retire to my room whenever I wished. Martin topped up my glass.

'Not bad stuff, is it?'

I took another sip. I had to admit that it engendered a relaxing effect. Perhaps, along with taking up smoking, I would set my sights on becoming a raging dipsomaniac. This seemed as worthy an ambition as any other. Martin suggested that I might be more comfortable if I took off my coat. He was, of course, correct, but as I did not know where such a wanton act might lead, I kept it on. He suggested putting on the gas fire, but I shook my head and said that that would not be necessary, as I would soon be going to bed. Martin nodded meaningfully, as if this constituted some kind of invitation. He drank more sherry.

'I hope this evening wasn't too much of a drag for you,' he said.

I assured him that it been perfectly pleasant and thanked him for inviting me. He kept his eyes fixed ahead of him. I noticed for the first time that he had inherited my father's Roman nose.

'Your friends are nice,' I said.

'They're idiots,' he said. 'I can't wait to get out of here.'

I finished my sherry and told him I was tired.

'I'm tired too,' he said. Then he leaned across and kissed me. He started on my cheek and then moved to my lips, which I kept clamped shut. It was not wholly disagreeable, however, and I did not turn my face away. Taking this absence of rebuff as encouragement, he placed his hand on my knee and squeezed it. My own hands remained on my lap. He started to snort like a little horse. Then he removed his hand from my knee and pushed it inside my coat. At this point I gripped his wrist and told him that that was quite enough. I stood up. He looked so crestfallen I almost felt sorry for him.

'Aren't you a little young for this sort of thing?' I said.

He protested that he had gone further with Cynthia.

I congratulated him but told him that he would not be going any further with me.

I performed my ablutions as normal and went to bed. I cannot be sure how much time passed or even if I had fallen asleep, but at a certain point, the bedroom door clicked open. Martin slipped into the room. In the dim light I could see that he was in his pyjamas. He took two or three paces towards the bed, then pulled back the blankets and got in beside me. He was in a state of what is termed 'arousal'. He started to kiss my shoulder and then my neck. His left hand fumbled at the hem of my nightdress. I held it firmly in place. He mumbled a request for me 'just to touch it'. I said I would do no such thing and told him that if he did not go back to his room, I would call his parents. Then his body went rigid as if he was having a seizure and I felt a sticky puddle form on my stomach. Once his breathing had subsided, he got out of bed and apologised. He begged me not to tell his parents. Of course, I had no intention of doing so, but I said I would have to think about it. Afterwards, I wondered whether it might, after all, have been so unpleasant to let him do what it was he wanted.

I became suddenly self-conscious and glanced towards Braithwaite. His hands were clasped across his paunch. As he did not appear to wish to interrupt, I continued.

The following day, I did not see Martin before I left, and I had the feeling that he was avoiding me. On the train back to London, I found a compartment with the window seat free. I sat down with my back to the engine. I like the sensation of being drawn away by an irresistible force, which one does not experience when facing in the direction of travel. A woman of spinsterish appearance occupied the middle seat of the three opposite. We exchanged a rudimentary greeting. Her choice of seat struck me as proprietorial. By choosing the central berth, she was establishing her jurisdiction over the compartment. Although the train had not yet moved off, she had arranged her knitting paraphernalia on either side of her. She was wearing a skirt that reached almost to her ankles and would not have been out of place in the Edwardian era. On the lapel of her jacket she wore a cameo brooch, and on her head a green felt hat with a feather in it. The skin of her hands and cheeks, however, was pink and had the elasticity of a younger woman. It was possible that, despite her septuagenarian garb, she was no more than forty. Whatever her age, she had the air of one who exists in a state of permanent annoyance. Life had let her down and to guard against future disappointment, all hope had been banished from her fiefdom. She was knitting a child's jumper. As she wore no wedding ring, I imagined it must be for a niece or nephew. How her sister must dread her bi-annual visits and raise a secret hurrah when the front door finally closed behind her. I wondered if once she had spurned the advances of a young man and ached with regret ever since.

I closed my eyes and leant my head against the window, as if I intended to go to sleep. A few moments after the train pulled out, the door of the compartment was yanked open. The sound caused me to look up. A young man with rosy cheeks, well-oiled hair and a fawn raincoat stood in the doorway. He had a suitcase in his left hand and an unlit pipe in his right.

'You don't mind, do you, ladies?' he said with exaggerated joviality. 'It's not a meeting of the suffragists, is it? Not that I'm against it, mind. All for it, in fact.'

The spinster looked at him without a trace of a smile. *She* was clearly not 'all for it'. I smiled welcomingly, if for no other reason than to disassociate myself from my fellow passenger.

He slung his briefcase onto the rack above our heads and, clamping his pipe between his teeth, pulled off his raincoat with such urgency that one might have thought it was on fire. Beneath, he was wearing a tweed three-piece suit of a cut that even my father would have discarded before the war. He struck me as the sort of young chap—a junior in an accountancy firm, perhaps—who thinks that by dressing in this fogeyish way, he might curry favour with 'Sir' and hasten his advancement.

Given the seating arrangements, it would have been customary for him to take the rear-facing seat nearest the door. Whether on omnibuses, park benches or in cafés, we humans instinctively position ourselves as far from one another as possible, and any deviation from this practice is rightly viewed with suspicion. Despite this, the young man took the seat next to me. This not only had the effect of cramping me but necessitating our travelling companion to shift her knees to accommodate his legs. She glared at him, before pointedly lowering her eyes to the knitting on her lap. The young man turned to me and pulled a face like a comically chastened schoolboy. I rolled my eyes in sympathy, and thus we were in cahoots. He took this as an invitation to introduce himself. His name, if I remember rightly, was George Borthwick. He passed his pipe from his right hand to his left and we shook hands awkwardly. As it would have seemed rude not to, I told him my name.

'A good solid name,' he said, as if it were a walking boot.

I must have made a face, because he then became flustered. 'I didn't mean to suggest that you were solid, only that it's a good solid name. Reliable, trustworthy, that sort of thing. I mean you yourself, you don't seem at all solid. Quite the contrary, if I may say so.'

His idiotic monologue trailed off and I diverted my gaze to the window. The outskirts of Clacton gave way to wheatfields, or fields of something at any rate. George was not at all discouraged by my inattention. Was I from Clacton? he asked. *He* was from Clacton, but was working up in London these days. He had digs in Elephant and Castle, but he had come up for the weekend to see his dear ol' muvva (this last phrase being pronounced in the most dreadful Cockney accent). He could see that I was a London girl, he said. I had that air. I was pleased to be told that I had an 'air', even if it meant little, coming from a provincial. George, it turned out, was not a junior accountant, but a clerk in an insurance firm. 'It might not sound it,' he told me earnestly, 'but it's actually damn interesting work.'

I told him that I was sure that it was, but if he didn't mind I was rather tired.

'Absolutely,' he said. 'Too much sea air and all that.'

'Exactly,' I replied with a smile. I then told him I was a little cold and could he be a dear and lend me his raincoat. He was only too happy to be of service. He fetched it from the rack and laid it over me like a father putting his daughter to bed.

I leant my head against the window and closed my eyes. George fidgeted beside me. He was filling his pipe. I heard the sound of a struck match and immediately the air was filled with an aroma of tobacco that made me feel as if my father had stepped into the compartment. I drifted for a time in a state between sleep and wakefulness. Contrary to what I had told George, it was warm in the carriage and the motion of the train was pleasant. Whether I dropped off, I cannot be sure, but I found myself recalling the previous night's events. The song Martin and I danced to had inveigled itself into my head. I recalled Martin pulling me close to him. Had he plotted the whole thing in advance? The idea that he might have, appealed to me. Under the guise of sleepily shifting my position, I slipped my hand beneath the waistband of my skirt. I began to amuse myself with the tiniest movements of my middle finger. The sensation was quite exquisite. I clamped my thighs tightly together like a child preventing itself from watering. Whether it was the motion of the train that pulsed through my buttocks or the proximity of George—lunk that he was—and the familiar aroma of his tobacco, I cannot say, but my crisis, when it came, was quite violent. I felt my throat constricting and could not restrain myself from emitting a series of short breaths, which I had the presence of mind to disguise as a fit of coughing. George leapt into action, giving me a few manly slaps on the back, before dashing off down the corridor to fetch a glass of water from the guard. The spinster stared at me. My cheeks felt flushed and I was sure she knew exactly what I had been up to. I was relieved when George returned, and I took the proffered glass of water gratefully.

'You must have had a bad dream,' he said.

'Yes,' I said, glancing demurely at him. 'I must have.'

I sipped the water. It would have seemed churlish after such a display of chivalry to refuse him a cup of tea when we pulled into London. I spent forty-five minutes with him in the cafeteria at Liverpool Street, listening to him explain the workings of the insurance business. He departed, poor fellow, thrilled to have obtained the telephone number of a girl with a Londony air. It shamed me that he would later discover that the number was as fictitious as the air.

Perhaps because I was prone on the settee, I had rather lost myself in the telling of this story. Dr Braithwaite had remained by the door throughout and had interjected no comments. I had almost forgotten he was there. In the ashtray on the table there were three cigarette ends, but I could remember neither lighting nor smoking them. This period of silence felt like a pause for breath after an exertion. I understood why people were willing to pay for the service of having someone do no more than listen to them.

Braithwaite looked at me for a minute or so. His expression was neutral. In my short acquaintance with him I had become familiar with the feeling that, even when no words were being spoken, a conversation was taking place; a conversation played out through the minute movements of hands and eyes. I swung my feet to the floor and sat upright. I did my best to still myself, but I was aware that he was reading me; that my twitches and tics were hieroglyphs revealing everything I wanted to hide.

In the event, it was he who spoke first. 'So,' he said, 'how much of that was true?'

'All of it,' I said indignantly.

He repeated my words in a sceptical tone.

'I couldn't swear to every last detail,' I admitted. 'It was a long time ago.'

He stood up and walked across the room, spun the wooden chair around and planted himself on it, his legs splayed apart, his chin on the backrest. 'So you made it up?'

'Certainly not,' I replied.

'The thing is, petal, it doesn't actually matter to me whether any of it actually happened. What matters is that this was the story you chose to tell.'

I started to protest, but he waved away my objections.

'Perhaps it's half truth, half fiction. But the real truth—the important truth—is that on this day, in this room, this is the story you chose to tell. Even if there is not an ounce of veracity in what you told me, that would still be true.'

I felt thoroughly confused and said so.

'And you don't like to be confused, do you, Rebecca? *Confundere*!' he proclaimed, his index finger pointing to the ceiling. '*Confundere*: the Latin root of confusion, meaning "to mingle together", "to stir up". And that is precisely what you dislike, isn't it, Rebecca? You do not like things to mingle. You do not like to be stirred up. You like everything to be in neat little compartments. That is what makes you comfortable. You retreat from interaction, from any contact with your fellow humans. Whether the events in your little story happened or not is neither here nor there. Every aspect of it was about your inability to mingle. It was about your fear of being stirred up.' At this, he stood up so abruptly that the chair toppled over. He seemed thoroughly pleased with himself.

For myself, I was growing rather weary of his mania for etymology. And I was growing weary of his ability to see through everything. 'Do you always have to be so mistrustful?' I said.

'If you weren't so untrustworthy, I wouldn't have to be,' he replied. 'I'm not sure I believe more than half a dozen words you've said since you started coming here.'

'Perhaps you don't even believe that my name is Rebecca Smyth,' I said recklessly.

'My dear, I couldn't care less what your name is,' he replied. He stepped towards me and bent over so that his face was only inches from mine. His breath was hot on my neck. 'You see? You're stirred up now, and you don't like it. But isn't that why you're here?'

I thought for a moment that he was going to molest me. I found the idea of his offally lips on mine repellent. I turned my face away. He straightened up and I began to gather up my things.

'That's it,' he said. 'Off you go, little spadge. Back to Daddy's nest.'

I stood up and put on my coat. As I left, I could not bring myself to look at him. I hurried past Daisy without a word. I could still hear him laughing as I hurried down the stairs.

The streetlamps glowed orange in the gloom. My breath formed a cloud in front of my face. I felt drained. It's hard to believe that merely talking could be so exhausting. Ainger Road was deserted. Here in the heart of London, I felt quite alone. I walked slowly in the direction of Primrose Hill. Braithwaite was right. I was stirred up. I lit a cigarette in an attempt to re-calibrate things. Everything felt crooked.

I entered the park by the gate at the foot of the hill. In recent days, I have started to deviate from some of my habits; motivated solely, I confess, by a desire to prove Braithwaite wrong. Yesterday at breakfast, for example, I first buttered then marmaladed my first slice of toast before repeating this process for the second. (My normal practice is to butter both slices before applying the marmalade.) Father made no comment about this aberrant behaviour, even affecting not to notice it. As I ate the second slice of toast, the satisfaction I gleaned from defying Braithwaite dissipated. I had succeeded only in getting marmalade in the butter dish and would have to suffer the admonishing looks of Mrs Llewelyn. The fact is that certain practices arise not out of fear of change, but because they are the most efficient way achieving the desired result. Abandoning well-established traditions simply to demonstrate that one is willing to embrace change is wholly vacuous.

On the other hand, it must be also admitted that some traditions are established solely through force of habit. Thus, I always sat on the uncomfortable settee in Braithwaite's office. Similarly, it had become my custom to walk clockwise around the perimeter of the park. I could equally well have walked anti-clockwise, or even along the path leading up the hill. So, it was with a sense of exhilaration that I began my ascent. Primrose Hill might not have posed much of a challenge to Sir Edmund Hillary, but I have never been a great one for physical exertion. At St Paul's I pled off gym as often as possible. Miss Scholl must have thought I had the curse every week.

After two or three hundred yards, the space around me became more expansive. I felt vulnerable. Perhaps this was why my previous instinct had been to cleave to the perimeter. One was invisible there, or more so, at least. Was it safer to conceal oneself close to the very shrubbery in which one's attacker might be lurking, or to flaunt one's presence by abandoning cover? Out here in the open, I was exposed. I imagined my body lying face down in the dewy morning grass, the back of my head bashed in, an indifferent crowd gathered around my corpse. How foolhardy, they would think, for a young woman to venture alone into the park at night. Nevertheless, here I was scaling Primrose Hill without so much as a Tenzing to carry my handbag. The wind freshened, prickling my cheeks. As the path steepened, I began to feel a little out of breath. Some distance ahead, a young man was sitting on a bench, his hands pushed deep inside the pockets of his coat. For a moment I thought it was Tom (I had lately been seeing him everywhere), but his shoulders were too narrow and he wore a beard. I do not trust men with beards, particularly young men with beards.

We are accustomed to seeing old people sitting on park benches or loitering at bus stops from which they have no intention of travelling. The old have nothing better to do with their time. But when one sees a young man alone on a park bench, one takes note. A solitary young man is one of two things: he is melancholy or he is menacing. This young man was not reading a book or a newspaper (it was, in any case, too dark for this). He was just sitting; hunched forward, his ankles crossed beneath the bench, coiled up like a spring. He watched me approach, his head to one side like a pigeon eyeing a scrap of food. I suppose there was nothing inherently threatening about this. He must have heard the click of my heels on the tarmacadam and turned his head towards the source of the sound. He might even have felt that, had he averted his eyes, he was deliberately ignoring me; that by *not* watching me approach, he was somehow snubbing me. Nonetheless, I felt disconcerted. As I passed, he formed his mouth into a sort of smile and said good evening. I responded in a manner intended to suggest, without being uncivil, that I had no desire to prolong the conversation. This was unsuccessful, as he followed up his opening gambit by stating that it was a chilly evening.

'Indeed,' I said. This time I employed a tone clearly suggesting that I found his remark barely worthy of rejoinder.

This exchange had been enough to carry me past him. He followed me with his eyes. Had we been in a busy thoroughfare, this would have troubled me less. I might, on the contrary, have felt insulted had he not thought me worthy of a second glance. But here in the murk of the park, I felt unsettled. After I had walked no more than ten or twenty yards, there was a sound behind me. I looked back. The young man had risen from the bench and was following me. I say he was following me, but perhaps he was merely walking in the same direction. It was, I told myself, perfectly reasonable that given his comment about the cold, he did not wish to linger. But why would he have chosen to wait for me to approach and pass before getting up? I did not want to look round again lest a glance over my shoulder be interpreted as a come-hither look. Men with wives at home do not loiter on park benches. They hurry home to a nice pork chop and mashed potato at the kitchen table. By the same token, however, my pursuer might suppose that young women with husbands at home do not wander alone in parks at night, and that a woman doing so must be amenable to a certain kind of attention. Perhaps, I thought, I should explain to him that I had no ulterior motive; that I was merely taking a turn around the park in order to clear my head, and that if he was following me in the expectation that I would accept an invitation to his grotty bed-sitting room, he was labouring under a misapprehension.

I freely admit that I was scared, but, wishing to deprive him of the satisfaction of knowing he was frightening me, I did not quicken my pace. If it seems surprising that the mere proximity of another human being could provoke such fear, it must be remembered that he was not just another human being: he was a man. I had been brought up to think of men as predators and myself as a victim, and no application of logic could gainsay this dogma. Did I think that he was going to molest me there on the open expanse of Primrose Hill, or that he was going to take a blunt object from the inside of his coat and bludgeon me to death? I felt a dreadful churning sensation in my stomach. It was the anticipation of the initial blow that most terrified me. Once that had been dealt, I would crumple to the ground and resign myself to whatever it was he wanted to do. It would be a relief to have it all over and done with.

The incline steepened towards the summit. Perhaps I was drawing away, or perhaps I could simply no longer hear his footsteps over the sound of my own breathing. At the top of the hill was a metal railing, silhouetted across the night sky like a tiara. A solitary figure was standing, looking out over the city below, a woman in an ankle-length coat with a scarf tied around her hair. I raised my arm and shouted, but she did not hear me. I broke into a run. I reached the top of the hill and called again. The woman turned and looked at me. I staggered towards her, a great wave of relief overtaking me.

'There's a man,' I gasped, this being, I supposed, sufficient explanation of my eccentric behaviour.

'A man?' she said.

'Yes. He was following me.' I gesticulated in the direction from which I had come. There was no one to be seen. I frantically scanned the park.

The woman looked at me. 'I wondered why you were running,' she said. She had a clipped manner of speech and a low, attractive voice. It was only then that I realised it was Miss Kepler.

I am not sure I have ever experienced such a swift transformation of emotions. I said her name breathlessly and instinctively grasped her hand. She took a step back and stared at me. Her eyes widened. She did not seem to recognise me. In the moments that passed I took her all in. She was even more striking than I had previously thought. The scarf tied around her hair accentuated the shape of her face, which was long and narrow with pronounced cheekbones. Her mouth was wide and downturned, with thin dark lips. But it was her eyes that most captivated me. The irises were black and glistened like wet pebbles. I realised I had startled her and embarked on an explanation of how I knew her name. She listened with commendable calm. I daresay I must have seemed quite mad. She wrested her hand from my grip and held it up to stem my monologue.

'And what might your name be?' she asked.

'Rebecca,' I said. 'Rebecca Smyth. With a Y.'

Miss Kepler now held out her hand, palm down, fingers slightly curled. As I took her fingers, I automatically inclined my head. I may even have curtseyed.

'Any friend of Collins is a friend of mine,' she said.

I replied that I wouldn't exactly call myself his friend.

'So what are you then?'

'Just one of his visitors,' I said.

Miss Kepler pursed her lips, as if the distinction meant nothing to her. 'So you followed me here?'

'Good gracious, no,' I said. 'I always take a turn around the park after seeing him. To gather my thoughts, I suppose.'

'And what kind of thoughts do you have?'

'Oh, I don't know,' I said airily.

'Gloomy thoughts?'

'Sometimes.'

'Of course you do. You wouldn't be seeing Collins if you didn't have gloomy thoughts.'

'No, I don't suppose I would.' I asked if she had gloomy thoughts.

She gave a small shrug and turned to look out over the vista. 'Are there any other kind?' she said. She took a packet of Consulate cigarettes from the pocket of her coat and I immediately resolved to switch to this brand. She offered me one and then lit them both with a gold lighter. We smoked silently for a few moments, before she spoke again. 'You do realise he's a genius, don't you?'

'A genius?' I said.

'Yes. A genius,' she said with conviction. She turned to face me. Her hip was resting against the railings. She held her cigarette between her index and middle finger, inches from her cheek. Her gloves were of dark suede. The indentation of her upper lip was a flawless Cupid's bow.

'How long have you been seeing him?' I asked.

She exhaled a little puff of breath. 'Years,' she said. 'Not long enough. Have you ever met anyone like him? Everything he says hits the mark. He sees through one's lies before one sees through them oneself.'

'So you lie to him too?'

'My problem,' she said, 'is not that I lie to Collins. My problem is that I lie to myself.'

I nodded. It was exactly the sort of thing that Braithwaite would say. 'Doesn't he scare you?' I asked.

'Scare me? Collins? Good heavens, no.' She laughed at my question.

'Don't you feel he could make you do whatever he wants?'

'I already do whatever he wants, my dear,' she said. She turned her profile towards the horizon and exhaled a long stream of smoke. She gazed out across London for a few moments, before turning back to me. 'Perhaps we should leave before any more phantoms appear.'

We walked towards an exit at the side of the park. She linked her arm into mine. Our breath hung in a cloud around us. Miss Kepler was a little taller than me. It was pleasant to walk arm in arm with her. I felt safe. Any number of men could have dawdled behind us and I would have been unafraid. I experienced a sense of sisterhood. I looked sideways at my companion. Her lips were slightly parted, her chin raised, like a fox alert to everything. I have always enjoyed observing women. The pleasure I derive from this activity is purely aesthetic and could not, I think, be characterised as deviant. I have yet to meet a woman who engenders the sort of feelings stirred up in me by a man like

Tom. I like the bulk of a man. I like their smells. If the underground is crowded and I find myself pressed against a man, I like to inhale the odour of his sweat. I can stare for minutes on end at a working man's hands, imagining their callouses prickling my skin. I have never suspected that I might be Lesbian. Naturally at St Paul's, there was often talk of such mischief amongst the boarders, but I never took these rumours to be anything other than malicious gossip. Indeed, I have tended to believe the existence of this species to be no more than a myth. Now, however, I wondered if Miss Kepler might be such a creature. There was something mannish in her features and bearing, a certain self-possession uncommon in our sex. Perhaps Lesbianism was the disorder for which she was consulting Braithwaite.

We came to a halt just before the gate. Thinking that we were soon to part, I said, 'It might sound foolish, but when you missed your appointment this afternoon, I feared the worst.'

She looked at me. There was a faint smile on her lips. 'Whatever do you mean?' she said.

'I thought perhaps you might have done something silly.'

'Something silly?'

'I mean that you might have done away with yourself.'

Miss Kepler looked at me seriously. 'There is nothing silly about suicide,' she said firmly. 'It seems to me that if you assumed such a thing about me, it must be because you have such thoughts yourself.'

'I do have dark thoughts,' I said.

'So if it had been you that had missed your appointment, it would be because you had chosen to not go on.'

'"To not go on",' I repeated. It was a pleasing way of putting it. We are all the time urging each other to go on. The greater one's misery, the more one is reminded to keep going. Just keep going, we cry, knowing full well that it is the last thing we want to do ourselves. But if like me, one faces no apparent adversity in life, nobody thinks to tell you to keep going. It is assumed that you will keep going, like an automaton. Why wouldn't you? It requires an effort of will, an act of violence, to cease going on. But what a relief it would be.

'If I miss an appointment now and again,' Miss Kepler said, 'it is simply because I sometimes prefer my own lies to Collins' truths.'

She stepped out of the park and indicated which way she was going. It was not an invitation. She held out her hand and I took it, this time without any display of subservience. I told her that I hoped we would be able to talk again. With the smallest movement of her head, she indicated that this might be possible. I felt that Miss Kepler was someone to whom I could unburden myself.

As she turned to go, I whispered, 'I'm not really who I pretend to be. Rebecca is not my real name.'

She paused and drew down the corners of her mouth. 'I wouldn't worry,' she said. 'We're all pretending to be someone else. And Rebecca is such a beautiful name.'

I watched her walk off. Her heels made no sound on the pavement. I remained inside the wrought iron perimeter fence. I looked back at the park. The lights of the city formed a halo around the summit of the hill. When I looked back along the street, Miss Kepler had already disappeared, and I had the feeling that she had never been there at all.

Braithwaite III: Kill Your Self

By the autumn of 1965, when the author of the notebooks contained in this volume presented herself at Ainger Road, Braithwaite was approaching the height of his notoriety, but his ascent had not been a smooth one.

On completion of his doctoral thesis, Braithwaite turned down a lecturing position at the university. He had had enough of Oxford. Ever since his run-in with Colin Wilson three years previously, he had felt that life was elsewhere. In June 1959, he hitch-hiked to London, found himself a bed-sitting room in Kentish Town and took a series of menial jobs. These ranged from labouring on building sites to warehousing, but Braithwaite was incapable of regular time-keeping or accepting authority and was invariably sacked after a week or two.

By the end of the year, the novelty of this aimless lifestyle had palled and he wrote to R.D. Laing, who was at that time Senior Registrar at the Tavistock Clinic, a psychotherapeutic facility in Beaumont Street. In his letter, Braithwaite described how he had been inspired to return to Oxford to study psychology after seeing how Laing went about his work at Netley. He would, he said, like to train under him. It was a unique moment of deference on Braithwaite's part. Laing replied recommending that if he was serious about a career in psychiatry he should first take a degree in medicine. Laing's letter was courteous and his advice reasonable, but Braithwaite felt that he was belittling him. He wasn't used to such treatment. He had assumed that Laing would recognise his talents and immediately offer him a job. He wrote back outlining some of the ideas from his thesis, and expressing the view that in order to understand the mind, he didn't need to know how to cure a child of diarrhoea. Laing did not reply.

At the beginning of 1960, Braithwaite ran into Edward Seers, whom he had first met in the company of Colin Wilson. In the parlance of the day, Seers was a 'colourful character', well known around Soho. Even at the height of summer, he dressed like an Edwardian aristocrat, sometimes in plus fours, never without a cravat or bow tie. He was no more than 5'5" and, when inebriated enough (which was often), was not averse to propositioning men in bars, despite the very real risks such behaviour then entailed. According to Braithwaite's account in *My Self and Other Strangers*, this was how Seers reintroduced himself in a pub in Dean Street. Braithwaite, who was at that time earning a pittance working at Covent Garden fruit and vegetable market, told him he could do what he liked as long as he bought him a pint. The two men retired to a corner of the bar and fell to talking. While Braithwaite was not exactly in the vanguard of political correctness, he was open-minded regarding matters of sexuality ('Why should it bother me what another man wants to do with his cock? I do what I want with mine.'). As long as Seers was buying the drinks, it did not seem to bother him if his hands wandered over his thighs or crotch. There is no reason to believe that things went any further than that, but by the time the bell had rung for last orders, Seers had offered him a job in Methuen's editorial department. Braithwaite accepted and presented himself at the publisher's offices the following Monday. He assessed manuscripts, did some proofreading and found that no one, least of all Seers, objected if he took long liquid lunches from which he did not return.

Zelda hitch-hiked down from Oxford every two or three weekends. Braithwaite's bedsit was filthy. As it overlooked the busy thoroughfare of Kentish Town Road, the windows were grimy, and during the day there was a continual rumble of buses outside. There was a wash hand basin, which also saw service as Braithwaite's urinal; an underemployed two-ring hob; a single bed with a thin stained mattress; and a desk and chair. The bathroom was on the floor above, but as there was rarely enough hot water for a bath, Braithwaite's ablutions were generally restricted to taking a 'French wash' at the sink. When Zelda arrived, she would throw open the windows, empty the ashtrays and clear up the bottles accumulated since her last visit. She was not exactly the home-making type, but there was only so much even she could put up with.

Zelda remembers these weekends fondly. They would fuck on the single bed, smoke joints and take walks on Hampstead Heath, nudging each other whenever they came across single men loitering suspiciously. As a legacy of his time following the grape harvests in France, Braithwaite was an enthusiastic practitioner of al fresco sex, and when the couple were now and again caught in the act, he was not in the least bit cowed.

According to Zelda, Braithwaite was as close to being happy as at any time she knew him: 'He didn't fit in at Oxford. He was always itching to be somewhere else, but Kentish Town agreed with him. It was shabby and he was shabby.' He was earning a decent wage, they could afford to eat out and go to the theatre now and then. Braithwaite appeared to enjoy his loosely defined role at Methuen. He had a keen editorial eye and, had things worked out differently, he might have had a successful career in publishing.

In April 1960, R.D. Laing published his seminal book *The Divided Self.* It was not, as is often thought, an overnight sensation*, but it certainly had an immediate impact on Braithwaite, who bought a copy in its week of publication.

Ronald David Laing was born to lower middle class parents in the Govanhill area of Glasgow in 1927. His father was an electrical engineer who regularly beat him. His mother was a possessive semi-recluse. In the early years of his life, Laing shared a bedroom with his mother while his father was banished to the box room of the family's small flat. Laing took refuge in his schoolwork and won a scholarship to the prestigious Hutchesons' Grammar, before studying medicine at Glasgow University. After his posting to the army facility at Netley, Laing took a job at Gartnavel Royal Mental Hospital in Glasgow, where he worked on the female ward. Insulin-induced comas, electroconvulsive therapy and lobotomy were routine treatments, and most of the patients had been there for over a decade. Here, Laing set up the 'Rumpus Room', a therapeutic experiment in which a dozen schizophrenic patients were allowed to wear their own clothes, interact as they saw fit and were given materials for handicrafts. Within eighteen months the patients had shown enough improvement to be released, although a year later they had all returned. Still, Laing was recognised as someone with daring ideas and the courage to put them into practice.

At the end of the 1950s, he moved to London to be at the centre of developments in the psychiatric world. He was thirty-two when *The Divided Self* came out. Braithwaite read and re-read the book (subtitled 'An Existential Study in Sanity and Madness'), in a fury over a weekend. From the very opening pages he recognised himself and his own way of thinking in

* Prior to 1965, when it was reprinted by Penguin with its iconic cover, it had sold only around 1,500 copies.

Laing's description of the 'schizoid' individual as one who 'does not experience himself as a complete person but rather as "split" in various ways'. Laing goes on to explain how this condition of 'ontological insecurity' can lead to the development of a system of false selves: an assemblage of masks or personalities that one presents to the world in order to safeguard the 'true self' from feelings of engulfment or implosion.

It was characteristic of Braithwaite that, rather than feeling that he had found a kindred spirit, he concluded that Laing had stolen the ideas he had expressed in his letter at the end of the previous year. Perhaps Laing had even read and plundered his doctoral thesis. Never one for circumspection, Braithwaite penned a furious letter calling Laing, among other things, 'a thieving Jock' and a 'thrupenny charlatan', and threatening him with legal action. His accusations were groundless. Laing had completed the manuscript of *The Divided Self* in 1957, long before he had ever heard of Braithwaite, but even had this not been the case, the idea that he would have appropriated the opinions of a random correspondent was absurd.

Braithwaite posted his letter (to which there was no response) on his way to the Methuen offices first thing on the Monday morning. He went straight to see Edward Seers, who sat him down and poured him the whisky he clearly needed. Braithwaite ranted for half an hour, pacing round the tiny office like a caged bear. Seers had heard of neither Laing nor his book. He did not take anything Braithwaite said seriously, instead waiting for the storm to blow itself out, which it eventually did. When Braithwaite resumed his seat, and with a second whisky in his hand, he told Seers that he proposed to write a book himself—'a proper fucking book'—about his ideas. If Seers was sceptical, he kept his doubts to himself. Braithwaite reminded him of the run-away success of Colin Wilson's *The Outsider* and Seers agreed to look at anything he produced. At the time, Braithwaite spent all his free time drinking his wages and seemed unlikely to muster the self-discipline required to write a book, but, for the next six weeks, after putting in a perfunctory appearance at the office, he took himself to the nearby British Library reading room, where Wilson had also worked. When Seers voiced mild objection to this, Braithwaite flew into one of his customary rages and told Seers to go ahead and sack him. He would take his magnum opus elsewhere. Seers just shrugged. He found Braithwaite's tirades amusing.

When Zelda arrived around lunchtime one Saturday in May, she was surprised to find Braithwaite not sleeping off a hangover, but hunched over his little desk, covering the pages of a notebook in his scruffy handwriting. The window was open. No bottles lined the skirting boards, and there was a box of eggs and a loaf of bread next to the hob. It was half an hour before he even spoke. Zelda was accustomed to such theatrics. What she was less used to was that when he stirred from his trance, he declined the opportunity to have sex, instead frying up some eggs, before getting back to work. Zelda went out for a walk. When she came back in the late afternoon, Braithwaite was still at his desk, but he soon called it a day. They made love noisily (Zelda remembers this because one of the other tenants banged on the door to tell them to keep it down) then went to the Moreton Arms, where Braithwaite was in an ebullient mood. He talked animatedly but incoherently about what he was writing. When he was like that, Zelda recalled, 'he was good company. His mind raced from one topic to the next with no discernible logic. There was no point trying to follow his train of thought, but it was entertaining.' He didn't even seem to mind when she suggested that he might soon be able to afford more salubrious digs.

A month or so later, Braithwaite presented Seers with the results of his labour. The manuscript, held in the archive in Durham, is a thing of wonder; so illegible that, at first glance, one cannot even be sure it is written in Roman script. Words are often no more than undulating lines, interspersed by the flamboyant tails of Fs, Gs or Ys. It is like trying to read normal handwriting from the window of a speeding train. The evidence of the haste with which the book was written is visible in every line. There are frequent crossings-out, with revisions written above or below the line. These annotations are often more legible than the original, the limitations of space perhaps acting as a brake. Finally, there are numerous arrows connecting different paragraphs or pages, and further notes scribbled vertically in the margins. The overall impression is of a creative but disorderly mind struggling to capture something, but not having the patience or stealth to do so.

The following day Seers called Braithwaite into his office. Braithwaite expected him to extol his genius and offer him a large advance. Instead, Seers told him that the person to whom he had passed the manuscript had said it was unreadable. Braithwaite was furious both at this perceived slight on his work and because Seers had passed the manuscript to a minion rather than read it himself. Seers attempted to placate him by telling him that, due to his fondness for Braithwaite, he would not have been able to be objective. In any case, Braithwaite would have to have the manuscript typed up. This done, Seers decided that it would, after all, be best if he read it himself. He would later privately dismiss the book as 'gibberish', but he was astute enough to understand that psychiatry was entering mainstream culture and there might be a market for such ideas. He baulked at publishing a book with such an inflammatory title, but on this and every other editorial suggestion, Braithwaite was intractable. It was published in March 1961.

Kill Your Self is a product of its time, both in the sense that it captured the zeitgeist, and in the fact that it was so hastily written. Let there be no mistake: the book is a mess. It is a mishmash of passages from Braithwaite's thesis, ruminations on various cultural phenomena and thinly veiled swipes at Laing. It is replete with unsubstantiated claims and generalisations and is often derivative or simply unreadable. At its best though, it fizzes with energy, and Braithwaite's talent for sloganeering would come to mean far more to his counter-culture readership than anything as square as intellectual coherence. In the preface, Braithwaite attempts to make a virtue of his book's failings: 'It was suggested that I re-write some passages of this book. I refused. To do so would be to censor myself, to impose an order that does not exist. That would be to defeat the purpose of my own work.' If anything, the impenetrability of certain passages only served to confirm the author's genius.

The infamous passage in the opening chapter is a case in point. Braithwaite takes as his starting point the idea that if one is going to talk about the self, one should begin by defining what one means. He quickly descends, however, into claiming that defining the self at all is a fraudulent act: the Self does not exist as an entity or a thing; if it exists at all, it is no more than a projection of the self (the book is full of such paradoxes). There is a tiresome discussion of an opaque passage from Kierkegaard's *The Sickness Unto Death*. 'The self,' Kierkegaard writes, 'is a relation which relates to itself.' The self, Braithwaite elaborates, consists of a dialogue between two competing versions of the self: one that is present-in-the-moment; and one that is seen as persisting over time and, by virtue of this, regarded as being 'true'*. The present-in-the-moment self is subjugated by the persisting-over-time

* Throughout the book, Braithwaite indicates this latter idea of the self as an independently existing entity by capitalising it, while the present-in-the-moment self remains in lower case.

Self. The latter is thus set up as a kind of tyrant, preventing individuals from fully engaging with the experience of the outside world and causing feelings of guilt and inauthenticity. This guilt is characterised by Kierkegaard as despair: 'To want to be rid of oneself is the formula for all despair.'

Braithwaite's discussion of this rambles on for half a dozen impenetrable pages. It's questionable how many of his readers persevered through his labyrinthine sentences and leaps of logic, but it ends with the declaration that was to make the book famous:

To escape despair, don't kill yourself; kill your Self.

As so often in Braithwaite's work, it is the triumph of assertion over argument. Few cared about the preceding pages when the conclusion was so ripe for scrawling on a toilet wall.

Kill Your Self can be seen as a kind of dialogue with Laing's book. The two men agreed on a great deal more than divided them. They shared a suspicion of the medical establishment and the rush to diagnosis that characterised conventional psychiatric practice. Electroconvulsive therapy, Braithwaite claimed, 'is like treating fear of flying by pushing someone out of an aeroplane: the patient may soar for a while, but the benefit is short-lived.' Both men shared a belief that psychotic delusions were, at least for the person experiencing them, real, and that these experiences should be engaged with rather than dismissed. They further shared a desire to deconstruct the traditional assumption that the patient's experiences and statements are subjective and false, while the therapist's interpretation of those experiences is objective and true. 'There is no reason to believe that the therapist is saner than the patient,' Braithwaite writes. 'In fact, any impartial reading of psychiatric literature shows us that the opposite is more often the case.' The goal of the therapeutic relationship should not be for the patient 'to *become sane*, but to become comfortable with his insanity'. Much of this could have been lifted directly from the pages of Laing's book, but it was on the question of the self that the two men differed:

> *Dr Laing clings to the notion of a 'true self' like the deluded Lear over Cordelia's lifeless body. He wants to liberate the insane, but the idea of the 'true self' is the straitjacket that keeps us all in the asylum. There are only personas, and the quest to return to some state of true being rooted in childhood is the very source of the troubles he describes. The route to liberation is to accept that we are bundles of personae [...] To elevate one of these personae above the others is to create a bogus hierarchy that is the origin of what is termed 'mental illness'. In this regard, those we brand schizophrenic are, in reality, the vanguardistas of a new way of being.*

He describes this new way of being as 'schizophrening'. As the decade wore on, this would become an idea perfectly in tune with the be-whoever-you-want-to-be mood of the time, and copies of *Kill Your Self* would be soon found in the back pocket of every student and bar-room philosopher. 'Phrening' (or sometimes 'phreening') passed into beatnik argot, and the slogans 'Don't be yourself: phree yourself!' or the more succinct 'Don't be: phree!' were graffitied on the walls of university campuses up and down the land. The concept also gave rise to the short-lived Phree Verse movement in which often acid-fuelled performers channelled their various selves into a spiralling cacophony, until the different personae melded into one incomprehensible but 'authentic' stream of consciousness. Ironically, more than one participant in these happenings would later find themselves recovering in psychiatric facilities.

Braithwaite's ideas filtered into popular culture too. Towards the end of 1966, prior to the recording of the album that would become Sgt Pepper's Lonely Hearts Club Band, Paul McCartney wrote:

> *I thought, Let's not be ourselves. Let's develop alter egos so we're not having to project an image which we know. It would be much more free. What would be really interesting would be to actually take on the personas of this different band … it won't be us making all that sound, it won't be the Beatles, it'll be this other band, so we'll be able to lose our identities in this.*

Whether the reluctant Beatle had read *Kill Your Self* is not known, but it was McCartney rather than John Lennon who moved in London's counter-cultural circles, and he would more than likely have been privy to discussions of the book. Both he and Braithwaite were present at the launch party of the avant-garde magazine the *International Times* at the Roundhouse in Camden in October 1966. Whether they actually met or not, McCartney's comments illustrate the pervasiveness of the ideas to which Braithwaite had given voice.

All this success was in the future, however. In the days following the publication of *Kill Your Self*, Braithwaite scoured newspapers and magazines for reviews. Colin Wilson had been hailed as the voice of his generation within a week. Braithwaite expected nothing less. Eventually a single review appeared in the *New Statesman*. Edward Seers had been at Westminster School with the magazine's new editor, John Freeman, and persuaded him to cover the title. He should not have bothered. The review concluded that 'the only notable features of this book are its irresponsible title and disdain for common sense'. With customary audacity, Braithwaite sent a copy to Laing with a note sarcastically thanking him for his role in the book's conception. Whether Laing read the book at the time is not known. Certainly he did not dignify it with a response.

Over the next year, the book sold a few hundred copies, a respectable enough number for an obscure work by an unknown author. To Seers, and anyone else that would listen, Braithwaite railed against an Establishment conspiracy to suppress his ideas, but in private he was devastated by the world's indifference. Zelda had never seen him so morose. At weekends, he would lie in bed chain-smoking until late afternoon. In the evenings, if the couple went out, he would drink even more heavily than usual and pick fights with anyone foolhardy enough to engage him in argument. More than once he ended up trading blows on the pavement outside the Moreton Arms. Zelda's visits became less and less frequent, but she could not bring herself to end the relationship. For the first time she felt that Braithwaite needed her for more than sex.

In his memoir, Braithwaite entirely glosses over this period. In a flagrant misrepresentation of reality, he writes: 'I had dared to say what no one had said before, at a moment when the world was ready to listen.' Whether this was the product of his talent for self-mythologising or a genuine misremembering is impossible to say, but, certainly, he had a flexible relationship with the truth.

In any case, this fallow period was not destined to last.

In September 1961, at a party at the home of the film producer Michael Relph, a friend of Seers, Braithwaite was introduced to Dirk Bogarde. Bogarde had recently starred in the film *Victim*, in which he played a barrister being blackmailed on account of his homosexuality. It was an important, campaigning film and

Bogarde, until that time a lightweight matinee idol, was praised for his courage in taking on such a role.

Bogarde was a complex character. Born Derek Jules Gaspard Ulric Niven van den Bogaerde, he was brought up in London before being sent as a teenager to live with an aunt and uncle in Bishopbriggs near Glasgow. He served in World War II and, at least by his own account, witnessed the horrors of Belsen first hand. Like most upper-middle class children of the period, he was raised under the credo of 'never explain, never complain'. Bogarde was an intensely private man. His biographer, John Coldstream, describes the 'tough outer skin which he had begun to develop in his teens; and which [in later life] hardened into a formidable carapace […] Dirk constructed a persona for public consumption.'

Bogarde lived for forty years with his partner, Tony Forwood, but always denied that he was gay. This was understandable in the 1960s when, as Coldstream puts it, the possibility of 'exposure' as a homosexual was to live with the 'very real fear of state-initiated disgrace'. Even after homosexual activity was decriminalised by the Sexual Offences Act of 1967, public opinion languished a long way behind the law. So Bogarde learned to live a compartmentalised life, oscillating between his public and private selves. Arthur Braithwaite, the ironmonger's son from Darlington, might have reinvented himself as Collins Braithwaite, but Bogarde's public profile meant that maintaining the carapace was a necessity in a way that it never could be for Braithwaite. The stakes for Bogarde were considerably higher.

According to his own account, Braithwaite introduced himself to Bogarde with the words 'You're a very good actor.' Bogarde thanked him in a perfunctory way—he must have heard the sentiment expressed a thousand times—but Braithwaite persisted: he was not referring to Bogarde's professional work.

He had been observing his interactions with various guests at the party. 'Everything you say and do is false,' he said. 'It's an act.' At this point, Bogarde looked at him with the supercilious smile familiar to anyone who had seen him on screen. Before he could reply, Braithwaite continued: 'See, even now, you're acting. You're smiling, but your smile is a mask.'

There is no mention of Braithwaite in Bogarde's seven volumes of memoirs, but he spoke privately to one or two friends about the meeting and his later relationship with him, describing him as an 'extraordinary fellow'. Something, it seemed, in Braithwaite's 'gargoyle-like' features and the brazenness of his approach caused his guard to drop. Perhaps it was simply a case of one poseur recognising another.

The two men retreated to an alcove conveniently situated next to the sideboard set out with booze. Bogarde began to question Braithwaite about who he was, a strategy the latter interpreted not as genuine curiosity but as a means of deflecting the conversation from himself. Bogarde had not heard of *Kill Your Self*, but Braithwaite outlined its main ideas. Bogarde, he reports, 'listened attentively, his eyes lowered. It was clear that he recognised himself in what I said. For a few minutes, the veneer fell away, and I was speaking not to Dirk Bogarde, film star, but to Derek van den Bogaerde.' The moment did not last long. The conversation was interrupted by the party's hostess, who dragged Bogarde off to say hello to another guest. Before he left, however, Bogarde—public persona restored—told Braithwaite that he must send him a copy of his book. Braithwaite did so, and a few days later received a note inviting him to the actor's sprawling home, Drummers Yard, near Amersham, twenty miles north-west of London.

Braithwaite arrived an hour late, but Bogarde did not seem to mind or notice. 'He feigned indifference,' Braithwaite wrote, 'as if he had forgotten he had invited me.' It was a type of affected absent-mindedness he recognised from the upper-class types he had rubbed shoulders with at Oxford, for whom it was 'important to always appear that one had higher things on one's mind than the plebeian business of punctuality'. The house was vast, but Bogarde showed Braithwaite into a small study, his 'wee den' as the Glasgow-educated actor called it. It felt like a sanctum.

Braithwaite's portrait of Bogarde in *My Self and Other Strangers* is acidly funny and minute in its attention to the actor's mannerisms and foibles. The Bogarde he describes is at once vain, evasive, charming, generous, acerbic and vulnerable. He was, in Braithwaite's blunt taxonomy of the human species, a 'fuck-up'. What Braithwaite appeared to do for Bogarde was to rid him of the guilt he felt for pretending to be someone he was not; to convince him that the self he was simulating was as real as the self he was concealing. He explained his interpretation of *The Double*. Who is to say which is the original and which is the imposter? The two men's acquaintance does not appear to have lasted more than a few weeks, but it was to have a lasting impact on both of them. 'It was a relief,' Bogarde told a friend, 'to be told it was all right not to constantly "be yourself"; that it was fine to be your own doppelganger.'

In the weeks that followed, Braithwaite received a number of calls from other actors and people connected to the film and theatre business. Braithwaite loved actors. They were the living embodiment of his ideas. Actors were revered for pretending to be someone they were not. In *Kill Your Self*, he quotes Camus:

> *'[The actor] demonstrates to what degree appearing creates being. For that is his art – to simulate absolutely, to project himself as deeply as possible into lives that are not his own … his vocation becomes clear: to apply himself wholeheartedly to being nothing or to being several.'*

Braithwaite goes on:

> *At the end of each performance, we rise to our feet to applaud. 'Bravo!' we cry, 'Encore!' The more convincing the illusion, the louder the applause. And yet, as soon as we step out of the theatre, people are derided for being fake, for not 'being themselves'. The quest to 'be oneself' is idolatry. Instead we should treat the world as a stage and perform whatever version of ourself we want to be. Only by inventing and re-inventing ourselves—by 'being several'—can we escape the tyranny of the fixed, immutable Self.*

This, for Braithwaite, was the route to happiness, and his newfound theatrical clientele proved a receptive audience. Actors, by the nature of their vocation, were misfits. From an early age they understood that they had to play-act in order to fit. 'It is not,' Braithwaite wrote in the argot of the time, 'that queers make better actors. It is that the persecution of this kink demands that all queers be actors.'

At first, Braithwaite visited his clients at their own homes, but by the autumn of 1962 he was able to give up his job and rent the house on Ainger Road. He lived on the ground floor and used the upper floor to receive his 'visitors.' If people were willing to pay Braithwaite five guineas an hour, there was no question of him turning them away. He was soon making his weekly salary at Methuen in three hours.

Zelda, who had now completed her own doctorate, moved in at the end of the year. For a while, the arrangement was relatively harmonious. Zelda had an income of her own and was never in thrall to Braithwaite, in the way that Sara Chisholm or other girlfriends had been. She spent the winter writing what would become *Another Woman's Face.*

At the beginning Braithwaite took his accidental role as therapist seriously. He spent his evenings reading volumes of case studies. Nothing, however, altered the views he had expressed in *Kill Your Self*. He was dismissive of the psychoanalytic model, and even sceptical about the existence of the unconscious. Dream analysis was 'mumbo-jumbo, practised by pseudo-shamans'. Still, whatever he was doing in the upstairs room of Ainger Road seemed to have an effect. His diary was soon full. He had a partition wall built to create an anteroom and employed a secretary to manage his appointments and billing. The first of these, Phyllis Lamb, remembers a 'cavalcade of beautiful girls and bohemians'. People often turned up at Ainger Road without an appointment and had to be turned away, or would just sit and wait until Braithwaite was free. Between sessions, Braithwaite would often go downstairs to smoke a joint or gulp down a bottle of beer.

Zelda's novel was published in late 1963. The *Observer* called it 'an astute and intimate portrait of the new womanhood'. *The Times Literary Supplement* compared it to Virginia Woolf. Now, when the telephone on the ground floor rang, it was more often than not for Zelda. 'Of course he was jealous,' she recalled. 'Collins didn't have it in him to be happy for anyone else's success.' Braithwaite scoured articles about her for mention of his own name and, when he didn't find any, would throw the newspaper or magazine across the room. 'He seemed to think that I somehow owed my achievements to him.' The couple spent the weekends throwing parties or attending other people's. The carousing at Ainger Road often spilled into the next day, ending only when the last guest had slumped unconscious on the floor. More than once, the police were called, and it would be up to Zelda to persuade them that nothing untoward was going on.

Sales of *Kill Your Self* had picked up and Edward Seers invited Braithwaite for lunch, to ask him to write a follow-up. Braithwaite was reluctant. He was making far more money from his clients than he ever had from the publication of his book. 'Yes,' Seers retorted, 'but if you hadn't written a book, your clients wouldn't be coming to see you.' The world moved quickly these days, he went on. If Braithwaite didn't produce more work, his clientele would move on to the next nine-day wonder. Cannily, he pointed out that in the intervening period Laing had produced a further two volumes*. Braithwaite remained unconvinced. He didn't have time to write another book. He'd said what he had to say in *Kill Your Self*. Why repeat himself? Seers' real concern was not for his former employee's career, but to exploit the growing market for books on psychiatry. He suggested that Braithwaite produce a volume of case histories as a kind of companion to *Kill Your Self*. There were those, he reminded him, who called him a fraud. This would be an opportunity to prove them wrong. 'But they're not wrong,' Braithwaite had replied. 'I am a fraud.' Seers knew it would be futile to try to persuade him to change his mind, but before the meal was over he mentioned the considerable advance he would be willing to pay.

A week or so later, Braithwaite telephoned Seers and told him he had an idea for a new book. It would be a series of case studies that would form a kind of counterpoint to *Kill Your Self*. The studies would, he said, 'perform the same function as the parables in the Bible'. No mention was made of the previous conversation. Seers told him it was a splendid idea and a contract was quickly drawn up.

Untherapy was written in the final months of 1964 and published in spring 1965. It was an immediate success. Aside from the abstruse preface, it is highly readable, salacious and often

* These were *Self and Others* (1961) and *Sanity, Madness and the Family* (1963).

insightful. The portraits of his clients are acutely observed and droll. The book is also shamelessly self-serving. Braithwaite never misses an opportunity to repeat a compliment paid to him by one of his 'visitors'. Naturally, each of the cases ends triumphantly, with the client in question leaving Braithwaite's office relieved of whatever psychological burdens he or she had been carrying. Gone are the bewildering discussions of Kierkegaard and Camus of *Kill Your Self*; in their place, a parade of human foibles and eccentricities, liberally seasoned with prurient descriptions of the subjects' sexual peccadilloes and masturbatory habits. Braithwaite dismissed it as a pot-boiler: 'People just like to read about those more fucked up than themselves.' But the press lapped it up. Julie Christie was forced to deny a rumour, cunningly started by Edward Seers, that she was 'Jane', the sexually promiscuous, valium-addicted starlet of the book's opening chapter. John Osborne issued a statement insisting that he had neither met nor consulted Collins Braithwaite. The Right Reverend Robert Stopford, Bishop of London, declared the book to be blasphemous (one client admits to being aroused by images of Christ on the cross) and called for it to be banned. A leader in *The Times* sniffily averred that while the book might indeed be a 'clarion of the permissiveness era in which we find ourselves ... that does not justify the publication of such material'. Needless to say, all this merely had the effect of bringing more clients flocking to Ainger Road.

It was only now that Ronnie Laing began to pay any heed to Braithwaite. Until this point, it had been Laing who had been the go-to shrink of London's bohemian set. Now his position was being usurped by an unqualified charlatan. According to his colleague Joseph Berke, the mere mention of Braithwaite's name was enough to send Laing into a tirade of Glaswegian invective, but he shrewdly refused to enter into a public feud, calculating that this would only fuel Braithwaite's notoriety.

The division between the two floors of Ainger Road began to blur. Braithwaite started inviting certain clients downstairs to share a joint after their session. At other times he would continue to smoke and drink through sessions. Appointments with different clients began to meld into one another. One client recalls turning up to find three other people already present. Braithwaite began to question her about intimate matters she had previously discussed with him and invited responses from the other visitors. She left and did not return.

Zelda did not approve of any of this. Apart from anything else, she was working on her second novel and did not welcome the constant intrusions. She had also become uneasy about Braithwaite's role and how he treated it. 'He had no concept of confidentiality. He gleefully repeated the most lurid details of what he was told upstairs.' But when he started holding his sessions downstairs she realised that the whole thing was a circus. 'It was,' she says, 'grotesque.'

The final straw came in October of that year, when a journalist, Rita Marshall, came to the house to interview Zelda for the *Sunday Times**. Braithwaite had been ordered to stay upstairs, but of course he could not bring himself to comply. He burst into the living room with a cheery 'Don't mind me', before fetching a bottle of beer from the kitchen. He then proceeded to hijack the interview, launching into a long description of his own work. Marshall nodded politely, before attempting to resume her conversation with Zelda. Braithwaite began to answer on her behalf. Zelda reminded him that he had promised to leave them in peace. 'It's my house,' Braithwaite replied. 'Can't I even get a beer in my own fucking house?' The journalist made her excuses and left. That evening, Zelda did the same.

* This incident is described in Marshall's article 'Zelda Ogilvie: Woman of the Age', published in the *Sunday Times* magazine on 24th October 1965.

The Fourth Notebook

Miss Kepler's words have haunted me these last few days. There is nothing silly about suicide. Of course, she is right. Her tone had not been one of rebuke, but I experienced it as such and regretted having expressed myself that way. Indeed, the whole encounter left me feeling like a dreadful chump. Miss Kepler must have thought me quite unhinged. I consoled myself with the thought that, as she was also visiting Dr Braithwaite, there must be a stain of madness on her too. Nevertheless, our conversation has led me to consider afresh my sister's demise.

Strange though it may seem, I have never given much thought to the details—to the *reality*—of Veronica's death. And if I had reflected on it at all, I had indeed been guilty of thinking she had done something silly; that rather than reaching the conclusion that she could no longer tolerate her existence, she had been overtaken by a momentary impulse. I now understood that this could not have been the case and that choosing to think of her act as a passing fancy was merely a way of making it bearable. It was what Braithwaite would call a 'defence mechanism'.

A few months before her death, Veronica came home from Cambridge for reasons that were not altogether clear. There was some muttered talk of 'exhaustion', but she did not strike me as being in the least bit fatigued. She appeared to have a great deal more energy than I ever had. In any case, Father was delighted to have her home. Over supper, Veronica would chat animatedly about intellectual matters while Father gazed adoringly at her. One evening, she explained something called the Red Shift Effect, using pieces of fruit as a model of the universe. The sun was an orange. The Earth was a grape. Many of the stars visible in the night sky, Veronica told us, had been dead for millions of years. She slowly moved an apple (I forget what this represented) towards the outer reaches of the dining table, prattling about wavelengths and frequencies as she did so. Even Mrs Llewelyn paused to listen, before shaking her head and muttering something about girls these days getting mixed up with things that didn't concern them. For once, I concurred.

Between Veronica and myself, there was little intercourse. I do not know how she spent her days during those weeks, or what her plans for the future were. I did not, truth be told, give it much thought. I daresay I assumed that at a certain point she would return to her gilded circle in Cambridge. It would not be true to say that we had grown apart, as we had never been intimate in the way sisters are supposed to be. I accepted, as I had always accepted, that she was my better and that, as such, she had little interest in me. Nevertheless, I was glad of her presence. It lightened the atmosphere in the house, and any suspicion that the dilution of our father's affections might have been a source of resentment is entirely groundless. It was, on the contrary, a relief not to be required to pass the time at supper entertaining him with fabricated anecdotes about my days at Mr Brownlee's.

One evening, I was in the parlour frittering my time on the latest Georgette Heyer. Veronica had been watching me for some time. She sighed and said: 'Oh, I do wish I could lose myself in a novel like that.' She was not paying me a compliment, but instead asserting the superiority of her mind. It was typical for there to be a discrepancy between what Veronica *said* and what Veronica *meant*. Over the years, this had been the cause of frequent misunderstandings between us. Around the age of twelve or thirteen, her tendency to say-the-opposite became something of a mania with her. If it was a bright sunny day, she would declare the weather to be 'miserable', or if it was pouring rain 'delightful'. This developed into a private argot shared only with my father. He called her Ironica, while she addressed him as Mother. If

Veronica reported that she had come top of the class in a school test, Father would declare that she was a disgrace and must be sent to bed without her supper. Veronica would reply that that would be splendid and that she should be caned, into the bargain. Father would assure her that it would give him great pleasure to soundly beat her. They would continue in this vein for hours on end. They formed between them a cabal that brooked admission to no others. If I took one of Veronica's statements at face value, she would roll her eyes and let out a great harrumph, as if I were the world's greatest clot. Likewise, if I attempted to take part in the game, she would declare that she had been being serious. With Veronica, you never knew where you stood. The threat of humiliation hung over our every exchange.

On this occasion, I gave her a sharp look, wishing her to know that I understood she was belittling me. She flushed, realising perhaps that she had over-stepped the mark. Father looked up from his crossword. 'We can't all be high-fliers like you, Veronica,' he said, then smiled at me as one might at a retarded child. I stood up and sarcastically apologised for lowering the intellectual tone. As I strode out of the room, they exchanged comedic looks of contrition, which only salted my anger.

If my relations with Veronica were not intimate, they were, for the most part, harmonious. Ever since I can remember, I had accepted Veronica as my superior. She was brainy; I was not. She exercised restraint; I did not. She did not behave gauchely in public or brazenly stare at the women my mother labelled Jezebels. If we were in an hotel, she used the correct cutlery and did not spill gravy on her blouse. She did not watch quiz shows on television or waste her time cutting out pictures of natty outfits from magazines. Veronica inhabited a different stratum and, because of this, our only rivalry was for our father's affection. If I made no effort to elevate my mind, I daresay this was out of fear that I would only succeed in proving my inferiority. By refusing to compete, I could cling to the illusion that we were merely different. Now and again, she would express jealousy about my 'little job'. 'You're quite the girl about town,' she would say, and I was happy to allow her to believe that working at Mr Brownlee's was a good deal more glamorous than it actually was. Father was of the opinion that Veronica would be bored in such a job, a view that was undoubtedly accurate. I myself have the ability to do repetitive tasks, or stare into space for long periods of time without feeling the least bit bored. There is always something going on if one looks hard enough. Tiny dramas unfold all around us. Intellectuals like Veronica are oblivious to this, however. They are too busy thinking to notice anything.

On the night Veronica died, the police called at ten minutes to nine. I know this because when one's doorbell rings late at night, one's first reaction is to glance at the clock. Father looked up from his crossword and said: 'That'll be her now. She must have forgotten her key.' Veronica's absence had caused some consternation over supper. Father speculated that she must have gone to the pictures or run into one of her clever friends from Cambridge (Veronica did not just have friends, she had *clever* friends), but I doubt if he believed either of these scenarios any more than I did.

I did not think for a moment it was Veronica who had rung the doorbell. I have a tendency to foresee calamity at the smallest provocation, so I was not in the least surprised when Mrs Llewelyn ushered two policemen into the parlour. The first—I cannot recall his name—was a detective dressed in a poorly cut brown suit and overcoat. He took off his hat and held it clasped in front him. His sidekick was a uniformed constable who looked barely old enough to be out of school. His cheeks were rosy and covered in pimples. Together they resembled a music hall duo and I half-expected them to break into a rendition of *Underneath the Arches*. The detective began by ascertaining that we were indeed Veronica's relatives. It seemed highly unlikely that we might be imposters, but I have learned that in times of crisis those in authority expend a great deal of time and effort verifying what is self-evident. This slavish adherence to protocol serves to create a distance between the protagonists and whatever upsetting events are to be discussed. One leaves one's self behind and becomes a cog executing its function. It is no longer personal. In the folderal following Mother's death, I came to enjoy being asked for the umpteenth time if I was 'the daughter of the deceased' (this phrase's weighty rhythm still pleases me). 'Yes, I am,' I would reply solemnly, taking pride in performing my role proficiently.

Having satisfied himself as to our identities, the detective then said that he had some bad news. He paused for effect, somewhat in the manner of a quiz show host, before informing us that Veronica had met with an accident. She appeared, he said, to have thrown herself from a railway overpass in Camden. He did not seem alive to the contradiction between his two statements, but it did not seem the moment to point this out. I did not dare look at my father. I suspected that he would be quite broken by this news and that it would fall to me to take charge of the situation. I composed my face into what I imagined was a look of distress and put my hand to my cheek. It would not do, I thought, to appear to have expected such news. I wondered if the detective took a certain pleasure in entering the houses of strangers and telling them that their relatives were dead. If he did, he betrayed no sign of it. He passed the brim of his hat through his fingers for a few seconds and then, apparently deciding that enough time had elapsed to get over the shock, asked us some questions: Did we know why Veronica might have been in that area? Had she seemed unhappy or upset? Had she been behaving in an unusual way? When my father had answered in the negative, the detective asked if he might 'stick his beak' into Veronica's room. I was irked by this deviation from bureaucratic idiom. This inappropriate colloquialism restored him to the status of individual rather than functionary. He no doubt regarded himself as a 'bit of a character', for whom telling some stuck-up types of a death in the family would soon be no more than a saloon-bar anecdote. Nevertheless, Mrs Llewelyn showed him upstairs.

The uniformed boy remained in the parlour, as if to keep watch over Father and me. I caught him looking at my legs and instinctively pulled down the hem of my skirt. For the sake of something to say, I asked how they could be sure it was Veronica. The boy answered hesitantly, as if unsure of whether he was exceeding his authority. Her handbag, he said, had been found at the scene. I made a mental note to carry out a thorough spring clean of the contents of my own bag before throwing myself in front of any trains. The boy began to say something about the identification of her body, but his voice trailed off. The knuckles of his right hand were grazed, and I wondered if he had recently been involved in some fisticuffs. I stood up and walked over to where Father was sitting. His newspaper had slipped from his lap and he had his hands over his face. I placed my hand on his shoulder. He laid his left hand over mine and we remained in this position, like figures in a tableau, until the uncouth detective returned. He explained the procedures that would follow and then, with a sharp tilt of his head, indicated to his young colleague that they could now skedaddle.

At the inquest, a young man named Simon Wilmot described how he had seen Veronica climb the balustrade of the overpass. Until then, I had successfully managed to avoid thinking about the reality of her act. I had tricked myself into believing that it had been an accident; that she had somehow slipped and fallen. Of course, the word 'suicide' had flitted through my mind, but I swatted it away like a troublesome fly. Certainly, I had not considered the notion that Veronica had acted deliberately; that she had purposefully chosen to end her life. The idea was preposterous. Simon Wilmott recalled how Veronica had hesitated for a moment and he had run over and grabbed her by the ankle. She leapt off and he had been left holding nothing but her shoe. That shoe, along with her other clothing and the contents of her handbag, were later returned to us. The second shoe was never recovered, but as her feet were two sizes larger than mine, I could not in any case have worn them.

My initial reaction to Veronica's death was, it shames me to admit, entirely selfish: I would never again have to compete for my father's affections. I would no longer be made to feel foolish at supper, or that my existence was somehow inconsequential. I had, by virtue of outliving her, for the first time won out. I am aware that these were petty and contemptible sentiments, but they are entirely worthy of me. I have understood from an early age that I am an unpleasant and spiteful person. I am unable to see events in any terms other than their benefit or injuriousness to myself. I distrust those who claim to act in the interests of the public good or who spend their free time on charitable activities. This avowed altruism seems to me to speak only of a desire to be thought admirable. Some weeks after Veronica's death I began to feel differently, however. On the one hand, this re-assessment was perfectly in accordance with my previous egoism. My father's grief was vast and enduring. For months, I returned home to find him in tears. He ate little and seemed to be wizening away to nothing. His pallor was grey. His hair thinned. Mrs Llewelyn kept up a façade of cheerfulness, but even her wheedling could not bring him to eat. Naturally, we did not speak of the cause of his distress. It would have seemed a pointless cruelty to mention Veronica's name. So we talked of other things, as if nothing had happened. It was in this way that an alteration in my feelings about Veronica's death came about: my father's unhappiness made me unhappy.

Then something else occurred. One evening as we sat at supper, I turned to the place Veronica had lately occupied and was about to say something to her, before I checked myself. For the first time, I keenly felt her absence. From that moment, I saw her death in a different light. There was a Veronica-sized void in the world. As well as her physical presence, the contents of her mind were gone. The question I had been about to ask would never be answered. Everything she had learned, the memories she had accumulated, her future thoughts and actions had all been snuffed out. The world was diminished by her non-existence. A sob heaved in my gullet. I swallowed it, but it would not be stifled. I disguised it as a fit of choking and rushed from the room.

When I arrived at Dr Braithwaite's for the fourth time, Daisy gestured silently for me to take a seat. Miss Kepler's sable coat was on the coat stand. I was pleased that order had been re-established. As I took my place, it struck me forcibly that Veronica must have perched on this very chair, waiting for Daisy to give the sign to enter. She would have sat straight-backed with her hands on her lap and her knees together, just as I was now doing. I wondered, however, if she would have noticed the little wallpaper tongue on the wall above Daisy's shoulder. I do not imagine it would have troubled her as it troubles me. Nor would she have thought to compliment Daisy on her cardigan. Daisy's cardigan would have been of no concern to her. Veronica was a practical, no-nonsense sort of person. She distinguished herself in her disregard for matters of fashion. She dressed in ill-fitting skirts, clumpy shoes and, sometimes, in what appeared to be men's tweed trousers. I occasionally wondered if she might have preferred to be a man. It would not have wholly surprised me had she taken to smoking a pipe.

Daisy was unusually concentrated on her work. I expect that after we had been caught confabulating the previous week, she wished to discourage me from engaging her in conversation. Perhaps Braithwaite had given her a dressing down in his office. I imagined the punishments he might have meted out to her. Nevertheless, I was suddenly taken with an idea and, knowing that if I think for too long about anything I will find a hundred reasons to prevent myself from acting, I came straight out with it.

'I wonder if you remember one of Dr Braithwaite's former clients?' I said. 'Her name was Veronica.' I made a gesture with my hand, intended to convey that this was no more than a casual thought and that her answer was a matter of no consequence.

She looked at me. Then her eyes flitted towards the door to the study. She furrowed her brow and hunched her head into her shoulders. 'You know very well that I can't discuss other visitors with you,' she said. Her previously chummy demeanour was all gone.

'I was just curious to know if you remember her.'

'Whether I remember her or not is neither here nor there.' She was speaking in a stage whisper. 'You mustn't ask me such things.'

She resumed her typing, forcefully striking the keys to make as much noise as possible.

I began to describe Veronica. 'Dr Braithwaite even wrote about her in one of her books,' I said over the din. 'He called her Dorothy. I always thought that was rather a good name for her.'

I fancied I saw a glimmer of recognition cross Daisy's face, but she suppressed it so swiftly I could not be sure.

She stopped typing and looked at me. 'I haven't read any of his books.'

I had the impression she was frightened. 'It's just that, in a way, it's because of her that I'm here,' I continued.

'Your reasons for being here are not my concern.' Her cheeks had coloured.

At that moment, the door to Braithwaite's study opened. Miss Kepler appeared. She did not look her usual composed self. Her face was flushed and her mascara was smudged. Her hair was dishevelled and, as Daisy helped her into her coat, she distractedly pushed a strand behind her ear. Her eyes alighted on me, but blankly, as if nothing had ever passed between us. I was wounded, but as she must have had reasons of her own for behaving in this enigmatic way, I conspired in her silence.

Moments after she left, Dr Braithwaite appeared in the doorway. It was like one of those dreadful country house farces so beloved by amateur dramatic societies. Although he is not of great physical stature, he is like a small country whose empire extends far beyond its borders. He seemed to fill the whole frame of the door. He glanced at me, but did not greet me with so much as a smile, and I feared that he had overheard my interrogation of his secretary. He informed Daisy that he was going downstairs for a few minutes and exited. I heard his footsteps on the stairs.

Daisy, no doubt to deter any further conversation, indicated that I should go inside. I closed the door behind me and surveyed the room. It was a peculiar experience to be alone there. Despite being granted permission to enter, I felt like an intruder. I stepped softly across the thin carpet and stood by the settee, removing my gloves. My eyes alighted on the filing cabinet behind the desk. What secrets must be contained there! As usual, the uppermost drawer gaped open. I glanced towards the door. Braithwaite had said he would be gone for a few minutes. No more than thirty seconds could have passed. I placed my handbag on the floor. My scalp prickled. Did I have the nerve? I told myself that this was a moment for action rather than contemplation. Hesitation would sink me. I stepped across the room, four, five, six paces. I gazed down into the open drawer. There were no neatly alphabetised dividers, just a haphazard pile of notebooks. I strained my ears for the sound of footsteps before opening the topmost one. On the first page the initials 'SK' were written in eccentric capital letters. K for Kepler, I supposed. My heart pounded. My eyes scanned the page. Braithwaite's handwriting was illegible. I wondered if perhaps it was a form of code or shorthand; that the thoughts expressed were so incendiary they had to be encrypted. In any case, it made no more sense to me than hieroglyphics. Still, somewhere in the cabinet there must be a notebook devoted to Veronica. If I was able to purloin it, I might later be able to decipher what was written there. I trotted back across the room to fetch my handbag, in which to secrete it. I rummaged through the contents of the drawer, opening notebooks randomly, then forced myself to pause. Almost two years had passed since Veronica had been coming here. I slid the drawer below open. It was even more disorderly than the first. I forced myself to systematically open each notebook, looking for Veronica's initials or some other clue. I paused and strained my ears. Nothing. I resolved to open five more notebooks before retreating to the settee. I had the first of these in my hands when I heard the click of the door behind me.

I dropped the book back into the drawer and slowly turned round. Braithwaite was standing in the doorway, kneading his hands in front of his chest, like a strangler priming himself for action. His face was impassive. I could feel the drawer against my back. He stepped slowly across the room and stood in front of me, so that our bodies were almost touching. He placed his hands on the corners of the filing cabinet, hemming me in with his arms.

'Perhaps you'd like to tell me what you're doing?' he said quietly.

'Nothing,' I said, in a voice that would shame a mouse.

'Nothing will come of nothing. Speak again,' he said in a clipped voice. His mouth was level with my forehead. His breath smelt of alcohol.

'I was curious about what filing system you use,' I said. 'At Mr Brownlee's, I file things both alphabetically and chronologically, but I see that you—' I allowed this drivel to peter out.

'Mend your speech a little, lest you may mar your fortunes,' he said. His chest rose and fell beneath his shirt. He placed his left hand under my chin and tilted back my head, so that I was forced to look him in the eye. His tongue moistened his fat lips. Then he placed his fingers gently on my exposed throat. My insides turned liquid.

'Well?'

I swallowed. His hand was warm on my neck and, had the circumstances been different, the sensation might almost have been pleasant. 'I was only curious about what you might have written about me,' I said.

Braithwaite removed his hand from my neck and massaged his jowls in his characteristically obscene way. His right hand rested on my shoulder, like a fat steak.

'But you know what curiosity did, don't you?'

'It killed the cat,' I said obediently.

'And we wouldn't want that to happen, would we?'

'No, we wouldn't.'

He lifted his hand from my shoulder and took half a step back. I scuttled to my place on the settee. 'I'm sorry,' I said. 'I shouldn't have looked in your cabinet. It was wrong of me.' I lowered my head in a display of contrition.

Braithwaite was now leaning against the offending item of furniture, his hands clasped behind the small of his back. The flies of his trousers (the same shapeless corduroys he had been wearing the previous week) were open, but it did not seem the moment to alert him to this fact. I reminded myself that I was Rebecca Smyth and did my best to compose myself. I reached towards the floor for my cigarettes, but my handbag was marooned at the foot of the filing cabinet. I had never before so keenly felt the need for nicotine.

'And what is it that you think I might have written about you?' he asked.

'I haven't the faintest idea,' I replied. 'That's why I was curious.'

'Then I'll tell you,' he said. 'Nothing.'

'Nothing?' I repeated.

'Not a word.' He looked terribly pleased with himself. 'And I'll tell you why. There's nothing to write about. I don't believe I've ever encountered anyone quite as hollow as you. I'm beginning to wonder if you really are who you say you are.'

'I often wonder the same thing,' Rebecca responded, rather deftly, I thought. (She is so much brighter than me; I sometimes wonder whether I shouldn't let her take over completely.)

'You affect this worldly air and yet you're all fiddle and fidget. Then there are your little tête-à-têtes with Daisy out there. And now Miss Kepler has informed me that you besieged her in the park last week. It seems the monstrous regiment of women is gathering its forces against me.'

'Besieged her?' I repeated. I felt quite offended that Miss Kepler could have cast such a complexion on our conversation.

He pushed himself away from the filing cabinet and, pulling up the straight-backed chair, straddled it in front of me me. His flies gaped open like a teenage boy's mouth. I stood up and retrieved my handbag. I lit a cigarette and felt I was returning to myself. There is nothing as vexing as a craving unsatiated, which is why I try insofar as possible to live without desires. If one has desires, one exists in a state of perpetual craving. Except with smoking. Smoking is a craving over which one holds sway. One can allow the longing to slowly intensify, then banish it with a single puff.

'Well, besieged or not,' Braithwaite went on, 'given your affected air, your wheedling away at Daisy and now your rifling through my papers, I can't help but conclude that you're plotting something.'

'I've never plotted anything in my life,' I said.

Then he started laughing to himself. 'You're a journalist, aren't you?'

'A journalist? Good heavens, no.' I was genuinely shocked at this suggestion.

'I've had plenty sniffing around here, believe me,' he said.

'I can assure you, I am not a member of that tribe,' I said.

'Then what? What are you, Miss Smyth?'

'I'm nothing. Nobody,' I said. 'Just Rebecca.' As he did not reply, I felt a little emboldened. 'And I really didn't besiege Miss Kepler,' I went on. 'I simply ran into her in the park.'

'She said you followed her.'

'After I left here, I took a turn around the park to clear my head. How could I have known she was going to be there?'

Braithwaite pursed his lips and looked at me. He appeared to accept the logic of what I had said. 'But you did speak to her?'

'Yes, I did,' I went on. 'I recognised her from the waiting room and said hullo. It would have been rude not to. It was all perfectly innocent.'

'You said hullo. Any more than that?' He massaged his temples.

I felt I was being interrogated and said so.

'The thing about Miss Kepler,' he said, 'is that she's given to, shall we say, flights of fancy.'

'Evidently,' I said.

'My advice would be to not get too involved with her.'

'I wasn't planning to get involved with her.'

'So, what did you find to talk about?'

I shrugged. 'Nothing much. The weather, I suppose.'

'Anything else?'

'Naturally, your name was mentioned.'

'And what did she say?'

'If I told you, it would only go to your head, and I rather think your head's quite big enough already.'

He looked at me quizzically. Notwithstanding my meagre knowledge of men, I do know that they are none of them immune to flattery. Men have egos. When one's husband comes home from work, one should always tell him how clever he is and how handsome he looks. This is our responsibility as women, and those who neglect such duties find themselves left, like me, on the shelf.

'If you must know,' I said, in a tone intended to convey that I did not concur, 'she told me that you were a genius.'

Braithwaite could not conceal the smile that played across his lips.

'As you say,' I continued, 'she is clearly given to flights of fancy.'

'Even the most psychotic cases have moments of clarity,' he said. 'And that was it, was it?'

'Actually,' I said, 'we did talk about something else.'

He widened his eyes questioningly.

'Suicide,' I said.

He repeated the word in an approving tone. 'And how did that weighty topic arise? It's not the usual tittle-tattle of two young women who happen to meet in a park.'

'Perhaps we were under your influence,' I said.

He remained silent.

I put my cigarette to my mouth and exhaled slowly. For the first time, I felt that I succeeded in piquing his interest. 'As a matter of fact,' I said, 'for some time now I have been entertaining thoughts of self-destruction.' I confess that I was rather pleased with this phrase, but Braithwaite did not seem the least bit impressed, either by the elegance of my wording or the sentiment expressed.

'Well,' he replied, 'if you decide to go through with it, make sure you call Daisy first to cancel any appointments.'

I suspected he was joking, but I looked down at my hands as if he had offended me. 'I'm afraid I don't think you're taking me seriously,' I said quietly.

'I assure you I am,' he replied. 'There's nothing that infuriates me more than a broken appointment.' He straightened his back and adopted a serious expression. He formed his fingers into a steeple, his elbows resting on his thighs. His forefingers tapping the furrow of his upper lip. He asked me how long I had been having these thoughts. I glanced at him, unsure if he was still teasing me.

'Some months,' I said. 'Perhaps even longer. Sometimes I find myself standing by the Thames wondering why I don't just throw myself in.'

'And what's stopping you?' he said.

'I'm sorry?'

'What's stopping you?' he repeated. 'Most folk think about doing themselves in now and again—God knows, I do—but most of the time they don't do it. Something stops them. So what's stopping you?'

I looked at him. 'I suppose I feel I haven't thought it through properly.'

'So, your continued existence is merely down to lack of planning?'

'No,' I said, 'it's not that. It's more that I feel I might regret it. That if I were to throw myself into the river, I might have second thoughts, but by then it would be too late.'

'And that would be your chosen method, would it? Throwing yourself from a riverbank. Not exactly fool-proof. There's every chance some young fellow will make a hero of himself and dive in to save you, or instinct will kick in and you'll swim to the bank.'

'I can't swim,' I retorted. (The idea of immersing oneself in a body of water has always struck me as wholly unnatural.)

'Even so,' he went on, 'not for you the gas oven or the handfuls of pills, the noose or the blowing out of the brains. Gunshot, of course, is a man's game. Hanging, if you get it right, is gruesome. And if you get it wrong, well, you've shit the carpet for nothing. Either way, not a pretty way to go.'

'You haven't mentioned trains,' I said, my scalp suddenly prickling at the thought of the overpass I had crossed little more than an hour before.

'Of course!' he exclaimed. 'The leap in front of a train. Excellent pedigree, thanks to Anna Karenina. Little chance of anything going wrong and no time to change your mind. But London is full of trains, and you haven't jumped in front of any of them yet.'

'No, but whenever I'm standing on a platform, I can't help thinking about how easy it would be to bring an end to it all.'

Braithwaite gave a little snort, as if what I had said was perfectly reasonable. 'And don't you think that all the other folk on the platform are thinking exactly the same thing?'

'No,' I said, 'I don't suppose they are.'

'Well, they are. Every last one of them.'

'But they don't act on it,' I said.

'No, they don't,' he said quietly. For the first time in our acquaintance, he seemed lost for words.

'I suppose they have some reason to go on,' I ventured.

'Such as?'

'I don't know. A husband. Children. A job.'

'You have a job,' he said.

'My job's idiotic. A chimpanzee could do it.'

'What about your father?'

I shrugged. 'I rather think it would be a relief to him if I wasn't around.'

'Well, when you put it like that, it does make me wonder why you haven't gone through with it.'

There was a pause for some moments, a minute perhaps. I became conscious of fat drops of rain noisily striking the windows. I had neglected to bring an umbrella and would get soaked. I don't imagine someone who is really suicidal much cares if they get soaked. It had been raining the day Veronica killed herself. I don't suppose she was concerned about ruining her coat. Braithwaite was observing me. There was a curiosity in his eyes, as if I were some kind of exhibit at a freakshow. Maybe he really did think I was mad. Then I wondered if I actually might be mad after all. I daresay the mad don't know they are mad, so it cannot be possible to know for sure that one isn't. The thought amused me. It would be rather fun to be mad. One can do whatever one likes if one is mad. People make allowances.

He clasped his hands behind his head. 'You know, Rebecca,' he said, 'it's really not my job to stop you killing yourself. If that's what you want to do, go ahead. Aside from your five guineas a week, it's really neither here nor there to me. But the thing is, I don't believe for a minute that you've got any intention of doing yourself in.'

I insisted that I did.

He crumpled his face and shook his head. 'I don't believe you. I see you come in here with your air of worldliness. You tell me your little stories, but all you're doing is deflecting attention from yourself. Everything you do is concealment. And it's not that you're concealing something from me. You're concealing it from yourself. You're buried under a landslide of fakery. The way you dress is fake. The way you speak is fake. Even the way you hold your cigarette is fake. You're a phoney.'

I lowered my eyes, as if he had offended me, which he hadn't. It was Rebecca he was insulting, not me. 'Perhaps I am,' I said.

'Good,' he said. 'We're all phoneys. You're a phoney, I'm a phoney. The difference is that I accept I'm a phoney. You'd be a lot happier if you accepted it too.'

'But what's the point in being someone you're not?' I said.

'What's the point in being whoever it is you think you are?'

It was true. There was no point. I got up in the morning, went to my silly job, came home, watched television or read a novel. I went to bed, got up and repeated the process ad nauseam. I was little more than an automaton.

'I can't imagine changing,' I said. 'Or changing in any way that would not be equally meaningless.'

'Why are you so concerned with meaning?' he said. 'Of course everything is meaningless. Accepting that life is meaningless is the first step to liberating yourself.'

'If everything is meaningless, what's the point in changing?' I said. I had become quite immersed in the conversation.

At this point Braithwaite got to his feet. He paced the room with an air of exasperation. 'Your problem, Rebecca, is that you think too much and act too little. You've crippled yourself.'

'So what should I do?' I said.

'Stop waiting for other people to tell you what to do.'

I retorted that it seemed reasonable to expect some advice in return for my five guineas a week.

'So if I told you to jump in front of a train, would you do it?' he asked.

'Are you telling me to jump in front of a train?'

'I am neither telling you to jump in front of a train nor telling you not to jump in front of a train. It's up to you.'

'And what if I did jump in front of a train?' I said.

'You won't. Jumping in front of a train requires an effort of will, something of which you appear to be incapable.'

'Perhaps I'll do it just to spite you,' I said.

'That,' he replied, 'would be something of a Pyrrhic victory, wouldn't you say?'

He stood up and pushed aside his chair so violently that it toppled onto its side. He knelt on the floor at my feet, so close that his chest was almost touching my knees. 'Forget about meaning,' he said. 'Life's not about meaning, it's about experience.'

The corduroy furrows of the thighs of his trousers were worn away. One would have thought that at his hourly rate, he could have invested in a new pair.

'Imagine you're in a park,' he said softly. 'It's a summer's day. You're walking by the Serpentine. You can feel the sun on your skin. You take off your shoes. The grass tickles the soles of your feet.'

He spoke slowly, allowing me time to absorb each image. His voice was hypnotic.

'You buy an ice cream.' He mimed holding a cornet, then put out his tongue and licked the imaginary confection. He gestured for me to do the same. His face was inches from mine. I held my hand in a loose fist in front of my chin and licked the air above it.

'How is it?' he asked.

'Nice,' I said. I took another lick.

'What flavour is it?'

'Vanilla.'

'I've got rum and raisin,' he said. 'Want to try some?' He proffered his cone towards me. As there was little danger of infection from an imaginary ice cream, I took it from him and put out my tongue. (At the time, it did not seem half as preposterous as it does now that I am writing it down.)

'Lovely,' I said, handing it back.

He shoved the remainder into his mouth, then wiped his lips with the back of his hand. I let my hand drop to my lap.

'You've spilled some on your blouse,' he said. He leant over and took a tissue from the box on the table and handed it to me. I obediently wiped up the mess I had made of myself. I laughed at the absurdity of what I was doing and felt anew that Collins Braithwaite was a very clever man who could make one do whatever he wanted.

After this silly episode, the mood had altered. Something had passed between us. I breathed slowly and evenly through my nose. Outside, the rain had abated. It was dark and silent. I had the impression that time had come to a halt. We sat for some moments in silence. In the normal course of things I would have lit a cigarette, but I felt no temptation to do so. After some minutes he stood up and declared that he would see me the following week, before adding with a laugh, 'If you haven't killed yourself before then.'

He watched as I gathered up my things. As I headed for the door, he called me back. He rummaged in his trouser pocket for a shilling and handed it to me. 'Buy yourself an ice cream,' he said.

'Perhaps I will,' Rebecca said. For a horrible moment I realised she was flirting with him. Outside on the pavement, I reminded her that it was November and hardly the weather for ice cream. I lit a cigarette. Rebecca insisted that she could still taste Braithwaite's rum and raisin on her tongue. I told her she was being suggestible. Couldn't she see that he was manipulating her? Why, she asked, did I always have to be so suspicious of people's motives? Why couldn't I just enjoy things for their own sake? That sort of mindless hedonism only led to trouble, I retorted. She imitated my mother's voice: 'We don't want another Woolworth's on our hands, do we?'

I shrugged off her remark. I was beginning to think she was attracted to Braithwaite.

And what if I am? she replied.

I wondered if Braithwaite had tried his ice cream ruse on Veronica. She would have had no truck with it. She was not the susceptible type. And she had never even liked ice cream. On the day of my tenth birthday, when we visited Richmond Park, Veronica refused an ice cream. Father had cajoled her, but she had insisted with the irrefutable logic that she always employed, that the consumption of ice cream on a hot day was counterintuitive as the temperature dictated that one must guzzle it down as quickly as possible. If one liked ice cream, it was more rational to eat it on a cold day, when it would take longer to melt, and one could thus prolong the pleasure. In any case, ice cream, she had said with a glance in my direction, was for children. Father insisted that ice cream was for everyone, but Veronica was not to be moved.

I set off in the direction of Primrose Hill, half hoping that I might encounter Miss Kepler again. Braithwaite was right to deride my propensity to establish a routine in a minimal amount of time. The virtue of routine, however, is that it eliminates the need for thought. One simply does what one has always done. There is comfort in familiarity. Nevertheless, I felt somewhat queasy now. I fingered the shilling in the pocket of my coat, but it was not Braithwaite's advice to buy myself an ice cream that lingered in my mind. Instead it was his blunt question: 'What's stopping you?' What indeed? No one would lament my passing. Father had replaced me with Mrs Llewelyn. Mr Brownlee might notice if I did not turn up to work, but an advertisement would be placed and another willing Girl Friday swiftly recruited. I was disposable. I was neither clever, talented nor funny. Neither beautiful nor plain. Nor was there anything about me that would make a child stop and point in the street. I was an in-between sort of person, a mediocrity. It was not so much that no one would lament my passing, more that it would barely be noticed.

I became aware of a presence on the pavement behind me. I told myself that Ainger Road was a public thoroughfare and the presence of another person was hardly noteworthy. Yet I felt quite definitely that I was being followed. Because, you see, I am, despite everything, a dreadful egotist. I cannot conceive of the actions of another person not being somehow performed for my benefit. I neither looked round to confirm my suspicions nor quickened my pace. I abandoned myself to fate. The footsteps, the heavy footsteps of a man, grew nearer. I relaxed my shoulders, awaiting a dull wallop to the back of my head, my knees giving way beneath me. The word 'cudgel' flitted through my mind, a weighty Anglo-Saxon word. I repeated it under my breath as I anticipated the blow.

Instead, I felt a hand on my shoulder.

It was Tom. Of course it was Tom (or whatever his name was).

'Rebecca,' he said. 'I was calling you.'

I repeated the name as if it meant nothing to me.

'It's me,' he said.

I must have looked blank. My eyes were level with his chest. The topmost button of his coat was dangling by a single thread. I was about to offer to repair it (I always carry a needle and thread in my handbag), but Rebecca stopped me: Tom was not interested in a prissy little home-maker. He embarked on a lengthy explanation of how he had tried to telephone me, but I must have written down the wrong number. The person who answered ('some old battle-axe') had told him that no one by the name of Rebecca Smyth lived there. It was an imposition, he knew, to ambush me like this. Normally he would never think of doing such a thing.

I looked at him in astonishment. His usual self-assurance had been replaced by the gaucheness of a teenager. He was wearing a fisherman's cap, which, because of his thick hair, sat too high on his head and looked ridiculous. He was looking at me with some unease. I realised that, by having seemingly given him the go-by, I had acquired some power over him (or, at least, Rebecca had). A handsome fellow like Tom would not, I imagine, be accustomed to such treatment. And the effect of this cruelty? He was standing before me like a supplicant willing to bathe my feet.

'That would be Mrs Llewelyn,' I explained. 'I have so many callers, sometimes I tell her to say that.'

'Ah!' Tom said, as if this was a perfectly plausible explanation. 'I'd have hated to think you'd fobbed me off with a false number.' This cleared up, he seemed to shake off his awkwardness. 'Well, now that we're here, we might as well have a drink. What do you say?'

I shrugged. Why not? We turned and walked back towards the Pembridge Castle. The pavement was slick from the earlier rain. Tom pushed his hands deep into the pockets of his coat. I hooked my hand around his elbow. It was soothing to hang onto his arm. My cheek touched the coarse material of his coat. It prickled like my father's chin before he shaved. We must have resembled the couples one sees in advertisements for his-and-hers rainwear or breath-fresheners.

Tom asked how my session with Braithwaite had gone.

'Let's not talk about that,' I replied.

'Yes, of course,' he said solemnly.

I asked what he had been doing with himself. He talked about various jobs he had been working on, but I barely listened. I was stranded in the hinterland between myself and Rebecca. I found myself wondering who Rebecca was. Certainly she resembled me. She wore my clothes. She spoke with my voice, although she had a more pronounced, clipped manner of speaking (I have a tendency to mumble, so that people often fail to hear what I have said). Her thoughts, in general, were my thoughts. The difference was that she had the gall to express them. I was not sure I liked her. She was brazen and, I suspect, somewhat indecent. In the unlikely event that my father met her, I was sure he would not take to her. But Tom seemed to like her. Tom seemed to like her very much. It was Rebecca he had pursued and Rebecca he was taking to the Pembridge Castle. It was Rebecca he wanted and Rebecca he must get.

We crossed Regent's Park Road and approached the pub. He held the door open and made a flamboyant spiralling gesture with his hand, as if ushering Princess Margaret into a ball. I stepped inside. The solitary man with his newspaper was at the same table by the door, a pint of some kind of ale untouched. The two solicitors had been replaced at the bar by similar types, one of them enormously fat, with mutton chop whiskers and a bowler hat sitting precariously on the back his head. Harry, the landlord, was standing with his back to the gantry, his fingers lightly clasped across his stomach. The table at which we had previously sat was occupied by a man staring at a crossword, a cigar clamped between the knuckles of his left hand. He glanced towards us as we entered. Aside from Rebecca and myself, there were no other women present. I allowed Tom to lead the way. He located a table in the 'snug' and suggested I make myself comfortable while he fetched what he called 'some lubricants'.

The snug was in the corner to the right of the bar and was shielded from prying eyes by panels of frosted glass bearing the insignia of the pub. There were two tables, both unoccupied. I sat down at the one beneath the window. If the snug constituted a partial haven from the surrounding decadence, it was also a secluded spot in which debauchery might be attempted. There had been plenty of other places to sit, and I wondered what Tom's motives were in thus isolating me. Of course, I was familiar with the mantra that men were only after one thing. In my experience, however, they were not after it with me. Perhaps that was about to change. Tom had not only telephoned me, but had then gone to some effort to track me down. He would hardly have done so if he did not have certain acts on his mind. I felt an awful prickling in my stomach. I had got myself into a proper fix. I stuffed my gloves into my handbag and wondered if I had time to effect an escape before he returned. From within the snug, I could not see the bar. I prevaricated. Perhaps I should have one gin and then excuse myself. Rebecca told me to shut up. I was going to spoil everything. I might not want Tom's hands wandering over me, but she did. She wanted to get sozzled. And if Tom wanted to prise open her legs, she would damn well let him. I might be happy to die a shrivelled-up virgin, but she wasn't. All I had to do was keep schtum and let her do the talking. Any other business that might need to be dealt with, I could leave to her. When I objected, she called me the most vicious names. Then she became wheedling. Why should I have it all my own way? Why not let her have some fun for once? I was about to tell her that she revolted me, but we were interrupted by Tom's return with the said lubricants. Rebecca greeted him with her broadest smile, reminding me as she did so that Tom did not even know that I existed.

He took off his coat and threw it carelessly onto the banquette, before sitting down opposite me. He kept on his silly fisherman's cap. 'This is cosy,' he said.

'Yes, it is,' said Rebecca. 'But don't get any ideas about where you might be putting your hands. The snug's a fine and private place, but none, I think, do there embrace,' she added archly.

She knew full well that by proscribing any such activities, she was only planting the thought into poor Tom's head. Not to mention letting him know that such thoughts had already crossed her mind. He held up the hands in question and swore that they would remain in full view at all times.

'If any hands are to go a-wandering, they'll have to be yours,' he said with a laugh. He raised his pint and we clinked glasses across the table.

Rebecca launched into a monologue about the frightful day she had had. The Shaftesbury Theatre was short of chorus girls. John Osborne was up in arms about the casting of his new play, and Mr Brownlee had abandoned ship at lunchtime to get drunk with that old queer Terence Rattigan. I listened to this stream of claptrap, unable to intervene. But Tom was rapt.

'It all sounds very exciting,' he said.

'Hardly,' said Rebecca. 'Men are such children. I might as well be a nursemaid. It's no wonder I'm seeing a shrink.' Tom seemed to find all this very amusing. She downed half her gin and tonic and gave herself a coughing fit.

'Let's get blotto,' Tom declared, in a preposterous approximation of an upper-class accent.

'Yes, do let's!' Rebecca agreed. She was incorrigible. Tom downed the rest of his beer and rose to get more drinks.

I said nothing. I had to admit that Rebecca knew how to enjoy herself. Maybe she was right. I should let her have her head for the night. Perhaps Tom was an ice cream that was meant to be licked. I lit a cigarette. In the centre of the table was a tin ashtray advertising Johnnie Walker's whisky. Save for the two cigarettes Rebecca had smoked since our arrival, it was empty. A striding figure in black riding boots, jodhpurs and a red fox hunter's blazer was depicted. In one hand he held a cane and in the other a pair of lorgnettes. I imagined myself in his outfit. Or rather, I imagined Rebecca, striding along Charing Cross Road, now and again taking her cane to some troublesome urchins.

The pub was rapidly filling up and there was a hubbub of conversation. Tom returned with a pint and whisky for himself and more gin for me. This time he slid onto the banquette next to me. I was alarmed by this escalation in hostilities, but Rebecca was unperturbed.

'Perhaps we should see a film together sometime,' Tom said. 'They're showing the new Godard at the Roxy. Do you like the *nouvelle vague*?' he asked. 'I'm fed up of that British kitchen-sink stuff.'

I had no idea what he was talking about, but Rebecca responded resourcefully, '*J'adore Paris*.' She even pronounced Paris the French way.

'I've never been,' said Tom. 'But I'd love to.'

'*C'est magnifique. Très romantique,*' she said, pushing my schoolgirl French to its limits.

Tom nodded earnestly.

'You should visit,' she said. 'It's full of pretty girls.'

Tom shrugged as if pretty girls were of no interest to him. 'I'd rather go with you,' he said. 'I'm afraid I don't speak the lingo, though. You'd have to be in charge.'

'I'm always in charge.' Rebecca smiled winningly at him. 'And, of course, the French are so in advance of us. Sexually, I mean.'

This caused Tom to puff out his cheeks and exhale slowly. Then he ran a hand across his brow. He took a deep swig of his beer and chased it down with a slug of whisky. Rebecca took a mouthful of gin. We had rather acquired a taste for it. That was one thing we had in common. Rebecca and I both loved gin. Gin brought us closer together. After two gins, I felt infinitely more well disposed to her. I found her amusing and admired her waspish remarks. It did not take a genius to see that my resentment of her was based on jealousy. The truth was, I wanted to be her. And she, perhaps because I was willing to sit quietly and not interfere, tolerated me more. She liked to be in control. And she liked an audience. In this, she was entirely my opposite. But that is often the way with chums. There is no room for two extroverts in a relationship, and two introverts never have the wherewithal to make friends in the first place. I took another glug. I had not forgotten my mishap of the previous evening, but I was now, I felt, more accustomed to alcohol. It seemed to be having no adverse effect on me whatsoever

Tom was discoursing on various French films. I had seen none of them, but Rebecca was able to pronounce authoritatively on them all. Yes, she loved Truffaut as well, but Chabrol was *too* dull. Tom's thigh was now touching hers, but she made no attempt to move away. Instead, she demanded another gin. While Tom was at the bar, she took the opportunity to touch up her lipstick. Her mouth made a lewd O in the mirror of her compact. When she had finished, she ran her tongue across her lips to make them glisten.

When he returned with the drinks, Tom finally took off his cap and sent it spinning onto the banquette. His hair remained rigidly cast in its mould. He took a deep breath, his chest impressively filling out his sweater. He turned and looked at me, trying to recall where we had been in the conversation. There was a prolonged moment of silence. Then Rebecca did something quite extraordinary. She raised her right hand and pushed her fingers into his thicket of hair. I told her to desist, but she pushed on until her fingertips made contact with his scalp.

'You have a wonderful head of hair,' she said.

'I can't claim any credit,' he said. 'My grandfather was a Portuguese sailor. It's Portuguese hair.'

Rebecca withdrew her hand. Her fingers were oily. Tom looked at her. He really was tremendously handsome. Rebecca pouted, then glanced modestly down at her lap. Some seconds passed. Then Tom let out a low whistle and returned his attention to his beer. I wondered how he could consume so much liquid. Beer is manly. Everything about it is manly: the hefty glass with its fist-sized handle, the dirty froth, the murky brown liquid, the foul taste. Even the word 'beer' is solid and manly. I could never imagine even raising a pint of beer to my lips. But I loved to watch Tom drink. He did it with relish. It was like watching a farmyard animal at the trough.

I would venture to suggest that a moment had just then passed between Tom and Rebecca. They had both been thinking of the same thing. But Rebecca, Jezebel that she is, still has her principles, and Tom—poor, handsome, dim-witted Tom—did not have the chutzpah to act. Now the moment had passed and his failure had created a barrier between them. Rebecca was disappointed in him. He was disappointed in himself. The silly conversation, which they both knew was no more than a preliminary to that moment, had withered away and the jolly atmosphere dissipated. A horrible silence grew. They were like actors who had suddenly forgotten their lines. The audience was shifting uneasily in the stalls. Tom glanced at Rebecca and gave a little laugh through his nose. Rebecca formed her lips in to a tight smile and took another sip of gin.

'Well, here we are,' he said, in a pitiful attempt to prevent the silence from thickening.

'Yes,' said Rebecca, 'here we are.' But although she merely repeated his words, she pronounced them in a way that invested them with far greater meaning. She spoke quietly, almost inaudibly, pausing after the first word so that Tom was forced to lean in closely to hear. Then, with Tom's ear only inches from her mouth, she enunciated each syllable as if it was quite precious, and placed an emphasis on the final verb, drawing it out so that it formed an elegant arc. Her meaning was unmistakeable, yet, were she to stand accused of coquetry, the written record would show no more than four thoroughly innocuous words. Tom needed to now do no more than turn his head slightly so that his mouth was in proximity to hers. Rebecca touched her lips with tip of her index finger and, before I could take any preventative action, they were engaged in a kiss. Tom tasted of beer, but the sensation of his lips on hers was obscenely agreeable. I felt a quickening between my legs. Then his tongue entered Rebecca's mouth and met the tip of hers. They jousted like a pair of nuzzling dogs. Tom's hand found its way onto Rebecca's knee. His finger slid under the hem of her skirt to the inside of her thigh. For a moment I was Constance Chatterley. I wanted it all. I wanted to be overpowered, to be crushed and debased under Tom's bulk. His great arm snaked around my shoulders and pulled me to him. I placed my hand on his chest and pushed him away. My breath came to me in short stabs.

He looked at Rebecca, awaiting further invitation.

'I want you to kiss *me*,' I said.

Tom's eyes darted from side to side. 'I thought I just did.'

'Not Rebecca,' I said. '*Me*.' My hand was still on his chest. I could feel it rise and fall like the swell of the sea. He wore a bewildered expression. Rebecca cursed me.

Then I told him my name. He repeated it questioningly.

'There is no Rebecca,' I said. 'There's just me.'

Tom blinked several times. He retracted his arm from my shoulders, as if I might be infectious.

'Rebecca's someone I made up so that I could visit Dr Braithwaite,' I explained. 'She's a character. She doesn't exist. I'm not a nut at all. Rebecca's the nut. I'm perfectly normal.'

Tom was looking at me as though I was very far from normal. 'But Rebecca,' he said, 'I never really thought you were a nut. Not a real nut anyway. And, in any case, I wouldn't mind if you were. I like nuts.'

'I'm not Rebecca and I'm not a nut,' I said firmly.

I leant forward to kiss him, but he placed his hands on my shoulders and pushed me away. Humiliated, I took up what was left of my gin and threw it in his face. Even without looking round, I could sense that people were observing this little drama through the entrance of the snug. The din of conversation in the pub had diminished. Tom sat dumbly on the banquette. He put out his tongue and licked gin from his upper lip.

Rebecca audibly called me a witless little shrew. I'd ruined everything. She rummaged in my bag and finding nothing else suitable, attempted to dry Tom's face with my gloves. 'You mustn't listen to her,' she said, as she dabbed at his cheeks. 'It was just a silly joke. She's the one that doesn't exist.'

Tom took her by the wrists and pushed her hands away. 'Funny kind of joke,' he said.

I looked round. The entrance to the snug now resembled the cast of a Brueghel painting. A narrow-faced man with round spectacles was painstakingly explaining what had happened to the Johnny-come-latelies. A second man dissented from his version of events and an argument ensued. The landlord's face appeared above the frosted glass partition of the snug to ask what was going on.

'Nothing, Harry,' said Tom. 'Nothing at all.'

'Doesn't look like nothing,' he said. He then asked Rebecca if everything was all right.

'Perfectly,' she said.

But everything was not all right. Tom stood up and put on his coat with as much dignity as he could muster. The crowd parted to allow him to exit. He apologised if he had offended me. I was rather touched by that. Then he turned and left.

Rebecca called his name imploringly, but he did not look back.

How I wished I had not thrown my gin in Tom's face. I craved the sensation of alcohol on my throat. Then I noticed that Tom had not touched his second whisky. Without any thought to whether I was being observed, I took the glass and emptied the contents into my mouth. It burned horribly and caused me to cough, but I felt a sort of relief in it. I lit a cigarette and did my best to appear unconcerned about the scene that had taken place. The figure in the ashtray now seemed to be looking at me accusingly. I stubbed my cigarette on his face. As I left the pub, the patrons nudged and whispered to each other. In the cab home, Rebecca kept up a stream of vitriol, which my apologies did nothing to staunch. My suede gloves from Heaton's were ruined. They were my favourite pair.

Braithwaite IV:
A Disturbance at Ainger Road

SHORTLY AFTER FIVE O'CLOCK on the afternoon of 17th August 1968, police were called to a disturbance at Ainger Road. Raised voices had been heard, followed by banging and a woman screaming. The official record of the incident states that it was attended by PCs Charlie Cox and Robert Pendle. Shouting and crashing continued from within the house, even as they were let in by a young woman named Angela Carver. Miss Carver stood aside in the hallway as the two policemen rushed into the ground-floor living room. Although it was a sunny day, the curtains were drawn. There they found Braithwaite grappling with another man, Richard Aaron. The men had their arms around each other's necks and, as the policemen entered, they lost their balance and collapsed sideways onto a coffee table, upsetting drinks and an ashtray. The two men remained locked together on the floor. Aaron was on top and he attempted to land some punches to the side of Braithwaite's head. The policemen pulled Aaron off and removed him to the kitchenette at the back of the house. Braithwaite got to his feet. He was bleeding from the mouth and his shirt was torn. He was wearing a pair of mustard-coloured corduroy trousers rolled up at the ankles and was barefoot. A second girl, Rachel Simmons, was slouched on the sofa, where she remained throughout. The girls, PC Cox noted in his report, were respectively nineteen and twenty-one years old. Rachel Simmons was in a 'state of intoxication' and 'scantily clad'. The room smelt strongly of marijuana.

Richard Aaron was in a violent temper, swearing and throwing crockery. PC Pendle was obliged to manhandle him into the tiny overgrown garden at the back of the property to calm him down. Charlie Cox returned to the living room. Braithwaite, who did not appear overly concerned about his injuries, joked that he would have had Aaron if the cops hadn't turned up. When Cox asked what had happened, he replied that he and Aaron had been engaged in a friendly wrestling bout. Cox replied that it had not seemed particularly friendly and that if Braithwaite could not provide a satisfactory explanation, he would be obliged to place him under arrest. Braithwaite laughed and pointed out that he had guests to entertain. Rachel Simmons, whose head was drooping slackly to the side, did not appear in the least entertained. Angela Carver stood with her back to the door. She asked if she could leave, but Cox refused, as she would be required to provide a statement. He then asked her if drugs had been consumed on the premises. Braithwaite told the constable to leave the girl out of it and that if he was looking to score he should have said so in the first place. Had he taken a less facetious attitude, things might have been sorted out on the spot, but, in the event, all four were taken to the police station at Holmes Road in Kentish Town.

Richard Aaron, thirty-eight, was a well-known actor who had recently enjoyed critical success in a revival of Pinter's *The Birthday Party* at the Old Vic theatre. He had previously appeared in Roman Polanski's *Repulsion* and alongside Michael Caine in *The Ipcress File*. At the Holmes Road station he alleged that Braithwaite had raped his wife, the actress Jane Gressingham. On hearing this, he had flown into a fury and had gone round to Braithwaite's to 'knock the living daylights out of him'. In the sober atmosphere of the interview room, he admitted that this had been the wrong course of action and he should instead have called the police. Still, what had seemed little more than a commonplace brawl now took a more sinister turn.

Jane Gressingham was the 'It Girl' of 1963. She began her career as a model, but landed minor roles in *Summer Holiday* and *From Russia with Love*. Gressingham was no one's idea of a great actress. Her roles required her to do little more than strike enigmatic poses. When called upon to deliver a line or two of dialogue, the results were wooden to say the least, but her angular gamine features and hooded eyes chimed perfectly with the age, and her face graced the covers of *Vogue* and *Harper's Bazaar*. She met Richard Aaron on the set of the long-forgotten comedy-musical *Those London Girls!* in the spring of 1964, and they married a few months later. They were unquestionably the celebrity couple *du jour* at a moment when London was becoming the most fashionable city on Earth. Gressingham was aware enough of her limitations as an actress to enrol in classes at the Royal Academy, but her career fizzled out. Her head was turned by the endless round of parties and premieres that London had to offer. Drink and drugs began to take their toll. The final straw came when she was sacked on the set of *Blow Up* for being 'drunk or stoned or both'. Richard Aaron was furious, as it was he who had persuaded director Michelangelo Antonioni to give her a part in this prestigious production.

Gressingham's real name was Susanne Kepler. She was the daughter of a German-Jewish émigré, Alfred Kepler, a set designer who fled the Nazi regime in 1938, and Doris Vaughn, a costumier. Alfred's two sisters and mother were murdered in Birkenau in 1944. Alfred himself drowned in the Thames in 1948. The inquest into his death recorded an open verdict, but it seems likely that he took his own life. Gressingham was nine years old.

On hearing Aaron's allegation, PC Pendle informed Detective Inspector Harold Skinner, who then took charge of proceedings. Braithwaite was informed that he had the right to call a lawyer, but he declined to do so. A car was dispatched to bring Gressingham to the station. This was a time when cops were not averse to earning a few pounds tipping off journalists about breaking stories, and when word got out that Richard Aaron and Collins Braithwaite were being held at the Kentish Town station, a posse of hacks rapidly assembled on the pavement outside. Unbelievably, Gressingham was driven to the main entrance of the station and taken in by the front door. Photographs of her attempting to conceal a blackened left eye behind a gloved hand appeared on the front pages of most of the following day's papers, along with insets of Aaron and Braithwaite. LOVE TRIANGLE GOES SOUR, declared the *Daily Express*. IT GIRL TO HIT GIRL, said the *Daily Mail*. The accompanying stories all mentioned the 'fracas' at Braithwaite's flat, but were otherwise composed of hearsay and speculation. Only the London *Standard* made mention of 'an alleged rape'.

Jane Gressingham, who knew nothing of what had taken place at Ainger Road, was offered a cup of tea and taken to be interviewed by DI Skinner. Gressingham was asked to give an account of what had occurred that afternoon. At first she was evasive. She appeared to be under the influence of sedatives or some other drug. DI Skinner assured her that she was neither under arrest nor herself accused of anything. As she continued to answer his questions vaguely, he asked how she came by her black eye. She said she couldn't remember. Skinner expressed surprise at this response; the wound looked painful and was clearly recent. He asked if her husband had inflicted it. She replied that he had, but it wasn't his fault. Pressed further, she admitted they had had an argument about her relationship with

Collins Braithwaite. Eventually, after much skirting around the topic, Skinner put Aaron's allegation to her. Asked if there was any truth to this, Gressingham reluctantly agreed that she had indeed said that. According to her version of events, Aaron had returned to their apartment to find her drunk. A row ensued in which he stated that her twice-weekly visits to Braithwaite didn't seem to be doing much good. Gressingham retorted that they were a great deal more beneficial than being married to Aaron and that Braithwaite was twice the man he was. Gressingham conceded that she had had sex with Braithwaite, at which point Aaron struck her. As he stood over her on the floor, Gressingham, fearing further blows, said that she hadn't wanted to do it, at which point Aaron said: 'So he raped you?' Gressingham had nodded and Aaron stormed out of the house. Skinner then asked Gressingham if the encounter with Braithwaite had been consensual and she replied that it had

When the allegations were put to Braithwaite, he readily admitted to having sexual relations with Gressingham on numerous occasions, but denied that any coercion had been involved. All parties were released around 11pm that evening. There did not appear to be any question of charging Aaron for his assault on Gressingham.

Despite the fact that no charges were preferred, the damage had been done. The press had never liked Braithwaite and they now scented blood. In the ensuing days, a number of journalists camped outside the house on Ainger Road. Braithwaite was unrepentant. He came and went as he pleased, even pausing to chat with the reporters on the pavement. In *My Self and Other Strangers* he wrote: 'I hadn't done anything wrong. Why should I hide myself away?'

Whether for this reason, or because those visiting a therapist do not generally want to be photographed doing so, his clients stopped coming. Braithwaite assumed this would be a temporary state of affairs, and spent the ensuing days carousing in the Colony Room and other Soho drinking dens. He even seemed to relish his notoriety.

This attitude did not go down well, either with the press or the police. The following weekend's *News of the World* featured the salacious accounts of former clients of the 'Primrose Hill Quack'. These stories described Braithwaite appearing from behind his desk in his underpants; lying on his back humming while his clients talked; smoking pot with clients; fondling himself; and asking lurid, irrelevant sexual questions. When asked why she had put up with such behaviour, one of the interviewees responded that she had never seen a psychiatrist before and assumed such things were normal. Another story in the *Daily Express* of 24th August branded the 'author of *Kill Yourself* [sic]' a 'cheerleader for suicide'. It featured an interview with a young woman who claimed that when she told Braithwaite she was having suicidal thoughts, he responded by asking what was stopping her. At the end of the session he requested that if she decided to go through with it, to be sure to settle her bill with him first.

There were calls for Braithwaite to be struck off by the British Medical Association, but as he had never had any medical qualifications in the first place, this could not happen. There was nothing to stop anyone putting a plaque on their door declaring themselves to be a psychotherapist. 'I never set myself up as any kind of guru,' he writes in *My Self and Other Strangers*. 'If people were daft enough to seek my counsel, who was I to turn them away?' Like so much that Braithwaite wrote, this is a self-justifying half-truth. While he never called himself a therapist, or claimed any medical credentials, neither did he correct those who assumed his title was that of a physician. And while he claimed that he was only reacting to demand, he purposefully set himself up in Ainger Road to accommodate his burgeoning business.

With customary hubris, Braithwaite assumed that everything would blow over in a few days. He was wrong. Although he had not been charged with anything, even among the bohemian circles from which his clientele was drawn, the word 'rape' carried a stigma. While there had once been a certain prestige attached to being a client of 'the most dangerous man in Britain', his cachet was rapidly waning.

And things were to get worse. Andrew Trevelyan, father of Braithwaite's erstwhile Oxford girlfriend Alice, read the newspaper reports with interest. The now knighted QC was by then working for the Crown Prosecution Service. He called Detective Inspector Skinner and asked to see the statements relating to the incident. Skinner explained that there was no need as no arrests had been made, but Trevelyan was insistent and that evening visited the station at Holmes Road. Skinner received him frostily. He was an East End boy who had risen through the ranks, and did not take kindly to interference from entitled bigwigs, or to the implied criticism of his decision not to press charges. Trevelyan read through the statements of the five witnesses, made a few notes and then asked to speak to Cox and Pendle. Later, he visited Angela Carver and Rachel Simmons at the addresses they had given in their statements. Simmons was an art student living in a flatshare in Camden with three girlfriends. She had met Braithwaite some months before in a pub and he had invited her and a friend back to his house. There, they listened to records, smoked dope and she had sex with him. It was 'no big deal'. Collins, she said, was cool and he always had plenty of pot. She had never met Angela Carver before the incident of 17th August and had not seen her since.

Angela Carver was the daughter of one of Braithwaite's clients, Mervyn Carver, a restauranteur and nightclub owner. She had met Braithwaite at a party given by her parents at their home on St Anne's Terrace in St John's Wood a few weeks previously. When Trevelyan rang the bell of this same address, it was Carver's wife, Beatrice, who opened the door. Trevelyan gave her his card and explained that he would like to speak to her daughter. Angela was called downstairs and it was only after some persuasion (Trevelyan was famously silver-tongued) that Mrs Carver allowed him to speak to her daughter alone, in Mr Carver's study. Trevelyan began by explaining that she was not in any trouble. He simply wanted to ask her some questions about the incident at Ainger Road. Angela, whose name had not appeared in the newspapers, was visibly nervous and kept glancing towards the door of the study. Her parents would kill her if they knew that she had been involved. Trevelyan assured her (falsely, as it turned out) that their conversation would remain strictly confidential.

Angela was not nineteen as she had told the police, but seventeen. She had fallen into conversation with Braithwaite at her father's birthday party. He had been funny and taken an interest in her studies and what she planned to do when she left school. Braithwaite had guessed her star sign (Libra) and they had talked about astrology and free will. No adult had ever spoken to her in this way and she was flattered by his attention. When Braithwaite's secretary called a few days later and invited her to a get-together at his house, she accepted without telling her parents. When she arrived at Ainger Road at two o'clock that Saturday she was surprised to find that there was only one other guest, an older girl called Rachel. Braithwaite assured her that more people would be arriving soon. He offered her a glass of wine, which she accepted. Braithwaite was smoking a joint, but he did not offer it to her. As the afternoon wore on and no one else turned up, she became uneasy. Braithwaite played records and danced around the room with his shirt open, pausing only to roll joints or fetch more wine from the kitchen. She had drunk two or three glasses of wine and danced with him. When Rachel tried to persuade her to share a joint, Braithwaite told her to leave her be. She was just a kid. Trevelyan asked if he had made any sexual advances towards her. Angela said that he hadn't, but that he had kissed Rachel on the sofa and become aroused. She had distracted herself by browsing through the bookshelves. It had almost come as a relief when Richard Aaron burst in.

Trevelyan told Skinner that a warrant would be issued to search Braithwaite's home for drugs. Although Braithwaite had not made a favourable impression, Skinner considered busting beatnik types for smoking dope beneath him, but he had no choice but to comply. Two days later he accompanied Cox and Pendle to Ainger Road to exercise the warrant. A substantial quantity of marijuana was seized and Braithwaite was arrested for possession with intent to supply. There was, however, no evidence for the latter and the charge was reduced to one of possession. While such an offence would now result in no more than an official caution, at this time it carried the very real risk of prison. That same year, Keith Richards of the Rolling Stones was sentenced to twelve months on a charge of allowing his home to be used for the purpose of smoking marijuana. The sentence was subsequently quashed on appeal, but Braithwaite would not be able to count on the same public sympathy were he handed a custodial sentence.

The trial was held at the Inner London Sessions Court on Newington Causeway. The public gallery was packed with journalists and curious onlookers. Against the advice of his solicitor, Braithwaite insisted on entering a plea of not guilty.

Andrew Trevelyan took personal charge of the prosecution. Angela Carver and Rachel Simmons were called as witnesses. Braithwaite did not deny that the drugs in question were his, instead declaring that he did not recognise the jurisdiction of the state over what substances he chose to put in his body. While this defence might have garnered approval among the counter-culture crowd, it held no sway with Justice of the Peace June Aitken. Nor did it have any basis in law. Braithwaite's attitude to the court (he took off his shoes and studiously picked at his feet during Trevelyan's closing statement) and general arrogance did not enamour him to the jury. Trevelyan portrayed the case as being one of symbolic importance. There was a cabal of people, he said, who believed that their celebrity placed them above the law. 'The defendant may think that the law is an ass,' he continued, 'but that does not give him, or any other individual, the right to flout it.' According to the *Daily Express*, he went on to 'eviscerate Braithwaite's character at such length that Mrs Aitken had to intervene and caution him to adhere to the facts of the case'. In her summing up, she reminded the jury that it was not the defendant's character that was on trial, but his actions; their only role was to apply the law to the evidence they had heard. The jury took less than fifteen minutes to find Braithwaite guilty. On hearing the verdict, Braithwaite turned and sarcastically applauded the jury for 'upholding the apparatus of their own repression'. Mrs Aitken sentenced him to sixty days, now taking her own turn to scold the defendant for his unbecoming and disrespectful behaviour during the proceedings.

In his autobiography, *Both Sides of the Bar*, Trevelyan recounts that, as a student, Braithwaite had an affair with his daughter that had left her 'hospitalised', a phrasing which drew a discreet veil over Alice's attempted suicide and implied that Braithwaite had physically assaulted her. His pursuit of

Braithwaite was not, he loftily claimed, motivated by revenge, but by a desire to protect the public from a 'dangerous charlatan'. He had watched Braithwaite's rise in the intervening years with horror, 'shocked at the naïvety with which otherwise seemingly intelligent people appeared to embrace his mumbo-jumbo as some kind of hippy scripture'.

Ronnie Laing, who would himself be arrested and charged with unlawful possession of LSD a decade later, greeted the news of these developments with glee, telling his friend John Duffy that the 'odious conman' should have been banged up years ago.

Braithwaite served forty days in Wormwood Scrubs. He found society in jail, he wrote, 'a great deal saner than that on the other side of the bars [...] I learned more about human behaviour in six weeks in prison than I did in six years among the toffs of Oxford.'

On his release, Braithwaite found that he had been evicted from Ainger Road. His furniture, clothes, books and papers had been packed up and stored in a warehouse in Acton. He found temporary refuge at the Notting Hill home of Zelda Ogilvie and her new boyfriend, the playwright Joe Carter, but she made it clear that she would not tolerate him for more than a few days. In the event, he stayed for a month, drinking and unrepentantly smoking pot, until Carter found him a small flat in Finsbury Park and 'almost forcibly removed him' to it.

Braithwaite made no effort to re-start his business. Royalties from his two books were still coming in and he told anyone willing to listen that he was fed up listening to 'over-privileged mediocrities mithering about their identity crises'. It was time to write another book. Laing was, at the time, touring European and American campuses, lecturing to large audiences of adoring students. Braithwaite, who had never travelled further than

France, fancied a piece of the action. When he eventually managed to persuade Edward Seers to take him for lunch, he did not find him receptive to the idea. Seers suggested that he might be better off writing a novel. 'A novel?' Braithwaite retorted. 'What's the use in bloody novels?' When Seers refused to extend the lunch into an all-day drinking session, Braithwaite told him he would take his book elsewhere. Seers paid the bill and told him he was welcome to do so.

The Fifth Notebook

I have not been into work these last two weeks. The malaise I affected at the outset of this ill-advised enterprise has become extant. I feel quite overwhelmed. I should have kept my gloomy thoughts safely under lock and key. Silly me. Silly, silly me. Yesterday, I stayed the whole day in bed. I have lost all inclination to take care of my toilet. My hair is in knots and my poor face has not seen a spit of make-up for days. My skin is dry and papery. I know that even a short walk in the fresh air might perk me up, but I have not the energy to even open the curtains, and I refuse to let Mrs Llewelyn perform this service for me. I do not want to be reminded that the world continues to exist beyond my room.

Mr Brownlee telephoned three times last week, but I refused to speak to him. Mrs Llewelyn told him I was unwell, but her tone of voice betrayed her feelings on the matter. A few days ago, I received a letter from him, expressing sympathy for my condition, but that he could not manage without me. If I was not able to let him know when I was returning, he would, regrettably, have to find a replacement. I am heartbroken. I am fond of Mr Brownlee and know that he has come to rely on me. I am saddened to think that The Great Dando will miss my applause as he scrabbles on the floor to retrieve his magic florin. Rebecca tells me that I am wasting my time on such duds. Mr Brownlee is no more a theatrical agent than The Great Dando is a magician. They are as misguided as the credulous no-hopers that present themselves at my desk. She is right, of course, as she is right about everything. Even so, I miss them. I miss taking the bus to work. I miss my walk along Charing Cross Road. I miss window-shopping on my lunch hour and gazing at the beatniks and the kohl-eyed girls in the espresso bars. I miss pretending to be part of the world, even though I have always known I am separate from it. It has taken Rebecca to show me the error of my ways.

Two nights ago, I was persuaded to come down to supper. I did not think to dress and sat at the table naked beneath my soiled nightgown. Poor Father did not know where to look. Mrs Llewelyn fetched my robe and I put it on, suddenly ashamed of my state of undress. Father gently enquired as to whether I was feeling better and, as I could see he was concerned, I assured him that I was. Other than that, the meal passed in silence. I ate only a few morsels of food, and this for appearance's sake only. I gagged on every mouthful.

Afterwards, Mrs Llewelyn took me upstairs and ordered me out of my clothes. I had not the will to resist. She ran a bath for me and sat on the rim gently washing my hair. It was pleasant in the warm water and I gave no thought to my nakedness. I stood on the bathmat shivering like a child while Mrs Llewelyn dried me and then pulled a fresh nightgown over my head. In my room she sat me on the stool front of my dresser and brushed my hair. I was grateful for this kindness, and all the more so as it was carried out without comment or admonishment. When she had finished she put me in bed, pulled the blankets up to my chin and wished me a good night's sleep. I should have thanked her, but I could not bring myself to utter the words.

Throughout all this, I have had Rebecca needling me. I have assured her that I do not need her to tell me that I am a worthless good-for-nothing, but she nonetheless amuses herself by finding ever more elaborate ways of expressing this sentiment. What is worse, however, is the resentment she harbours towards me. I am dragging her down. Without me, she would be out enjoying herself. If it wasn't for me, she would have f—ed handsome Tom by now (her language is atrocious). I remind her that I have apologised and promised that next time I will keep out of it. Thanks to me, she retorts, there won't be a next time; she would be better off without me. I cannot demur. We would both, I agree, be better off without me. Variations of this dialogue play out constantly. Sleep is my only relief from her hectoring. I loathe her, but despite my care never to express this, she seems to read my thoughts. 'It's not me you hate. It's yourself, you spineless milksop.' She regularly reduces me to tears, which only provides her with further ammunition with which to ridicule me. There seems only one way to get rid of her and that is to follow her advice and do away with myself. The worm that has established itself in my brain nourishes itself on such thoughts. Like a maggot in an apple, it grows replete.

If there is one thing that has saved me thus far, it is that I have always been dreadfully lazy. I lack the will to diligently apply myself to any task. Lethargy, however, hardly seems a proper reason not to do oneself in. To go on merely because one is too idle to do otherwise is neither noble nor romantic. Yet this appears to be the point I have reached: I can no longer be bothered living, but neither have I the wherewithal to end my life. Even in my state of lassitude, I can laugh at the irony. The default in life is to go on. Without intervention, life continues, as if it is an entity that exists independently of its custodian. To terminate a life requires an effort of will. Suicide (if we are, for once, to call it by its proper name) requires a certain resolve. It requires planning and decisiveness. These are qualities in which I am entirely lacking. Suicide is not for ditherers and I have always been a ditherer. That is yet another difference between Veronica and myself. Veronica had the ability to fix on a course of action and see it through. I should be more like her.

On Monday, or perhaps Tuesday morning, I forced myself from my bed. It took me such an effort to perform my ablutions and dress myself that I was astonished I had hitherto achieved these feats with nary a second thought. It seemed easier to let the water drain from my bath and evaporate from my skin than to stand up and make the effort to dry myself. Sitting at my dressing table, the powder puff felt as heavy in my hand as a stone.

Father was delighted to see me at breakfast. 'Ah, splendid! You're feeling better,' he said.

'Yes, much better, Daddy,' I assured him.

Mr Brownlee would be happy to have me back, he said. He and Mrs Llewelyn had been worried about me.

I smiled wanly. I was sure that he was not in the least bit fooled by my act. I know that he too harbours melancholy feelings. He never parades these sentiments, but I sometimes see their shadow pass across his face, or sense his weariness in the moments when his eyes, under the guise of blinking, remain closed for a few seconds too long. I spread some butter and marmalade on a piece of toast, which I then slipped into my handbag while Father's eyes were on his newspaper.

I am sure it is unnecessary to say that I had no intention of going to work. For the sake of appearances, however, I set off along Elgin Avenue. By the time I reached the bus stop, all the energy I had mustered was spent. I stepped into the Lyons there and sat down, exhausted, at the table nearest the door. When a Nippy appeared, I was startled, as if she had roused me from a deep sleep. She was a skinny girl of no more than eighteen. She had chestnut brown hair, fixed in a parting by kirby grips, and spoke with a soft Irish accent. I wondered whether it was the limit of her ambition to wait tables at a Lyons, or whether, like the succession of waifs that presented themselves at Mr Brownlee's, she had the urge to flaunt herself in front of the leering men of

Soho. She was pretty enough, but she had not the body for it. Instead, she would find a young man charitable enough to overlook her flat-chestedness and trade her ambitions for a lifetime of domestic drudgery. The interval between her addressing me and my response was long enough for her face to adopt a concerned expression. She widened her eyes and thrust her head forward a little. Perhaps she thought I was a foreigner and had failed to understand her question. Remembering the script one follows on such occasions, I gave a little shake of my head, as if banishing a daydream, and ordered a pot of tea. It was only then that I realised I was sitting in the window, exposed to all and sundry. There was no danger of my father walking by (he rarely leaves the house), but Mrs Llewelyn might pass on her way to do her marketing, and my little subterfuge would be exposed. It was, however, too late to move to a table at the back of the room. The Nippy would be aggravated by my fickleness and I would be forced into some convoluted explanation of why I had inconvenienced her. And if I failed to account for my behaviour, she would think me the stuck-up type to whom a waitress is not worthy of the courtesy of an explanation.

As it was still early, most of the tables were unoccupied and there was little of the normal clatter of cutlery and china. The Nippies stood around in bored pairs, waiting for customers. One absent-mindedly fidgeted with the topmost button of her blouse. Another stole glances at herself in the mirror behind the counter, before touching her fingers to her hair. The furthermost leg of the table next to mine was supported by a folded piece of cardboard. I wondered if it was the table leg that was too short or the floor that was uneven. I placed my palms on either side of my own table and pressed down. It was quite stable. The tables were all of the same type, which one finds in Lyons everywhere, so I concluded that there must be a localised indentation in the floor beneath the nearby table. This unevenness in the floor was no reason to think that the building was in danger of imminent collapse. Nevertheless, that is what I imagined. It begins with a gentle tremor, enough to shake the teacups and glasses in the cabinets. The Nippies glance at each other. Customers look up from their scones. Cracks appear in the cornicing. Lumps of stucco fall to the floor. A woman is struck on the head and falls face first onto the table in front of her. The tremors grow more violent. The plate glass windows shatter and the entire ceiling crashes down. The Nippies scream and run for the door. Beams and masonry rain down. I am knocked unconscious and my body is buried by rubble. The following day a newspaper photograph shows the aftermath. A woman's leg is sticking out of the debris of the building. My father sees it as he turns the pages of *The Times*, but he has no reason to suspect that it is mine, as I was purportedly at work when the incident occurred.

The waitress, oblivious to the impending drama, returned and placed my pot of tea and the cup and saucer on the table. She even made a comment about how pleasant the weather was.

'Yes,' I replied. 'It's most unseasonal.' The last word, however, somehow became trapped between my tongue and palate and petered out before the final syllable. The girl smiled in an automated way, as my inability to successfully articulate even the simplest sentence had confirmed that I was foreign and thus worthy of her pity. This interaction completed, I had nothing with which to distract myself from my surroundings. I had neglected to bring a paperback. Had I been a man, I would have sent one of the Nippies out to buy me a newspaper, but I have never been able to muster any interest in affairs of state, and now did not seem the moment to rectify this.

A woman in a horrid maroon coat three tables away was looking at me. She pushed a portion of scone into her mouth.

A crumb broke off and landed on her scarf, where it clung precariously. A daub of jam remained on her upper lip, giving her the appearance of one who has been smacked in the mouth. She continued to masticate while she talked to her companion and I could clearly see the mouthful of scone form into a ball of dough. Had my stomach not been empty, I would have vomited. I averted my eyes. The large clock on the back wall read twenty past nine. Everything was muffled, the way it is when you submerge your head in the bathwater. I felt dreadfully self-conscious. What would I say if questioned about why I was there? What plausible explanation could there be for my presence? I lived only a short distance away. Why would I have left my home, where there was an ample supply of hot beverages, to sit alone in this café and pay 3/6 for a pot of tea I did not even want?

I poured some of the liquid from the pot into the cup provided. It emitted a curl of steam and a weak aroma. I lowered my nose to it. I have drunk a great many cups of tea in my lifetime, but at that moment the yellowish-brown liquid was no more appealing than if the waitress had urinated in my cup and presented it to me. I reminded myself that it was a Cup of Tea, a familiar, comforting thing. I poured some milk from the little jug decorated with the Lyons logo and observed the fusing of the two liquids precipitated by the agitation of my spoon. Yes, there it was, a nice cup of tea. 'Have a cup of tea,' I told myself. A cup of tea would make everything all right. But it was not all right. I raised the cup and touched the liquid to my lips. It was incomprehensible that I had previously consumed such a concoction not only willingly, but with enthusiasm.

I turned my attention to the street outside. Even if I could not move from my table, I could at least keep my eyes peeled for Mrs Llewelyn. The earlier bustle of people hurrying to work on the pavements outside had dwindled. Now, housewives made their way to the butcher's to buy a chop for their husband's supper. Such women have no need to hurry. This is their task for the day: to buy a chop. Later, they will cook it with some cabbage and potatoes. They will set the table and await dear hubby's return from the world beyond. Between then and now, nothing. Perhaps they will pause a while in a park or treat themselves to a pot of tea in a Lyons. They might read a novel, or put the chain on the door and lie on their beds amusing themselves, their eyes determinedly fixed on the ceiling. Regardless of what short-lived pleasure such activities may bring, they have but one purpose: to distract from the doleful passing of time.

On the pavement outside was the telephone box from which I had responded to Mr Brownlee's advertisement. A man stopped and checked the change in his trouser pocket before stepping inside. The hem of his coat caught in the door and there was a minor kerfuffle while he freed it. He was in his thirties. His hat was pushed back on his head, as if at some point he had paused to wipe sweat from his brow. He seemed flustered. He lifted the receiver and cradled it between his cheek and shoulder while he dialled, his left hand poised with the coin on the slot, anticipating the click. He must have been calling someone familiar, as he knew the number by heart. The business of dialling accomplished, he took the receiver in his right hand. As he awaited an answer he cast his eyes about, as if to ascertain if he was being observed. He was not. No one was paying the least attention to him. He waited. Perhaps he was calling to check that his wife was at home. Perhaps he was calling his mistress to arrange a tryst. In any case, in a room somewhere, a telephone was ringing. Perhaps the room was empty, or perhaps a woman was staring silently at it, wondering whether to answer. I began to feel a rising tension. Then the man gave a start. His finger pushed the coin into the slot. I read the word hullo on his lips.

He said it three times, but evidently there was no reply. He held the receiver in front of his face, and then, as if it was to blame, repeatedly and with some violence struck it against the dial of the telephone. He then replaced it on the trestle and adjusted the collar of his raincoat. Outside on the pavement, he looked around to see if anyone had witnessed his act of vandalism. Satisfied that they had not, he strode off down the street. There was a greasy stain on his raincoat from where it had become trapped in the door.

My tea had gone cold. I put it to my lips and pretended to drink. I had forgotten to put on my watch, but I glanced down at my wrist, as if to check the time of some future appointment. I was overtaken by a feeling of clumpiness. It was, I felt, out of the question that I would succeed in standing up without upsetting the table and causing a general disturbance. The Nippies would fuss about me. The manager would be summoned and I would be asked to pay for the broken crockery. The front of my skirt would be soaked with cold tea. Outside, passers-by would avert their eyes. The longer I remained, the more ossified I became. I gazed out of the window for as long as I felt I could respectably stay. Mrs Llewelyn did not appear and no further dramas were played out in the telephone box. Eventually, I could bear it no longer. I took my purse from my handbag. It was smeared with marmalade from the toast I had earlier secreted there. I left the correct change in the pewter salver provided for this purpose, calculating that my failure to leave a tip would be attributed to the fact that I was foreign and had no knowledge of the customs here. With a great effort of concentration, I managed to extricate myself from the table without incident. Outside on the pavement, I felt light-headed. I forced myself to walk a few yards, hoping to suggest to anyone observing me that I had a definite purpose in mind. I crossed the road carelessly, half-hoping to be hit by a bus. I imagined the commotion around my body. A young man would kneel by me and grasp my hand, telling me to hold on, that an ambulance was on its way. I would smile weakly, then close my eyes and slip away.

I made my way along the pavement. I got in everyone's way. The leash of someone's dog became tangled round my ankle. I wanted to kick the horrible little mutt. The idea of passing several hours in this manner was unbearable. I paused on a bench in the gardens off Randolph Crescent. Presently, a woman of about seventy sat down next to me. She remarked that it was a pleasant morning. It was the sort of banal comment that barely necessitated a response, but I forced my mouth into a smile and said: 'Yes.' She clasped her hands on her lap and gazed straight ahead at the bare trees and the backs of the houses. She was wearing a wedding ring, but it was clear that her husband was long gone. I suppose she passed a little time here every day. Perhaps she would sometimes find a companion more talkative than me, and I felt guilty about the inadequacy of my response. I longed to get up and leave, but I did not wish to offend her and I had, in any case, nowhere else to go. After some minutes, she produced a brown paper bag from somewhere inside her coat. From this she began to sow handfuls of breadcrumbs across the pathway. Within seconds, a horde of pigeons besieged us, like urchins scrambling for pennies. They appeared from all directions, as if conjured by The Great Dando. I subtly shifted my feet beneath the bench, not wishing to display my discomfort. The pigeons bustled around self-importantly, turning their heads to the side to eye a crumb before stabbing down on it with their beaks. One particularly tatty specimen remained on the fringes, unable to force her way into the throng. One of her feet was curled beneath her breast, like a withered hand. Her plumage was oily and ragged. I kicked my foot out into the multitude. There was a momentary, indifferent dispersal, before they once again inundated my feet. I turned my face away. The woman observed the scene with disinterest. It did not appear to bring her any pleasure. The birds were merely performing a service for her. After a while, she looked inside the bag, and then held it upside down to empty the remaining contents. There was a final flurry of activity, then the horrid creatures dispersed as swiftly as they arrived. Only the tatty bird with the withered foot remained, pecking vainly at the tarmac. There was nothing left for it.

Yesterday, or perhaps the day before, Mrs Llewelyn knocked softly on my bedroom door. She has lately been treating me with a kindness unmerited by my previous behaviour towards her. I take this as a sign that she knows I am not much longer for this world. When I gave her permission to enter, she told me that Dr Eldridge had called to see me. Of course, he had not 'called to see me'. He had been summoned, but I nevertheless consented to see him. He left a short interlude before entering, I suppose to allow me time to make myself decent. I propped myself up on my pillows and teased my hair into some semblance of order. I was mortified both by my appearance and by the disorderly state of my room. The air was stale. Dr Eldridge showed no sign of noticing any of this. He took two or three steps inside and asked if I was happy to talk to him for a few minutes. When I agreed, he closed the door behind him. Dr Eldridge has been our family doctor since my parents returned from India. It is quite possible that he was present when I entered the world (a difficult birth, as my mother never failed to remind me), and I expect he will be around when I take my leave of it. In the time I have known him, he appears not to have aged in the slightest. He was wearing what appeared to be the same dark tweed three-piece suit as he was when I was taken to his surgery at the age of five with mumps. I have never been one for running to the doctor at the least excuse. We were brought up to think that illness was a weakness and not something to be indulged. Childhood coughs and colds were dismissed as sniffles, and complaints about other ailments were invariably regarded as malingering. As a result, my acquaintance with Dr Eldridge is negligible. He has, however, a reassuring presence. I expect that if I told him I was thinking of doing away with myself, he would do no more than purse his lips and utter a little tutting sound.

He walked over to the window. 'Why don't we get a bit of day-light in here, eh?' he said, pulling open the curtains.

It surprised me that it was light outside. I had lost all track of time.

He sat down on the edge of bed. 'Your father tells me you've been feeling poorly,' he said.

I affected not to know what he was talking about. 'I've just been a little tired,' I replied. 'I always get this way at my time of the month.'

Dr Eldridge gave a little snort to this. If I had thought to throw him off with mention of women's troubles, I had not succeeded. 'Even so, since I'm here I might as well make sure everything's shipshape, hmm?'

He took my hand and then gently clasped my wrist, his fore-fingers resting on the tendons I would never have the courage to cut. He took the fob watch from the pocket of his waistcoat and waited for the second hand to reach the hour. It was pleasant to feel the touch of his fingers on my skin. I suppressed an urge to grasp his hand in mine. After thirty seconds or so he laid my hand back on the blankets, palm upwards, and gave a little nod to himself. He rummaged in the Gladstone bag at his feet and took out a device with a wide canvas strap, some rubber tubes and a gauge. He told me that he was going to take my blood pressure. He secured the apparatus round my upper arm and pumped it with a little rubber ball until it tightened.

'Just a little pressure, my dear, nothing to worry about,' he murmured. He looked at the gauge impassively, before tearing back the Velcro strip that secured the band. He took out his stethoscope and asked me to open my nightdress. My ribs showed through the skin. He inserted the earpieces and placed the diaphragm on my chest. The metal rim was cold. His face was only inches from mine. His cheeks were latticed with broken capillaries. I could feel the warmth of his breath on my ribs. He smelled of tobacco and carbolic soap. His face was as untroubled as if he were listening to a Chopin concerto. My hand lay palm upwards on the blanket, where he had left it. I turned it over and lightly ran the tips of my fingers along the coarse material covering his thigh. He instructed me to take a deep breath. Then, as if waking from a short nap, he leant back.

'Well, the good news is that you're still alive,' he said.

I emitted what probably seemed like a laugh. 'Can I listen?' I said.

He turned down the sides of his mouth and raised his eyebrows, tipping his head vaguely to the side. He took the head-set from around his neck and allowed me to put the little speakers in my ears. The sounds of the street outside became muffled. Then he repositioned the diaphragm on my chest. I placed my hand over his, and there it was: my own heart, blithely carrying on as if nothing were amiss. I kept my hand over the doctor's, listening to the gentle, reassuring rhythm. I loved my little heart then for keeping going; for being oblivious to the worthlessness of its custodian. It deserved better than me.

Dr Eldridge was watching me. I suppose it was usually only children who asked such things of him. I removed the earpieces and handed them to him. I don't know if he felt that something had passed between us. That has always been my problem. I never know if others are feeling what I am feeling. For him, no doubt, all this was no more than routine. He was carrying out procedures he had performed thousands of times. He packed his equipment carefully into his bag but did not stand up.

'So this fatigue,' he said, drawing out the middle syllable as if it were a foreign word he had never heard before. 'Tell me about this fatigue.'

I did not tell him that when I awoke in the morning (or the afternoon or whenever it might be), I felt the blankets covering me to be so heavy I could not imagine moving them. I did not tell him that every moment of my life up to this point seemed utterly devoid of purpose or meaning, and that I saw no prospect of that ever changing. I did not tell him that while I could (just) imagine the pleasure of feeling the sunshine warm my skin for one last time, I had not the energy to even think of going outside.

Instead, of course, I made light of it. I was just being silly. There was nothing wrong with me. I was a lazy good-for-nothing. I'd be as right as rain (I actually used that idiotic expression) in a day or two. I was sorry, I told him, that he'd been put to the trouble of coming to see me. He assured me that it was no trouble. He looked at me for a few moments with his placid expression. I longed for him to tell me what nonsense I was talking. I longed for him to tell me that I was terribly ill and needed a prolonged confinement. Dr Braithwaite would have seen right through my lies. But Dr Eldridge did not. He pursed his lips and nodded slowly. Then he picked up his bag and stood up.

'Try to get a bit of exercise,' he said kindly. 'Go for a little walk. We all feel a little tired sometimes. But it doesn't do to lie around in bed all day. And you must eat. You're much too thin.'

Then he left me. I longed for him to stay. I started sobbing and pushed my face into the pillow to prevent anyone from hearing. Rebecca hissed into my ear: I was pathetic. It was no good crying now. Nobody could hear me.

I imagined my father waiting anxiously downstairs for the prognosis. Dr Eldridge would tell him in a hushed voice that he could find nothing wrong with me, physically at least. He would then ask a series of questions, which Father would answer, embarrassed on my behalf. No, she never goes out. She hardly eats. She hasn't any friends. After a few minutes I heard the front door click closed and he was gone.

I have decided to visit Dr Braithwaite one last time. It was Rebecca's idea and I lack the will to resist her. When I awoke this morning, she was in one of her wheedling moods. She could not take any more of this. I might have given up on life, but she had not. It wasn't fair, she said. I could see her point. It *wasn't* fair. Why should she suffer on account of my failings?

She tried to cajole me out of my torpor. I reminded her of all the hateful names she had called me. She apologised. She had spoken only in frustration. I could hardly blame her. Who could put up with being shackled to me?

I pushed aside the blankets and placed my feet on the floor. The carpet felt coarse on my soles. I retrieved my dressing gown, which lay on a crumpled heap by the bed, and put it on. I could smell the sickly odour of my armpits. I walked to the window and drew the curtains. It was raining outside. Well, what did that matter? Rebecca said. A little rain never hurt anyone. She told me to take a bath. On the landing I met Mrs Llewelyn. She looked at me with surprise and then smiled. Rebecca asked her if she would be so good as to run her a bath. They had never met before, but Mrs Llewelyn complied without dissent.

'I'd be glad to, my dear,' she said.

I sat on the seat of the lavatory while Mrs Llewelyn ran the water, testing the temperature now and again the way one would for a child. When she turned off the taps, Rebecca thanked her in a manner that made it clear she was no longer required. I undressed and stepped into the bath. I placed a flannel over my face and lay back in the water. It was dark and comforting. I could quite easily have let myself slip under, but Rebecca made me sit up and wash myself. I soaped my armpits and private parts and rinsed them with a flannel. Rebecca liked to be nicely turned out. She would never allow herself to let herself go, the way I had. Nor was there to be any lingering in the warm, soapy water. She ordered me out of the bath and dried me vigorously, making my skin tingle. I imagined Mrs Llewelyn downstairs informing my father that I was up, and decided I should breakfast with him. I pulled on my robe and went downstairs. Father was in his usual place at the head of the table, cracking open his boiled egg.

'Good morning, dear,' he said. 'It's nice to see you up. Feeling better, are we?'

'As a matter of fact, we are,' Rebecca said. Speak for yourself, I thought. 'Nice weather for ducks,' she went on.

Father looked at her curiously. He sprinkled a little salt on his egg and started to butter his toast. Rebecca expressed the desire to have an egg of her own. Two eggs, in fact. I myself have never eaten a boiled egg for breakfast, but Father immediately got to his feet and, placing his napkin on his newspaper, went to the door and instructed Mrs Llewelyn to put two more eggs on to boil.

Rebecca, unaware of the difficulty my father and I had maintaining a conversation, had not calculated that the time required for the boiling of the eggs would result in a period of strained silence. This seemed to have no effect on her, however. She first spread a piece of toast with butter, cut it into four triangles and then began eating it in dainty little bites. Father did not appear in the least disconcerted by this uncharacteristic behaviour. Rebecca then asked what plans he had for the day.

'Plans?' he said. 'I expect I have a little correspondence to take care of this morning.'

'I do think it's important to keep oneself occupied, don't you?' she said. The remark was clearly aimed at me.

Father nodded his agreement. I told Rebecca that if she didn't behave, I could just as easily take myself back to bed. Before she could protest, Mrs Llewelyn arrived with her eggs. This proved a welcome distraction from making small talk. Rebecca set about the eggs with enthusiasm, skilfully shelling them before mashing them onto two more slices of thickly buttered toast. Clearly, Rebecca was not concerned about her hips. Father looked on in bemusement. She smiled at him and took an enthusiastic bite. Some yolk dribbled down the front of her robe, but she did not appear to notice. I took up a napkin and mopped it up as best I could.

The business of breakfast concluded, we retreated to our room. Rebecca set about choosing an outfit. It was a relief to let her take control of things. She began to berate me for the outmoded nature of my wardrobe, but, realising she was still somewhat in my hands, she checked herself. Instead, she suggested in a chummy tone that we might go shopping together sometime. I replied that I would like that very much. Despite everything, I was flattered that she might wish to befriend me. Perhaps I wasn't such a ninny after all.

She chose a white blouse and grey tweed suit. I was pleased. This was the same outfit I had chosen for her the first time we visited Braithwaite. She sometimes seemed to forget that without me she would not even exist, but as (for once) we were getting on, it did not seem wise to remind her of this. Were it not for her, I would still be languishing in bed, like the wretched idler I am. I must let her have her head. She was right, too, about Braithwaite. It might be easy to pull the wool over Dr Eldridge's eyes, but Collins Braithwaite would not be so easily fooled. If I had so far resisted him, it had been solely out of stubbornness. I had the strong feeling that only he could help me and I must submit to whatever course he advised.

I put on my underthings and sat on the stool at my dressing table. I looked at the familiar objects arrayed there: the set of hairbrushes with the cameo motif; the little tin I had bought as a child on holiday in Torquay and in which I kept my hairpins; the chunky little bottle of Chanel No.5 I had formerly worn in the hope that, just once, a man would tell me I smelled nice. I arranged everything precisely before I began. As I patted the powder onto my cheeks, I watched myself disappear. With the addition of a little rouge, Rebecca emerged. She smiled at me and I smiled back. I applied mascara to my lashes and then a red lipstick I had bought especially for her (it was far too daring for me). Rebecca rolled her lips inwards and pouted at the mirror, satisfied with the job I had done. She looked, I must say, quite marvellous.

She then dressed carefully and inspected herself in the mirror on the inside of the wardrobe door. She was ready. I asked only that I might write a few lines in my journal before we departed. We had not made an appointment with Dr Braithwaite, so it mattered little what time we arrived. Rebecca consented to this and I sat down at my little desk and unlocked the drawer in which I have kept these notebooks. Now that I'm done, I suppose it's time to go. I expect this will be my final entry here.

Braithwaite V: Tunnelling Out

The final years of Braithwaite's life were spent at the family home on Westlands Road in Darlington. After his brother George's death in 1962, the house had never been sold. By 1970 royalties from his books had all but dried up and Braithwaite had exhausted the patience of those prepared to lend him money to pay his rent or fund his increasingly alcohol-soaked lifestyle. His final months in London were spent in various Soho hostelries, propositioning women and haranguing anyone within earshot about stuck-up publishers, the Establishment, and 'that cunt Laing'. He was routinely asked to leave premises.

In a letter to Edward Seers of January 1971, he wrote that London was 'finished' and he intended to make a fresh start elsewhere. He had decided to write the novel Seers had suggested and asked for an advance. Seers did not believe a word of it, but the idea that he might finally see the back of Braithwaite was enough to persuade him to send a cheque for £50. He did not expect to hear from him again. Braithwaite caught a train to Darlington on 4th February 1971, his 46th birthday. The firebrand who had preached 'perpetual revolution of the self' ended up back where he started, sleeping in his parents' bed.

The Darlington of 1971 was separated from the London counter-culture Braithwaite had inhabited by a great deal more than 250 miles. It remained a traditional Northern town dominated by engineering and wool works. Post-war town planning dictated that parts of the town centre be demolished to make way for a new system of ring roads, but in general the streets had changed little since the thirties. Beyond the hemlines of women's skirts, the fabled 'Swinging Sixties' had had little impact there. Newfangled ideas were viewed with phlegmatism. It was like travelling back in time.

To some, a homecoming might constitute grounds for celebration, but for Braithwaite, stepping onto the platform at Darlington station was 'an admission of defeat'.

If he was concerned about what the local population might make of his humiliating fall from grace, he need not have worried. In Darlington, nobody knew who he was. As he did not have keys to the house on Westlands Road, he smashed a window next to the back door and let himself in. A neighbour, Mrs Agnes Bell, called the police to report that a burglary was in progress. When a local constable, Fred Hirst, knocked on the front door, he found a man who gave every appearance of being a vagrant. 'I am Arthur Collins Braithwaite and this is my house,' the tramp declared. After leaving the constable on the doorstep for ten minutes, Braithwaite returned with his driving licence. This, in itself, proved little, but despite his unkempt appearance, Braithwaite's behaviour was not that of a burglar, and Hirst had no alternative but to leave. The following afternoon, he telephoned Mrs Bell to inform her that the relevant checks had been carried out and the burglar was, in fact, the rightful owner of the house. Mortified by her mistake, she called round to apologise. A few years earlier, Braithwaite would have berated her, but instead he stood unsteadily on the threshold and looked at her curiously. He introduced himself as Arthur and explained that the house had belonged to his father. 'He shot himself, you know. The stupid bastard.'

Mrs Bell, now widowed, still lives in Westlands Road. When I called on her, she was happy to discuss her former neighbour, whom she remembered with a mixture of fondness and pity. She was, at the time, in her late twenties and had attractive features and a slim figure. She had not thought to change out of her apron before calling on her neighbour and, under Braithwaite's gaze, she felt suddenly self-conscious. 'He had,' she recalled, 'a way of looking at you unlike anyone I had ever met.'

There was no need to apologise, he assured her. If anything, he should be sorry for startling her. Mrs Bell said that was very generous of him and, as they were going to be neighbours, invited him for supper that evening. Braithwaite at first refused, but then, after some persuasion, accepted. He had, in any case, nothing in the house to eat.

The get-together was not a success. Braithwaite arrived with a clanking bag of bottles of brown ale, which he did not hand over as a gift but kept at his feet and systematically drank as the evening wore on. Naturally, it was Agnes who made the conversational running. She was a part-time librarian at a nearby Cockerton primary school. Her husband, Robert, was a book-keeper in the wool firm of Patons & Baldwins, one of the town's major employers. They had two young sons, Peter and Andrew, who were safely tucked up in bed by the time Braithwaite arrived. The house was fashionably furnished. The Bells were part of the generation eagerly throwing off the virtuous austerity of the post-war years. They were the children of Macmillan and Wilson, for whom revolution meant not the throwing open of the doors of perception, but access to Hire Purchase and participation in a new era of consumerism. 'Through the acquisition of *stuff*,' Braithwaite wrote unkindly, 'the Bells had so effectively subsumed their existential and sexual frustrations, they did not even know they were spiritually dead: they were the happiest people I ever met.'

Agnes had gone to some trouble to prepare some modish hors d'œuvres, and Braithwaite greedily tucked into them. He also enthusiastically partook of the sherry offered, helping himself to the bottle that was left on the coffee table between them. When Agnes disappeared to the kitchen to prepare the meal, the two men struggled to sustain a conversation: Robert was a keen football fan; Braithwaite had no interest in sport. Braithwaite evaded his neighbour's questions about what line of work he was in with a vague gesture of his hand. The only gambit Braithwaite volunteered was that Agnes was a 'nice bit of skirt'. Bell responded to this with muted thanks. It was a relief when Agnes reappeared and announced that supper was ready.

This was taken in the small dining room, connected to the kitchen by a serving hatch. Agnes served *coq au vin*, helpfully informing Braithwaite that it was 'a French dish'. Robert and she hoped to take the boys to France when they were old enough. It was important nowadays, she opined, to experience foreign cultures. Whether due to the food, the number of bottles of ale he had consumed, or simply because they had happened upon a topic of conversation that was of interest, Braithwaite loosened up. For the next half hour, he entertained the couple with stories from his time in France after the war, not omitting several anecdotes about his sexual conquests. After a particularly risqué tale, Robert protested that such talk was unsuitable for his wife's ears. Braithwaite fixed him with a look of mock innocence. 'You've got two boys upstairs,' he said. 'There must have been some point when she wasn't averse to a good fucking.' Agnes defused the situation by clearing the plates from the table. Braithwaite brazenly appraised her as she did so. She went into the kitchen to prepare dessert, humming a tune as she did so. The two men sat in silence. When she returned, she turned the conversation to the changes in the town that had taken place since he had left. Braithwaite said he hadn't noticed.

At a certain point, Robert went upstairs to check on the two boys. Braithwaite turned his chair toward Agnes and stared at her for a few moments. She found herself blushing. Then Braithwaite made an apology of sorts. He wasn't used to being in polite company and had not meant to cause any offence. Agnes assured him that she had not been the least bit offended. It was stimulating to have such a sophisticated guest. He must think them terrible fuddy-duddies. Braithwaite replied that he thought no such thing. The evening ended amicably enough, but he was not invited to supper again.

The house on Westlands Road was in a state of disrepair. The roof was missing several tiles and water had leaked into the loft, causing the ceiling on the upper floor to buckle. Sodden piles of plaster had dropped to the landing floor and rotted the carpets. The paper on the staircase was peeling off the walls. Everything smelt of damp. Braithwaite oscillated between his parents' bedroom at the front of the house and the kitchen, which he heated by means of a paraffin stove. His routine during these first few months consisted of little more than drinking. He rarely rose before midday. Breakfast was a Player's Navy Cut and a slug of Scotch from the bottle he kept by the bed, and which he was always mindful not to finish the night before. As there was no hot water, his ablutions were minimal. He never washed his clothes. He grew skinny and gaunt. Afternoons were spent in the Railway Tavern on High Northgate. There, he sat at a table in the corner, drinking pints of ale and staring into space. As long as he had money to pay for his pints, his tramp-like appearance did not bother the landlord, Brian Armitage. He was not hostile to the other regulars, but nor did he involve himself in their discussions about the day's news or local gossip. They, in turn, were content to leave him be. On the way home he would stock up on tins of sardines and peaches from the grocer's shop on Northcote Terrace. He spent his evenings in the kitchen, slouched on the sofa he had manoeuvred from the front room, reading and drinking whisky. Sometimes he fell into a stupor where he lay. Other times he made it upstairs.

'I was in every sense down to the bare bones,' he wrote. He compared himself to the disembodied voice in Samuel Beckett's novel *The Unnamable*, a stream of consciousness disconnected from the physical world. 'It was a kind of liberation. There was nothing to think about, other than physical survival. And yet, despite my attempts to drown it in alcohol, my mind kept up its ceaseless hectoring. On and on and on it went.'

Then spring came and things changed.

'I awoke one April afternoon,' he wrote, 'with a shaft of sunlight stabbing through the gap in the curtains. I looked around the room. Everything was filthy. The walls were stained. The carpet was stained. The bedclothes were stained. I was stained. I went downstairs to the kitchen. The floor was stacked with bottles. In the corner was a pile of cans. Mice scurried out of sight. I disgusted myself. I had allowed myself to fall into a state of dereliction.'

Whether on that same day or soon after, Agnes Bell realised that a clear-out was taking place next door. First, boxes of bottles and other rubbish appeared in the small garden at the front of the house. Then the back garden was stacked with furniture Braithwaite had broken down with an axe. He tried to burn it, but it was too damp to catch and sat for weeks, like a ramshackle sculpture. He then even started to clear the overgrown garden, often working from morning until evening. Agnes began to chat with him over the fence and sometimes brought him cups of tea. His conversation was often distracted, but he was friendly enough and refrained from making lewd remarks. At one point he asked if she had known his father, but she shook her head. He seemed disappointed when she said she did not remember the ironmonger's shop on Skinnergate. She was far too young. 'He was right proud of this house, and look at it now,' Braithwaite told her, before continuing to attack some undergrowth with a scythe. One Saturday morning, Agnes saw Braithwaite on the roof, attempting to repair the missing tiles. Fearing that he might fall, she sent a reluctant Robert out to steady the ladder. 'Are you going to hold that, or pull it away?' Braithwaite shouted down. Eventually, the furniture dried out sufficiently to burn and there was enough space at the back door to set out a small table and chair.

Over the months that followed, Mrs Bell would see him there, often bare-chested, hunched over a typewriter. When she asked what he was writing, he replied, 'A tragedy. A bloody tragedy's what it is.'

The typescript of *My Self and Other Strangers* runs to almost 500 pages. Even at this nadir, Braithwaite remained convinced of his own genius. If he had fallen low, this was due not to any failings on his own part, but to his enemies' determination to destroy him. This was, he contends, a natural reaction. For the Establishment to endure, 'those with a vested interest in its survival must destroy its opponents. This is true,' he writes, 'of all totalitarian systems, whether political or psychic.'

While there may be some truth in this observation, it demonstrates the hugely inflated view Braithwaite continued to hold of himself. The truth was less palatable: despite his short-lived notoriety, he was never important enough to merit the orchestrated campaign he alleges. Those involved in this crusade against him included the police, the media and the legal system, as well as individuals like Edward Seers, Richard Aaron and, of course, Ronnie Laing. No one is spared his vitriol. Dirk Bogarde, to whom he owed much of his success, is dismissed as 'a vacuum, [a man] so vain and affected he barely existed'. Seers is 'like all queers, a coward at heart, a mediocrity who victimises others to deflect attention from his own failings'. But it is for Laing that he reserves his most operatic jibes: 'There he sits on his dunghill Parnassus, his piss lapped up like vintage champagne by sycophantic courtiers.'

My Self and Other Strangers is rambling, bombastic, self-justifying and wildly cavalier with facts. It is also, by some distance, Braithwaite's finest and most entertaining work. When he is not settling scores or making grandiose claims about his own intellect, the bulk of the book is really a memoir, what might today be termed 'autofiction'. The long sections on his childhood and the period he spent in France are lyrical and evocative. The passages about Netley bristle with an indignation, for once, directed at a worthy target. Edward Seers' suggestion that he should write a novel was perhaps not as ill advised as Braithwaite thought.

On working in his father's ironmongery, despite the indignity of being constantly ordered about and belittled for the tiniest transgressions, he recalls the tactile pleasure of feeling the curve of an axe handle in his palms, the satisfying weight of its head. 'To hold an axe,' he writes, 'is to feel it ache to be swung. Tools are an invitation to activities far more befitting a man than the wielding of a pen.'

Recalling a particularly vicious beating at the hands of his brothers, he empathises with them: 'I had committed the sin of being clever. They were thugs. I could hardly expect them to reason with me.' Such beatings took place with the tacit approval of his father, who 'presumably thought they would effect a cure for my malady'.

Throughout his account there is constantly the need to hide, both literally and metaphorically. His earliest memory, he claims, is of pretending to be asleep in the bedroom at Cartmell Terrace while his father, returning from the pub, forces himself on his mother. She protests that Arthur will hear them, but when she whispers his name to see if he is awake, he squeezes his eyes tightly shut. He lies rigidly in the dark listening to his father's grunts, feeling complicit in his mother's rape. Whether this episode is misremembered, embellished or fantasy, it is revealing: even as a four-year-old, Braithwaite was learning how to absent himself.

At the age of thirteen or fourteen, he takes one of his mother's nightdresses from her closet and takes it to his room. He puts it on and masturbates. He describes how the softness and aroma of the flannelette brings him closer to his mother. This might seem sordid, but it also the act of a little boy abandoned by his mother who has no other outlet for the emotions provoked. Later, he cuts out the lining of his trouser pockets so that he can surreptitiously masturbate while watching passing girls as he lies around on the banks of Cocker Beck. 'It never crossed my mind,' he writes, 'that I might have approached one of those girls and asked her to take a walk or go to the pictures with me, which was all I actually wanted. I had been brought up to see myself as inadequate, to believe that I was unworthy of any affection, so I buried any such feelings I had.'

Reading all this, it is easy to see the origins of Braithwaite's subsequent flaws: his inability to perceive other men as anything other than rivals; his overbearing arrogance and bombast; his dismissive treatment of women. It was all rooted in his fear of rejection.

The happiest passages of the book are those recalling his time in France. 'To be in another country, speaking another language, was to be another person, and in being another person I felt for the first time that I was myself.' Braithwaite enjoyed the camaraderie among the gangs of grape pickers. He enjoyed the physical exhaustion of a proper day's labour. He enjoyed the sun on his back and the salty taste of sweat on his upper lip. He enjoyed the free flow of wine at the trestle tables set out for lunch and the half-understood anecdotes that were exchanged. Most of all, he enjoyed the easy-going sexual milieu that all this engendered. 'I learned that fucking was not an act of aggression, something that men did to women, but an act to be enjoyed by two people with no obligation to anything other than pleasure.' Reading Braithwaite's descriptions of the orange soil and the smells of lemon, lavender and dung of Provence, it's surprising and perhaps tragic that he ever returned to England.

He does not write in any detail about individual clients. Maybe he felt that he covered this ground in *Untherapy*. More likely, he had simply become bored of listening to the smart set of London describe their 'dime-store angst' to him. 'If I learned anything,' he writes, 'it was that no matter how much material comfort you throw at a human being, we will always find something to be miserable about. We are programmed for dissatisfaction. We always want more. More furniture, more gadgets, more sex, more love. We covet what the other guy has, just as the other guy covets what we have. This is the driver to perpetual discontent.'

The work of the psychotherapist ('so-called') was the easiest in the world. 'I never had a single visitor who did not, on some level, understand his own problems. All that was required was to listen and watch, then put my observations to the individual in question: to give voice to what he already knew. A simple process, and yet, time and again, I was told of my perceptiveness, of how I understood. All I did was listen. When a visitor arrives believing you are some kind of guru, your thoughts are already invested with profundity. As a therapist, you are thanked for saying things that would earn a guy in a bar a punch on the jaw. And when someone is paying you five guineas an hour, your words have been pre-consecrated. Psychotherapy is nothing more than a transaction, a confidence trick, in both senses.'

It's a cynical view, and one to which both traditional psychiatrists and contemporary counsellors would no doubt object. It also perhaps downplays Braithwaite's talents as a therapist. There can be little question that he had an aptitude for identifying the roots of his clients' discontent and of speaking truths others might have shied away from.

> *When a woman [he writes] tells you she feels asphyxiated by her life, it does not take a genius to suggest that she should change it.*
> *'But I can't,' she will say despairingly.*
> *'Why not?' you reply.*
> *'I just can't,' she says. 'It's too complicated. I'm trapped.'*
> *'If you really wanted to, you could.'*
> *'I could?'*
> *What people—especially women—are seeking is permission. They are so crushed by the structures of family, decorum and responsibility that they are incapable of acting autonomously. They require external authorisation for their own desires. All that is required is to move forward, to refuse to be manacled to the past.*

The irony of writing this in the garden of his childhood home was not lost on Braithwaite. 'If I had five guineas to spare, I could do worse than to consult myself,' he writes, 'but I don't.'

During the summer of 1971, when he was writing all this, Agnes Bell noticed a change in him. Aside from his constant activity at the little table at the back door, he began to cook himself simple meals. He put on weight. He still drank, but his hands did not shake in the morning. His personal hygiene improved. He washed his clothes and hung them out on a clothesline improvised between two trees. If Agnes was hanging out her own washing, he would give her a hand. After a while, as the Bells owned a washing machine, she offered to take in his laundry, and he allowed her to do this. In return, he did odd jobs for her around the garden, at least while Robert was out at work. She sometimes even let 'Uncle Arthur' keep an eye on the boys when she had to run out to the grocer's or post office.

At times, Braithwaite was so immersed in his writing that he did not hear Agnes calling to him over the fence, but often he would stop, light a cigarette and chat amiably. He told her stories about growing up in the area. Agnes confided that she had only married Robert because she fell pregnant to him. He was a good husband and father, but she didn't love him. She expressed great curiosity about London, which she had visited only once when she was eighteen. Braithwaite told her it was full of charlatans and she was better off where she was. 'But it's so dull here,' Agnes had said. 'I feel like I'm in a cage.' Braithwaite replied that he had met many women in similar situations. He asked what she would do if the cage door was open. Agnes laughed and said she would probably lock it and stay on her perch.

Despite the closeness that developed between them, Braithwaite never made any inappropriate advances towards Agnes. Even when she confessed that she sometimes fantasised about having a lover, Braithwaite told her that she should go ahead, but he did not propose himself for the role.

Two or three evenings a week, Braithwaite took himself to the Railway Tavern. He still kept himself to himself, but he would exchange a few words with the other regulars when he was at the bar. One evening he was invited to make up the numbers in the pub's darts team. He had always been hopeless at sports, and he lost every leg he played, often missing the board completely, but his new teammates were magnanimous about his performance. He bought a board in a second-hand shop, hung it on the back door of the house and measured out an oche. He practised for an hour every morning and evening, and when one of the Tavern regulars died, he had reached a decent enough standard to take his place in the team. When he threw the winning darts in the match against their local rivals, the Slater's Arms, he celebrated by buying a number of rounds for both teams. Brian Armitage even permitted a rare 'lock-in'. Braithwaite left in the small hours of the morning, drunk but elated. 'I had not known such a moment of simple pleasure for a very long time,' he wrote. 'I experienced a feeling of companionship. I was accepted by a group of men who knew only my first name and had no interest in me beyond my ability to hit double tops. I had found a new level in life.'

In November 1971, Braithwaite sent the typescript of *My Self and Other Strangers* to Edward Seers. With all his old arrogance, he neither had a clean copy typed up, nor deleted the derogatory remarks he had made about the recipient. Seers greeted its arrival with dread, but he read it dutifully and then, in order to ensure that he was not allowing his own prejudices to colour his opinion, passed it to a colleague. Not wishing Braithwaite to think he had not given it proper consideration, he allowed six weeks to pass before replying. His reply, dated 12th January 1972, was courteous but firm. After some rudimentary praise for Braithwaite's 'customary chutzpah' and 'colourful prose', he concludes that 'regretfully I cannot envisage a large enough market to justify publication'. He was therefore returning the manuscript, with thanks.

Braithwaite, already infuriated by the delay in getting back to him, telephoned Seers the following day. Seers listened wearily to the predictable diatribe. Braithwaite, realising his former editor was not going to alter his position, boasted that several other publishers were eager to publish the book and that he had only sent it to Seers out of misplaced loyalty. Seers wished him luck and hung up.

Whether Braithwaite sent the typescript to anyone else is not known. If he did, it met with a similar response. The book was never published and the sole copy of the typescript resides in the archive at Durham University. Some weeks later, Braithwaite wrote to Seers asking him to send any outstanding royalties on his previous books. There were none. Both *Kill Your Self* and *Untherapy* had been allowed to fall out of print. Nevertheless, as a goodwill gesture, Seers sent him a cheque for £20. Around the same time, Braithwaite also wrote to Zelda. He congratulated her on her success (she had by that time published four novels, one of which, *A Passing Shower*, had been filmed by Lewis Gilbert) and asked her for the fifty quid she owed him. She ignored the letter.

My Self and Other Strangers ends thus:

I had spent my entire life hating Darlington. I hated the red-brick terraces. I hated the cobbled lanes and the stinking pubs. I hated the toffs of Cockerton and the vulgar mob of workers streaming out of Patons & Baldwins. I hated the munificent Joseph Pease looking down from his plinth on High Row. I hated the chummy nickname 'Darlo'. Darlo was not my friend. Darlo was my enemy. Darlo was a penitentiary from which my only desire was to tunnel out. To preserve your sanity, you have to escape. If you do not escape, your inevitable retreat is into the moronic municipal pride that is the refuge of those that never leave. It is only now, in returning here, that I understand that my hatred of Darlington was misplaced. Darlington is no better or worse than anywhere else. I hated Darlington only because it is where I come from. It is not Darlington I hate, but myself. It is myself from which I have tried and failed to escape.

On 14th April 1972, Braithwaite fetched a length of rope from the garden shed and hanged himself from an exposed rafter on the first-floor landing of the house. He had left the back door open and his body was found the following day by a distraught Agnes Bell. The typescript of *My Self and Other Strangers* was on the kitchen table. On it was a scrap of paper on which he had written:

If my enterprise upstairs has been successful, you may consider this my suicide note. ACB

Ten days later, Arthur Collins Braithwaite was buried next to his father and brothers in Darlington's East Cemetery. The funeral was attended by Edward Seers, Agnes Bell and two members of the Railway Tavern darts team. There were no other mourners.

Postscript to the Second Edition

Following the publication of this book in the autumn of 2021, I received a good deal of correspondence pointing out various errors in the depiction of London in the 1960s. Despite the fact that I had myself drawn attention to it in my preface, several readers point out that the pub visited by the protagonist is called the Pembroke, not Pembridge Castle. 'No one who had lived in London at the time,' wrote one correspondent, 'would make the mistake of placing a Lyons tea shop on Elgin Avenue.' The nearest Lyons was, apparently, round the corner in Sutherland Avenue. Another gentleman questioned the route that the protagonist walks from Chalk Farm Station to Ainger Road. The president of the Primrose Hill Historical Society wrote to inform me that there was not now, and never had been, a metal railing at the summit of Primrose Hill, as is mentioned in the episode there with Miss Kepler. Neither had there ever been a café named Clay's on Regent's Park Road. I answered these letters and emails patiently. The gist of my response was that these errors were in the original notebooks and even if I had known about them, it would not have been my place to correct them. They could be easily be explained by the author mis-remembering or simply embellishing here and there.

Nevertheless, the volume of correspondence was disconcerting and I felt compelled to carry out some further research of my own. Perhaps in my desire to believe in the authenticity of the notebooks, I had been guilty of confirmation bias: I had unconsciously sought to verify what I wanted to believe. I leafed through years of the *Woman's Journal* in the Mitchell Library in Glasgow, before finding the author's story, *An Agreeable*

Reception, in the May issue of 1962. It was, I wryly noted, published under the name of Rebecca Smyth, and was not half as bad as the author of the notebooks had claimed, though it did share some of her idiosyncrasies of style. Clearly, it was the work of the same person. I could find no trace of a theatrical agency by the name of Brownlee Associates, but that proved little either way. Given that the author had been so careful to protect her own identity, it was reasonable to assume that she had also changed the names of other characters.

However, no matter how often I told myself that it was of little consequence whether the notebooks were genuine, my scepticism grew. I decided to write to Martin Grey to ask if there was any further information he could provide to corroborate his story. Mr Grey replied, saying that he had been observing the reception of the book with interest, but he could think of nothing to add to what he had previously told me. To my surprise, though, he offered to meet me the next time I was in London. As it happened, I was going to be in the capital the following week. Mr Grey suggested that we meet in the Greenberry Café on Regent's Park Road, Primrose Hill. When I asked what he looked like, he told me not to worry; he would recognise me.

We arranged to meet the following Wednesday at 2pm. It was a sunny afternoon in April. I had walked around the area a good deal during my preparation of the book and had even once stopped in the café Mr Grey had chosen, wondering if it had been the prototype for Clay's teashop in the notebooks. I had even asked the owner how long there had been a café on the premises, but she was unable to tell me. I arrived at ten minutes to two. The proprietress did not appear to remember me from my previous visit. I ordered a flat white and a sparkling water and took a seat at a table in the window. The café was frequented by affluent young mothers with children dressed in designer clothes. One elegantly dressed lady in her seventies was sitting with a pot of tea at a table at the back of the room. I did not feel unduly concerned when two o'clock came and went with no sign of Mr Grey. By quarter past, however, I was becoming anxious. Perhaps there had been a mix-up and he was in one of the other cafés that lined the little high street, but it did not make sense to leave and start looking for him. He was sure to appear as soon as I had left the premises.

I ordered another coffee and kept my eye on the street outside. If, as I assumed, Martin Grey was the Clacton cousin of the author, he must be around seventy-five years old. At one point, an elderly man passed by on the pavement outside. I went outside and called his name, but the man merely stared at me blankly, then politely apologised for not being who I hoped he was. I drank my second coffee unenthusiastically, wishing Mr Grey had suggested meeting in the Pembroke Castle at the end of the street. I checked my email on my phone, but there was no message. I had given Mr Grey my number, but he had not reciprocated. It became clear that he was not going to show up. I felt disappointed and foolish. Evidently, the whole thing had been a prank. I had, as the author of notebooks might have said, been given the go-by. I paid and began to gather up my things. As I pulled on my jacket, the elderly lady at the back of the café rose and approached my table. She was dressed in a white blouse and knee-length tweed skirt. She wore a dark wool coat and had a turquoise scarf knotted around her neck. Her grey hair was loosely tied, so that some strands framed her face. Her eyes were alert and pale blue. She was quite striking. Perhaps it was the turquoise scarf that made me wonder if I had seen her somewhere before. Certainly, I experienced a brief sense of déjà vu.

'I believe you're waiting for someone,' she said. She had a pleasant, musical voice.

'I was,' I said. 'But I don't think he's coming.'

'No, he isn't,' she said. 'I hope you won't think ill of me. I'm afraid I have been rather toying with you. My name is Rebecca Smyth.'

I nodded and gave a little laugh. 'Of course you are,' I said.

We stood looking at each other for a few moments. I was processing what had just occurred. I expect she was gauging my reaction.

I made to resume my seat and indicated that she should join me, but she leaned in towards me and suggested, in a mischievous whisper, that we could instead go to the pub along the road. I readily agreed. As we walked the short distance to the Pembroke Castle, she clasped her hand in the crook of my elbow. She moved with a gait that belied her years and held her head haughtily, like a terrapin turning its face to the sun. Passers-by glanced admiringly at her and I was gratified to be seen in her company. She had the air of an aging but still elegant actress.

Acknowledgements

My deepest thanks to:

My publisher and friend, Sara Hunt for your unstinting support to me as writer. Your passion and commitment to this book has been overwhelming. I'm honoured to be published by you.

My agent, Isobel Dixon for your encouragement, good humour and astute editorial notes.

My editor, Craig Hillsley for your perceptive observations and meticulous attention to detail. And, yes, even for the commas.

My great friend and fellow traveller, Victoria Evans, always my first reader, your support means everything to me.

To Angie Harms and the small number of others who read all or part of the manuscript and offered words of support when most needed. The words 'Just keep going' are never wasted.

Finally to Jen Cunnion: in more ways than one this book would never have been written without you. It's for you really.

Quotations:

p.54 Quoted in *R.D. Laing: A Divided Self* by John Clay (Sceptre, 1997) p.48

p.179 Words of Paul McCartney quoted in *White Heat* by Dominic Sandbrook (Abacus, 2007) p.436

p.181 From *Dirk Bogarde: The Authorised Biography* by John Coldstream (Phoenix, 2005) p.8

p.183 From *The Myth of Sisyphus* by Albert Camus (Penguin, 2013) p.58

I also acknowledge the support of a three-week residency at Ventspils International Writers' & Translators' House, Latvia. Finally, my sincere thanks to David Holmes for invaluable legal advice. Any errors in the sections on Collins Braithwaite are entirely down to me. As to the remainder of the text, any inaccuracies beyond those already noted are the responsibility of the author of the notebooks.